AARON LUSTER

SCAVENGERS

Thank you to my Family for your unwavering support!

Promise fulfilled...

AARON LUSTER

SCAVENGERS

1
THE PRESS CONFERENCE

Number two glowed in a bright fluorescent red on the black display screen above their heads inside the elevator. The three of them, two military officers, who'd dressed as though they had prepared for an all-out war on a battlefield, and the second in command to the Global President, Nathan Dunne, all exited the elevator. Dunne's trim athletic physique filled out his hand-tailored dark navy suit to perfection. His eyes were dark and tear-filled as they made their way down the corridor. There was a nurse at a desk ahead of them that stood up as they approached. She recognized Dunne from the television and had been aware as to whom they were there to see. The coverage had been all over the news; the entire world was holding their breath. She was filled with a mix of emotions: fear at the sight of the armed military officers, excitement to see Assistant Global President Nathan Dunne, and sadness because of the events that were unfolding. She tried to speak, to direct them where to go, but the three men walked right past her with no acknowledgment of her presence. Had they noticed her, she wouldn't have been able to speak anyway with the lump that had formed in her throat.

As they marched down the hall towards the room for what seemed to take them an eternity, they eventually found themselves in front of room 236. Just outside of the room, two other military officers stood guard. They had cleared the rest of the floor for security reasons. Once outside of the room, Dunne's frantic pacing slowed. While all signs surrounding the room pointed towards him being in the correct room, he needed to reassure himself. He peered at the patient's chart just outside of the door.

It read, "Global President Mallory Hansen".

Dunne inhaled deeply to gather himself as a single tear trickled down his left cheek. He pulled out a white handkerchief from the inside of his blazer and wiped it away. The four military officers, still on high alert, awaited for their next instruction from Dunne. After a few moments, he gave a simple nod, signaling them to remain outside of the room before he entered.

Inside of a narrow, elongated, pristine white room, Dunne noticed a bed far off near an enormous window that had the curtains drawn. He couldn't quite make out if who he came to see was in it or not because there appeared to be a physician standing at the bed with his back towards the door. He approached slowly, hesitantly, heart racing, not knowing exactly what to expect. The physician turned to see Dunne walking towards the bed.

"Oh, Mr. Vice President, I didn't realize you were there," the physician said, startled.

"H-how is he?" Dunne asked worriedly.

The doctor sighed. A concerned look came across the physician's face before he spoke. His eyes squinted and his head lowered, as if he were trying to find the right way to break the news to him. To Dunne's surprise, however, the doctor's response differed from what he'd been expecting.

"When he was brought in," the doctor started, "they said there was an attempt made on his life."

Dunne's eyes widened as he looked at the doctor and nodded his head to understand what was happening.

"He... he ah... he was shot in the head," Dunne said.

"Yes, yes… I could see that," the doctor said, with his head still lowered, trying to make sense of what was occurring.

"How bad is it? Will he live? Is he—," Dunne couldn't dare utter what he feared the most, so he stopped himself.

"No… quite the opposite. He's progressing along rather fine," the doctor said, still with a sound of concern in his voice.

"Well then, what is it?" Dunne asked.

"It's just that… well, for someone whose gone through what he's gone through, being shot in the head, he's doing *really* well."

Now Dunne's eyes squinted. He couldn't understand what the doctor was saying, so he walked around him to see the Global President for himself. There he was, bandaged up, tubes going into him and out of him. At the sight, Dunne took a deep breath to hold back the surfacing tears.

"Hard to understand what you mean by 'he's doing really well.' Doc," Dunne said as he observed his leader.

"I know what it looks like; it looks bad, I know, but he's doing much better than how he appears. It's a rather… strange thing. We've run tests, we've gone through all the protocol, and he's responding well to everything, but…"

"What is it? Just say it!" Dunne said sharply, showing his frustration with the doctor.

"He's recovering all on his own. I've never in my twenty-five years of practice seen anything like this. Sure, what we're doing helps his recovery, but the rate in which he's healing is off the charts. When he was brought in, we noticed it was as if he'd already begun healing.

Frankly, what we're witnessing… it's… it's humanly impossible. I don't know what to make of this. I'll give you two some time alone."

Global President Mallory Hansen stood squarely in front of an enormous gold-trimmed mirror inside of the dressing area within his home as his tailor, Eugene, made a few minor adjustments to the break of his trousers before his speech that evening. He glared directly into the reflection of his own eyes, motionless. The suit itself had been handmade by his tailor of cashmere, wool, and silk. It'd turned out perfectly and Hansen, despite his expressionless appearance, had been well pleased with its outcome. The navy blue suit was dark enough to be mistaken for black by those who wouldn't be able to get near him, accentuating the high collared white shirt-which, of course, had been free from any blemish-that complemented the strong jawline of the Global President's smooth face. He'd found time for himself to select the fabrics.

Hansen took excellent care of himself-worked out regularly with one of the world's best trainers, ate the right foods as recommended by his nutritionist-and he appeared much younger than what he was. His face shone with no wrinkles. At least this was as it was told by his admirers. But, of course, there were some. His breathing was slow and rhythmically paced, much as it had always been, regardless of the situation. An occasion where he'd become unglued was incredibly rare and "not what this world needed to witness from a leader," as he'd expressed once during an interview. Hansen's calm and poised demeanor was unlike anyone had ever encountered from anyone in leadership. He'd almost been mechanical, which could be attributed to his high level of understanding of the seriousness of the role in which he'd held.

Humanity had been on the verge of complete annihilation, as every country had risen against the other. Whatever had once held humanity in place had been obliterated. It was country against country, region against region, state against state, city against city, and town against town. Humankind fed upon itself with an unsatisfying appetite, and while the hunger was constant, its belly never became full. It was a snake that had eaten its own tail.

Then came Hansen, who was once head of the United Nations, called upon to restore order and civility amongst them all and, in time, mostly, he could accomplish this. He brought many of the wars to a halt, Nations met and found means of finding peace all under Hansen's guidance making it virtually impossible for anyone to deny the restoration, balance, and order that his administration had put into place. They applauded him, cheered, and he was loved by the people. In a world that was lost and on the brink of meeting its demise, Hansen appeared and had become their savior.

The globe had been separated into four Quadrants, and two Regions divided by the equator and prime meridian. North America, Iceland, and parts of Brazil were inside of Region One, Quadrant One. Europe, Asia, Russia, and the northern part of Africa, as the prime meridian divided it, were inside of Region Two, Quadrant Two. Most of Brazil and the western portion of Antarctica, as the prime meridian divided it, were within Region One, Quadrant Three. Last, the southern portion of Africa, along the equator, Australia, divided it and the eastern part of Antarctica, separated by the prime meridian, was inside of Region Two, Quadrant Four. There were four Quadrant Presidents, an Ambassador for each Region, which had been Wells and Moreno, one Global President, and Nathan Dunne as his second in command.

Eugene finished up and President Hansen began making his way towards the helicopter that awaited him behind his secluded, immaculate home as he made his way to his upcoming press conference.

Nathan Dunne stood bedside, looking over at the man who'd reshaped a world that had been on the brink of complete annihilation. Leaders from across the world had risen and waged war against one another. They created a discord to the likes of which had never been witnessed before in history. There was an absolute collapse at the foundation of civilization causing the United Nations to step in to restore order and above all else, peace. The man at the realm of establishing order was Mallory Hansen.

Hansen passed down punishments, banishments, and judgments that were brutal. During the time, many felt that he was ruling too harshly, and some questioned his authority and position. Those who'd called his bluff and attempted to continue operating however they saw fit found out the hard way that Hansen meant business. He would say that he will restore the earth with peace through any measure required.

He made peculiar comments that most of the public didn't quite understand. He would say that with so much chaos, the world required divine intervention and that his presence and work were a divine order. People chalked it up to being more fancy talk given by another politician. But then, something happened. He began getting things done; he generated results, and he brought the war to an end.

Once the war had ended, there were more peculiar sayings from him such as that his divine calling had appointed him to establish a unification amongst the people. As much as he gave reason to people to critique what he was saying, his actions and what he was able to accomplish was far more impressive and therefore wound up completely overshadowing what he said.

Dunne touched Hansen's hand, causing his eyes to slowly open. When he'd seen that it was Dunne, his eyes lit up and he smiled slightly. His head was heavily bandaged, he'd appeared to be sedated, but the monitor next to bed showed him to have a strong pulse. Dunne hated to see him this way. Absolute darkness and hatred filled his heart for who'd done this to him. Luckily, that same hatred was passed along by those in the building where Hansen was shot during his speech. The culprit never made it out of the lobby.

"Why the long face," Hansen asked, jokingly.

"I can't believe that someone would try this, after all that you've done for them. How could they?" Dunne asked as he shook his head in dismay.

"It is… as it should be… as it should be," Hansen responded.

Dunne wasn't particularly sure what he meant by that.

The two men were silent for some time. There was only the sound of the rain hitting against the window seal outside and the monitor beeping next to Hansen. It was arranged that should anything occur whereas Hansen could not operate in the capacity as Global President, Dunne would step in his place. Hansen had always kept Dunne close, showing him the ropes. They were so close that some were convinced they were related because of the obvious habits and traits in which Dunne had picked up from Hansen, simply by being around him. Dunne looked up to him, cared for him, and relied on him to always be there for him. Today, however, out of all days, Dunne hadn't been there for him and that devastated him.

"With so much happening right now, I want to make sure that I didn't miss the opportunity to thank you for everything that you've taught me," Dunne said.

"Nathan… I'm not… dying today," Hansen said.

The two laughed softly.

Moments passed as reality set in once again.

"You should know… I'll be stepping down. You are to fulfill the duties and obligations of the Global President. I have laid the foundation for you to follow."

"Wait, what do you mean? Where will you be?"

"I'll be around. However, I'll only be available to you. I'll be here for guidance, advice, or whatever other things you may need. The days where my physical presence is being needed within the public eye are done."

"This doesn't make any sense; I didn't envision it happening like this," Dunne said, full of confusion.

"But you did envision it happening, perhaps, not in this manner, maybe."

"So… what does this mean? Is it finished?"

"We're rather far away from things being finished. This is only the start of our prophecy."

"Thank you, citizens, across the world, for joining me today in, what I feel is, a matter of urgency in taking the next steps towards the full unification of our planet. Over the past few years, we have taken enormous strides towards improving the livelihood of every individual on this planet, as many of you can all agree. For a moment, let us all look at what we have all accomplished. We have eliminated the needless casualties derived from warfare amongst one ourselves. Every country has become unified as one and has all become family, accepting of one another as well as all our differences. We have become more patient, more understanding, and more helpful as well as tolerant towards our fellow man."

President Hansen's voice was calming, reassuring, and yet powerful as his tall, athletic frame stood in front of the press delivering his speech. Although his words spoke of things of certainty, hope, and great promises, underneath, undetected, there lied something, yet to be seen; something that was hidden from the public.

"This administration and I have come together and feel that, during this phase, it is now time for us to elevate ourselves to the next level. We have carefully… diligently, prepared this world to evolve into something truly unique; in the eyes of some of my administration, a utopia of sorts. I find it rather astounding that, for so many centuries, humanity has consistently gotten it wrong. Taking care of one another, sharing, and loving has been foreign concepts and ideas since the very beginning of our time. And as we'd reached the very edge…" he paused, as his frustration had grown and had nearly gotten the best of him. "We'd reached… the edge of the cliff, but we stopped ourselves just before it was too late. What has happened, has happened; it is now time for us to look towards the future. We needn't look far because we are standing right where we need to be for us to leap into all that we have ever aimed to be.

"Look around you. We have so many resources and technologies right at our very fingertips, yet we are plagued with diseases, homelessness, and hunger. This is only naming a few of our struggles that are faced unnecessarily in the eyes of this administration. We are solution oriented. From the very start, we made it known that our goal has been to restore and uphold peace amongst all nations. We have accomplished that and now we found it is time to shift our focus and our efforts toward other areas.

"We pondered, how is it that every resource exists on this planet, yet millions suffer and go without each day. We asked ourselves, how could we solve the problems of poverty, hunger, homelessness, and be able to provide healthcare for everyone. Now we have come up with a solution. The plan is to eradicate greed. We will level the playing field and finally, once and for all, do what humanity has failed to do until this point and grant true equality amongst all men.

"You may ask, 'How are we to achieve such a thing?' You might even feel that this is something that has been promised by politicians from the very beginning of time… but it is quite clear that we have become the exception to all that has come before us. All of us are on one accord. We finally have a widespread leadership with a logical goal that is impossible to oppose. Show us the person who does not agree to peace. Point us to the person who stands against true equality. Expose the individual who has attempted to block your freedom. Such a person should be viewed as the enemy and should not be entertained, tolerated, or accepted in any capacity. The people and their government have become aligned. An enemy of yours is an enemy to all.

"It is an honor to represent the world as your Global President but, I must admit, the circumstances in which I've had to come into this role is rather unfortunate. However, that is all behind us, and our future is brighter than it has ever been. As I stand before you, I'd like to officially announce that this administration will implement a global currency system."

There were whispers and mumblings within the media audience intermingled with a rush of camera flashes at Hansen's announcement.

"We have proposed a highly effective strategy that will eliminate poverty, hunger, as well as homelessness on this planet. I cannot stress to you how pleased I am with the diligent efforts that this team has put forth in ensuring that this plan comes together smoothly. There hasn't been a single administration that has come nearly as close to accomplishing half of what this one has done. That isn't to stand before you in a manner of braggadocio, but to point out the differences in how we have approached accomplishing what has held all of humanity at the foot of its neck since the beginning of time. When politicians discuss change and making a difference, you must take a step back and ask yourself, 'What have they really accomplished?'

"Effective immediately, all global citizens will have the opportunity to register their identity in the global identity database to establish their citizenship. Each individual's fingerprint and or forehead will become imprinted with an invisible stamp of citizenship, which will hold information, including payment options, for the convenience of each individual. Those without food and shelter shouldn't worry. No matter what the circumstances were that have led you to such a predicament, the slate will become wiped clean. We will provide you with a home, food, as well as an opportunity for employment within your local government after a screening process has become completed.

"We have become far too complex and have wandered away from human decency and compassion for our fellow man. No one should be without the basic human necessities. We only have one life, and our time spent here shouldn't be one of struggling, misfortune, and anguish. This ridiculous illusion that only a certain type of person can live a life of fortune is absolute nonsense. Every human being will have access to a healthy, safe, and peaceful life. Everyone will have access to all of their necessities.

"Finally, as it relates to matters of religion; we have all seen the damage, discourse, confusion, as well as the interruptions to the lives of those who have lived in manners, in which another individual's religion may, perhaps, be against. How have we put up with this for so long? Yes, of course, through time, we have seen these institutions along with their hateful stances slowly fade, but they are still around. To this, I say, enough is enough! We must remove the head away from religion to reestablish freedom, equality, and love for all. Some may challenge and suggest that those who ascribe to these religions are part of their right and freedom to do so. To this, I say that we shall firmly stand against any institution whose foundation and actions are rooted in hatred and we shall view them as our enemy. From this very moment, I ban leaders and followers of all religious institutions. I will accept an allowance for everyone associated to get their affairs in order, after which, we will transition into a zero-tolerance policy, outlawing the public displaying and practice of any religion. Please, I warn you not to challenge this law."

Photographers and members of the press mumbled amongst themselves at Hansen's astonishing announcement while they continued to snap photos of their global leader.

Hansen then opened the floor for questions. Members of the media began probing him on the specifics behind the global information database and the banishment of all religions. One reporter who questioned how he'd planned to pull off "such a tall order" challenged him.

"What this administration has done and has continued to encourage citizens to do is consistently place the well-being of every individual in the forefront. This means that if there is an organization that falls under the category of being a religion or cult that stands on hatred and inequality, this lies in direct conflict with our mission of ensuring fairness, acceptance, and equality for all. To those who may question how we will pull this off, my answer is by developing a suffocating environment around these religions where it will be impossible for them to operate. It will be against the law itself, leaving them susceptible to all punishments arranged by the court system."

President Hansen was one to never waste his words. His speech was no different. There was far too much for him and his administration to oversee, so opportunities for wasted speech, bargaining, and negotiating were extremely limited. He continued to address the media, standing tall, backing up all that he had said without a waiver. Hansen continued to stress the importance of the Global Identity System and how it would completely reshape society and how everyone functioned. This would be one system that housed all of an individual's information for ease of access. The days would be gone where files, credit cards, and history would become lost; the only thing that mattered now would be the individual.

Then, without warning, there was a thunderous echo that vibrated between the walls of the press room causing a jolt among everyone, then there was a collective gasp, then... stillness...

For a moment, no one moved... except for Hansen.

His tall frame collapsed onto the floor. After silence, there came an uproar of shouts, cries, and screams of agony at the sight of what they were all witnessing.

Security scrambled to rush by their leader's side, yelling, making calls, all in hysteria. Chaos ensued near the exit towards the back of the room as security, along with members of the press, had gotten a hold of someone. They clawed and beat him, triggering a stream of red to run from him. Countless poundings against his ribs soon caused several of them to crack. A gun fell out of his pocket as one of the security guards snatched the shooter away from the ground, bringing him face-to-face. Although now slightly disfigured and battered, the face was still familiar, which sent the guard into a maddening fury.

A reporter.

He'd hidden a gun inside of his camera.

"He's evil! He's the Devil... he's the DEVIL!" the reporter muttered, what would be his last words. Despite his death, the torture and brutality continued against the reporter's mutilated corpse.

Those not involved gathered around Global President Mallory Hansen, tending to him until the medics arrived. Many quickly turned away at the scene; minds and stomach unable to process what lied before them.

The gash…

Skull fragments…

Ripped flesh…

A pool of blood…

Some kept their cameras rolling throughout the madness and broadcasted the entire scene worldwide, live. The screeching outburst of pain, unknown to many, pierced through the thick air. Palms trembled, visions became blurry; it had all been a gloomy haze. It happened so rapidly, unexpectedly. There wasn't time to process what had just occurred.

A moment thereafter, not a single soul could move; everyone had become frozen. Not only inside of the press room, but cars traveling on the outside, teachers, and students within classrooms, lawyers making their last arguments in cases, friends laughing amongst themselves, all became still throughout the entire world. One camera captured an unknown figure, seemingly male, who'd not been at the conference previously, kneeling beside Hansen. Its lips slowly, gently, lowered down towards Hansen's bloody ear to whisper words unheard, not meant for the living, but only the dead. Shortly after, the figure's face carefully rose, now possessing a mask of inhuman terror that no human could bear witness to while in its mortal form of flesh and blood.

The world, now, unfrozen gazed upon Hansen as they began to all bear witness to a miracle in the likes of which they'd never laid eyes on. There was an abrupt movement within his legs, which startled some, then there was twitching in one of his hands. His chest seemed to rise and fall as if he'd taken a breath. Then, something happened with the opened wound; it was as if time had rewound itself. Blood puddles retracted back into the gash within his head, the shattered fragments of skull mended itself, muscle and tissue cells underwent mutation and alas, the wound started healing.

The room filled with confusion, relief, and... *fear*.

2
NEW LEADERSHIP

After the events that'd taken place with Mallory, it was understood why the swearing-in of Nathan would take place in an undisclosed and private location. Although it was being broadcast worldwide, the number of members of the press was only around a handful. Once he was introduced, he couldn't help but think that it was all unfolding, in the same manner, the day they had nearly killed Mallory. He thought about how it may have all gone differently if the assassin had used a more powerful gun. He might've blown Mallory's head completely off. There may have been nothing left of his head to recover from at all, had that been the case. Still, with this all in mind, he approached the podium and became officially sworn in as the new Global President. For the most part, he'd been viewed by the public favorably and his stepping up into Hansen's place had shifted no one's opinion of him into a negative light of any kind.

He was composed, just as Hansen had been. All that he'd learned had come directly from the source, so he was on a mission to carry out the wishes and agendas already set in place by his mentor. After being sworn in, a woman slightly on the larger side, Dunne noticed, approached him, attempting to place a twenty-four-carat gold lapel pin of the earth into his blazer. Her hands were shivering, and she was taking more time than usual. Dunne stood as still as a statue, but his eyes slowly shifted over to the woman's trembling hands that were trying to complete such a simple task. Despite her never looking directly at him, she noticed he was looking down at her. She gave an embarrassed and equally shaky smile to make things less awkward. Finally, she managed to place the pin on him.

"There," she said before quickly scurrying off.

To Dunne, it was obvious; she was terrified of him and she wouldn't be the only person to possess that same level of fear for their new Global President.

After Dunne had been sworn-in, and was now officially recognized as being the new Global President, he shared a few words on his agenda moving forward. The Global President first brought up the tragic events which led to him getting his new leadership role and he spoke about the miraculous improvements in Hansen's health that had already been made. He discussed his plans to continue in the direction in which Hansen had already put into motion as well as implementing many of his ideas, along with help from the rest of his administration, which would aid in the unification of citizens all across the globe. He was an eloquent speaker and people worldwide had taken a liking to him already during his time when he'd been the Global Vice president, so he was a familiar favorite.

Over the next several days, Nathan had constructed a plan to continue what his predecessor had started. The most important thing was to implement a global identity system. He knew it would take more time to get everyone into the database, so he and his administration needed to start the conversion as soon as possible. Luckily, Hansen had already established much of the work, so it was only a matter of someone carrying things out successfully. Once the system was in place, everything else would fall in order. Wars between nations were officially brought to a halt, thanks to the brilliant effort on Hansen's behalf; now it was time to tend to the needs of the people. Poverty rates were becoming completely out of control and to go along with this, record numbers of individuals who had trouble finding food were being reported. This simply couldn't continue any longer.

Dunne stood within the office of his home, holding a glass of one of his favorite pinot noir red wines, overlooking the busy city during the night. He looked out onto the people wondering that if they were willing to make an attempt on the life of a man whose mission and track record was for the unification of all humankind, what would stop them from going after him, his successor, the one who would pick up exactly where Hansen had left off?

A large wooden rectangular table-dimly lit-was centered inside of an old, yet refurbished room. Shelving-filled with books on history, law, and warfare-aligned the room on either side with the same wood as that of the table. The room, which was absent of any windows, wasn't used very often and it was rare, outside of periodic dusting from housekeeping, that anyone ever entered inside. Today, however, was very different, as the tall, heavy wooden door slowly creaked open. Two gentlemen and one female, dressed sharply in tailored suiting, walked inside, removed their jackets, and sat around the table-one gentleman at the head and the other two across from one another. A stern look-as each of them sat silently for a moment's time-rested upon each of their faces as they prepared to commune within one another for as long as it would take. The gentleman seated at the head of the table placed his elbows on the table, hands clasped, with his forehead gently resting within them.

Humanity was at a loss after what had occurred with former Global President Mallory Hansen; he'd appeared to have been murdered in cold blood, but then, moments later, he'd been healed. There just wasn't a clear understanding or explanation of what had exactly taken place. In the simplest sense of the word, it had been a miracle. This was the talk amongst everyone worldwide, and leading this proclamation was Nathan Dunne. President Hansen had now taken a step away from the public scene, and now Dunne was officially named as the new Global President. He stood firmly on executing the plans or orders in which he and Hansen had already put into place, including the elimination of public displays of religious worship.

There was a light knock on the door just before it creaked open once again. A man entered, walked towards a bar area within the room, and carried a small steel tray holding a glass container, white cloths, and three small empty glasses to the table where the three individuals sat. He carefully placed a white cloth to the right of President Dunne, an empty glass to his left, poured water into the glass about halfway full, and then moved to Ambassador Lucinda Moreno and then over to Ambassador Vincent Wells, who sat across from her, repeating the same gestures. Still, there were no sounds other than the smooth pouring of water and the slight clinging noise of the glass water container being sat back onto the metal tray. He placed the metal tray onto the center of the table and exited the room. His departure was confirmed as the lock from the creaking door was flipped upward with a light click.

Dunne reached for his glass and took a slow, long drink as the two ambassadors anxiously, yet respectfully, watched on without uttering a single word. Dunne finished his serving and placed the glass back onto the table.

"Well, then… shall we begin?" Dunne asked.

Moreno and Wells both gestured in agreement.

"There's quite a bit for us all to process after what has taken place over the past couple of months since the attack on Hansen, but I would like to stress to you both that nothing has changed and that all of his wishes will continue to be met. We can already see much of this with the Global Identity System going into effect. A few more weeks are remaining before we go into a full conversion of this system, so if either of you are lagging in ensuring that citizens within your Regions are imprinted, I suggest you expedite whatever is causing any type of delays. We are also, still on schedule with the religious cleansing. There has been an excellent amount of progress, but we still are not quite where I would like for everyone to be. Please be reminded that we will move with full aggression on those who are noncompliant. Statues, figurines, books, absolutely anything that represents some type of god or deity are to be removed. Are there questions regarding this?" Dunne asked.

Wells looked over to Moreno. Neither stated any objection.

"Good. Let's move to—"

"Mr. President," Moreno interrupted, "forgive me, but much of what you are expressing to us is already understood. Hansen has given us his wishes and we see no reason to stray away from what he has envisioned. Simply look at all what he has done for this world. However... there are other questions that linger."

"Such as?" Dunne asked.

"Such as... what exactly happened that day? People are worried. They're worried about the condition of their former President. *I'm* worried. People saw him get murdered and then, somehow, *resurrect himself...* live across the air! People are scared! We've only been able to tell them so much because we know so little. You are the only one who has seen him since this happened." Wells stated.

"We just don't know what else to tell them. We've run out of answers." Moreno added.

Dunne was silent, glancing back and forth at the two ambassadors, creating a feeling of unease amongst them. Wells took a sip of his water to break the sense of awkwardness. It didn't help as Dunne continued staring at them.

"What do you tell them... when people question 'who is Hansen, really?'" Dunne asked them, finally breaking the pause.

"What do you mean, Sir?" Ambassador Wells asked.

"How do you answer them? What is your response?"

"Well, I tell them everything is normal, everything's fine, there wasn't anything out of the ordinary that'd occurred, and that he's just lucky to be okay," Wells replied.

"Hm," Dunne responded.

Wells gave a puzzled look over to Moreno, confused by Dunne's question as well as his response to his answer.

"What about you," Dunne asked, gesturing his head in Moreno's direction, "who do you say he is?"

"Basically, I tell them the same. Like I said, he isn't—"

"No, no, no. I'm afraid that won't suffice," Dunne jumped in.

"Whom… do you… say that he is?"

Moreno hesitated for a second. Was this a trick question?

"He's the President… well, *former* President, with you currently holding his seat. Excuse me if I'm misunderstanding where you are going with this."

"I'm only inquiring as to what your perception of our outstanding leader is."

Dunne's stance was clearly biased. What was Moreno to say in response?

"He certainly has been, *is*, a sensational leader. I don't recall there ever being anyone in history to accomplish what he has. How

Hansen has turned this world around has been truly remarkable," Moreno stated. She'd almost been fishing for the right words to say and dancing around any words that might become taken the wrong way.

"Oh, well, you two deserve some of the credit for how far we've come, right?" Dunne asked, chuckling.

"I don't know," Wells began, "Hansen just stepped right in and said, 'enough is enough' and we basically just followed his lead. There wasn't much else offered from us outside of executing his game-plan for restoring order."

"Ah. You're being modest." Dunne responded. He sat back in his chair, crossed his legs, and then stared up into the ceiling for a moment. Again, an awkward silence filled the room. Wells and Moreno looked at one another.

What was Dunne getting at? This had to be leading somewhere, surely.

"You know I've worked closely alongside him for quite some time now and I just... I don't know... marvel at some of the things that he sets out to do and manages to accomplish." Dunne said.

"Some of the things that he's done almost seem inhuman. It's as if he's... *God*." Dunne released an eerie gasping burst of laughter that carried on, causing the other two to nervously conjure up a laugh of their own.

There was something strange about his statement, behind the laughter, as though he'd genuinely believed that Hansen was God. The atmosphere had become uncomfortable, yet Wells, trying to add more "humor" and break free from their predicament, only made things worse by asking, "what would that make you". Moreno couldn't believe he'd asked him that and her irritated squinting eyes at Wells expressed that clearly.

"Well... I suppose that would make me the Messiah," Dunne answered.

The world grew closer to the final deadline of completing its full conversion into the Global Identity System and the banishment of all public displays of religious practices. Dunne worked endlessly to ensure that Hansen's vision was fulfilled with the help of Moreno in Region One and Wells in Region Two. President Dunne traveled back and forth between each Region, throughout each state, city, and town to monitor everyone's progression towards making its conversion and checking on the status of its housing development for "New World Citizens". There were countless meetings with farmers, builders, scientists, and engineers daily to prepare humanity for its next phase. Dunne had picked up precisely where Hansen had left off.

There had been so much carnage and destruction from warfare that humanity had to enter a stage of rebuilding in many places. There were some areas where there wasn't as much damage, while others were left with no hope. Dunne continued his development of Green and Red Zones worldwide. Green Zones were areas that could be of use for home building, crops, stores, or whatever was necessary for that section. Red Zone areas were of no use or hazardous and had become sectioned off, usually far away from Green Zones. With Hansen already restructuring the world between two Regions and Quadrants, implementing the Global Identity System was one of the last stages towards his world peace initiative. His accomplishments were undeniable, and it'd been difficult for anyone to say otherwise.

Rumors and speculations continued to spread as to whether Hansen had survived the assassination attempt or if the reporter had killed him. There was talk that, although he survived the day of the shooting, he'd passed away from complications in surgery a few days later. People inquired about why he'd stepped down and why he was no longer in the spotlight. For some, Dunne's constant reassurance that he was doing fine simply wasn't enough and his absence caused everyone's longing and desire to see their leader on the front lines once again to grow with each passing day.

"We just would like to know if he's really okay, you know?" a woman being interviewed stated, nearly in tears. "Dunne keeps us all updated, telling us he is, but... we don't know for sure. We just don't. He's done so much for us... I can't-no politician has done what he has. How are we to go on? Mallory Hansen rescued us; we were literally annihilating ourselves, but he saved us."

For many people, Hansen had been their greatest source of help that they'd ever seen, and he was someone that had been reachable; he was a physical being. As time passed, his absence caused the hearts of the people to realize what was once present amongst them. For others, the attempt on his life wasn't surprising. History had shown throughout time how many prominent leaders, serving a just cause, were always killed or, at the very least, an attempt would be made on their life. John Kennedy and Martin Luther King Jr. were frequently referred to as an example of what Hansen had meant to them.

Riots and protests were constantly held to reverse the decision handed down by Hansen, largely to no avail. Rioters were, usually, put into their place quickly by officers, who'd been amped up with exoskeletal technology, underneath their high-grade military uniform, making them much stronger than they were. It gave them a significant advantage over the public to withstand any scenario that might arise. The military officers marched and patrolled throughout the streets of every neighborhood and community, mainly suspected communities where individuals who were possibly not imprinted had lived, within both Regions and all four Quadrants, uniformed in all black, bulletproof vests and stern padding, and gas masks solidifying an intense feeling of intimidation amongst the public. The mere sight of a military officer struck fear and would cause many to flee away, mainly those not registered.

Talks had spread about the many unethical treatments against individuals who hadn't become imprinted; they were being treated unfairly and looked down upon. The worst treatment, however, had come from the officers. Cases were reported, yet went without an investigation, where officers harassed, beat, and sometimes murdered individuals who were not registered. Officers could quickly scan and detect whether an individual was registered or not through specialized helmets and handheld scanning devices, and if they had been, all of their information would instantly become displayed for the officer to see.

Early on, word had spread to avoid any face-to-face contact with military officers because they could scan you without your knowledge. It was illegal to scan an individual unknowingly, but much like other laws, officers overlooked it at their convenience. Whenever questioned by reporters about the practice of their officers, Presidents from each Quadrant, seemingly, were always able to cleverly deflect the question to another ongoing issue. All of the leaders were aligned according to Hansen's vision and Dunne's leadership.

Dunne paid a visit to Hansen's home, within an undisclosed area in Region Two, as he would from time to time, to brief him on all that was occurring as well as the progress that was being made since the attempt on his life had been made. Hansen was having a glass of an extremely rare and expensive Malbec wine within a dimly lit room in his study where he'd often come in to reflect, create notes, and free himself from the stresses of the world. His favorite chair, in which he currently sat, faced an enormous window that gave way to the bright city lights many miles away from where he'd lived.

His face remained in darkness, only appearing as a shadow, with the only light given off coming from a vintage lamp that sat off to the side atop of an expensive handcrafted wooden desk. Dunne sat to the right of him, also partaking in a glass of wine, while two men caught up. Dunne asked about Hansen's health and other topics of small talk and family. After this, most of the questions then came from Hansen. Dunne's admiration for Hansen was incredibly high, and he always remained respectful and humbled whenever he was within his presence. He always managed to simmer down his otherwise boisterous behavior whenever he came in front of Hansen.

"How are people responding?" Hansen asked.

"I would say well, for the most part." Answered Dunne in between a sip from his glass. "There's been significant progress made. We now stand close to seventy-two percent of people becoming imprinted."

"That's not enough," Hansen calmly responded. "I needn't remind you of the importance of ensuring that we reach one-hundred percent, yes? Time… is not something that we have much of."

"Understood, Sir," Dunne said softly. He then quickly tried to shift to more of the positive efforts that had been made by informing Hansen of the co-operation of the religious leaders in the removal of religious artifacts. This had been a major point of emphasis. However, Dunne had also been urged to push even more. Dunne obliged.

As time passed and more reminders were given, the deadline had come along with the fulfillment of all of Hansen's promises; Dunne had seen to it. Some had taken heed to what Hansen spoke of and removed religious texts, artifacts, and symbolisms away from plain sight and had ceased public displays of their faith. Some reconciled within themselves and figured, if their beliefs weren't shown and expressed outwardly, they'd be okay.

Then, some had been slightly more stubborn. Military officers within every country marched in throughout the streets of every city to correct those that did not comply with the new law. Each thunderous stride vibrated against the pavement of every street corner, roadway, and concrete step of sacred religious institutions. Those inside deciding to stand their ground were drug into the streets, torn, battered, beaten, and completely stripped away from the very core of their identity.

They broke the bold down into submission as tears and blood continued to be shed. Screams and outcries were heard from those trying to resist the new law, mixed with cheers for military personnel upholding Hansen's orders. The cleansing of hatred continued throughout the globe for those not in compliance. It had been one of Hansen's greatest orders, outside of his initial call for global peace. World peace had, once upon a time, been a fairy tale, but now as spiritual leaders, who'd been willing to fight to the very end, held their hands across their mouths as they wept at the sights and sounds of the burning pile of sacred texts, Hansen's vision of love and peace was closer to reality than ever before. Though hurt by the resistance of some, Hansen had expressed to Dunne that, overall, he was well pleased.

3
SEEKING JUSTICE

REGION TWO: SOMEWHERE AROUND ~~LONDON~~

Cynthia finished placing the food onto the plates of her family, and their youngest son, Noah, started a prayer to the best of his young ability. Andrew sat at the head of the table and his wife Cynthia sat at the other end, with Noah to her right and their eldest son, Trevor, seated to the right of his father. Everyone had their heads bowed, waiting patiently, as he stumbled through the prayer that his father, Pastor Andrew Dawkins, had taught him. Young Noah fumbled and asked for forgiveness, but his mother assured him that it was okay and encouraged him to continue. Once the prayer was complete, he finished with a bold, "AMEN!"

The family ate in silence, mostly, with Noah making an occasional grunt or playful noise to keep himself entertained. His family had done a good job of keeping him oblivious to the troubles that constantly lurked about them. Their home wasn't what they'd previously purchased; they'd lost it because of their unwillingness to yield to the new law and new ways of doing things. It was against their beliefs to become imprinted and registered into the Global Identity System, as ordered by Mallory Hansen and overseen by Nathan Dunne. The residence in which they'd lived was an abandoned home, hidden deep away within a wooded area along the outskirts of town. There was mold, in which they'd worked endlessly each day to keep under control, and mildew that never seemed to completely go away. The over-saturation and overgrowth of trees covered their *new* home, almost disguising it from appearing to be what it truly was. "This is a good thing," Andrew had told them. "This way, it will make us more difficult to become discovered."

This way of living was easy in trying to convince Cynthia, especially with their young son, but Andrew relied on Trevor, heavily, to help his mother and younger brother in remaining steadfast in their mission. Early on, however, it was also difficult in trying to bring an understanding of their choices to Trevor as well. "Why can't we just live like a normal family?" Trevor would challenge. "We're choosing to live a life of struggle when we don't have to." Andrew would regard such talk as blasphemy and would respond with biblical scriptures and God's promise of His return. Trevor was a believer as well, but during the cold and nights where his stomach ached and rumbled, it became incredibly hard to justify their stance.

They managed to get by the best way that they could without electricity and water. Somehow, they were able to survive by taking each day one day at a time and with the assistance, now and then, from those willing to help those who'd refused to confine to the new ways of society, despite them doing so themselves. These people were known, within the underworld, as *Helpers*.

The number of these people was small, and they weren't organized in any official capacity, but their impact was enormous. It had become a growing trend within the underworld throughout Region Two, with rumors that the same was happening inside of Region One as well. One advocate was a woman named Clara, who'd provided the meal for the Dawkins family that evening. She understood the potential dangers for them that could arise from the family traveling to meet her to get the food, so she didn't mind bringing it to them instead. If anything were to ever happen with their family, where they needed to suddenly evacuate, Clara arranged for them to meet with a fellow Helper, named Tracy, to ensure that they could escape.

That evening, however, she'd raised some suspicion from a military officer who'd, earlier, noticed her enter the woods with a basket covered with a cloth only to return, not long after, with it considerably lighter, judging by how she now carried it. The cloth appeared tucked inside of the basket as if it were now empty.

The officer's eyes squinted as he observed Clara from afar. What had she been up to? What was inside of those woods? Or perhaps, a better question, who was inside of those woods? He'd become quite curious. The military officer looked over to Clara, who'd entered a vehicle parked not too far away, and then he glanced over towards the woods again. He had to quickly choose as to if he was going to follow her or explore whatever it was inside of those woods. Quickly, he jumped onto his motorcycle and followed within a safe distance, behind Clara.

It became late in the evening; the sun had fallen, and the woods were nearly in complete darkness. Back at their home, the Dawkins finished up their dinner and Andrew had gathered his belongings, his jacket, a tablet, as well as his Bible that he'd always kept locked away, and placed it into a satchel, to depart and conduct his sermon for the evening. Cynthia looked on nervously.

"I didn't realize that you were having a sermon tonight," Cynthia said to him.

"It's Thursday; we always fellowship on Thursdays," Andrew responded.

For a moment, there was silence. Trevor continued to sit at the kitchen table watching his parents exchange glances and speak in an unspoken language to one another while Noah circled the home, creating airplane noises with his mouth. Andrew was aware of what his wife was thinking before she said it.

"Just thinking about how things have been lately; the police have been on high alert for anyone out of order," Cynthia said.

"We can't let that stop us; you understand this," Andrew said. "We have to keep the people encouraged, them seeing our consistency will be good for their faith."

"But it has become far too dangerous, Andrew."

"Yes, of course, but this only means that we need to remain careful. It doesn't mean that we should stop spreading the word to the people. We're thankful for Clara and the other Helpers assisting us. You know, should anything go wrong, Clara has made arrangements with Tracy, near the edge of town, to help us in escaping over to Region One. The artificial identification stamps have been arranged for all of us. It comes up inside of the database as if we are actually registered within the system. At any rate, while we're here, my son Trevor is with me; he's a solid fellow that will watch over his father's backside," Andrew joked.

Trevor smiled at his father. He'd always try to find the bright side of things. Despite his light-hearted humor, deep inside of Andrew there was indeed somewhat of a fear. He could never show it or express this to anyone, especially towards his family or congregation. Trevor rose from the table when he saw his father was ready to leave, and the two men said their goodbyes to Cynthia and Noah. Just before leaving, Andrew reminded his wife to blow out the candles.

The moon was full and provided more than enough light for the two to travel about through the woods while it was dark. Trevor, quietly, expressed his gratitude for the moonlight to his father, stating that it was as if the eye of God had been watching over them Himself, but Andrew wasn't entirely thrilled at the lowly hanging full moon.

"That moon… could very well be our betrayal." Andrew countered. "It could be a spotlight that shines down on us and be a giveaway to the officers. Truthfully, I'm a bit nervous to travel underneath it tonight, but we must press on. Your mother was right; the patrolmen have been becoming more aggressive as of late, so we must remain supremely careful." Trevor nodded in agreement with his father.

They walked on deeper into the woods, trying to avoid encountering anything that would make a noise, as the night grew darker and darker. As they traveled further, even with the moon's light, it still became more and more difficult walking along their path. During these outings, whether it was to get food, water, or hold a sermon, they never knew what to expect, which is why they both had sheaths on the sides of the waist to carry their blades. Now and then, whenever there was a creaking noise or an unexpected crackling sound of a branch, the two would suddenly stop, with Andrew reaching back towards his son's chest, signaling him to freeze, as both would reach down to the waist for their knives.

The officer parked down the road a bit from where he'd seen Clara park her car. He spotted her getting out, walking up to a home, scanning her right palm, and then entering. He removed his helmet, stepped away from the bike, and strolled down the sidewalk towards where he'd seen the woman enter the home. It was a quiet neighborhood within the Green Zone, part of the newly renovated areas where homes were provided to those registered in the global database. Your income status would determine the type of home that each citizen would be eligible for if they'd chosen to accept a home from the government and judging by this neighborhood, the woman must've been doing well for herself, the officer determined. What was she doing visiting all the way out in a Red Zone area, he wondered?

He casually walked near her place, noticing that her curtains were drawn, and saw her now reading on a sofa with a gentleman, possibly her husband, seated next to her, watching television. He'd also seen a young child playing on the floor in front of them. At a glance, there didn't seem to be any reason for a woman with a beautiful family with, as it appeared, a lot going on for them to be alone visiting the abandoned woods so far away from where she lived. The officer continued walking along the street, but he knew that something was off, and he didn't plan on letting things go any time soon.

Andrew and Trevor carefully approached a cave-like opening, which appeared to be completely still and abandoned from the outside entrance. Out in front, slightly blocking the entryway, there was an old, wrecked, and deteriorating vehicle that had formed rust all around it. The two checked their surroundings, looking along the sides of the cave and behind them, whence they'd just walked from, within the sheet of blackness that had now set around them.

"Do you see anyone?" Andrew whispered to the other. Trevor shook his head that he hadn't. Even if they were followed, it would be nearly impossible to know for sure. They slowly walked around to the other side of the car, stooped down slightly, and entered the cave. There was more darkness and silence save for the deep sound of breathing that came from the father and son and the occasional flutters and flapping of wings from unseen flying creatures. Their steps were soft and muddy from the drips of water onto the ground, which they'd become accustomed to whenever they would come here. Trevor found it uncomfortable, but it was a necessary part of their mission.

Before Noah was born, Cynthia would join along with them as well. But now that he was here, the journey along with him might put them all at risk, Andrew decided. With the wife and child not joining,

Andrew would teach them, at home, about whatever was discussed during the Thursday meetings.

As they continued deeper and further down into the cave, they began to see a flicker of light, a sign that they were nearly at the place where they were expected. Soon, their pathway opened up to a large area where torches burned from the walls and a large group of unregistered citizens gathered around, faces filled with fear, eyes widened, hoping the on-comers were someone that they'd known and not someone who'd opposed them. After a moment, they could recognize their leader and his son and welcomed them both with a warm embrace and a kiss on each of their cheeks. Each time, their presence brought forth relief, as there was never a guarantee that they would make it to the congregation safely.

After everyone greeted them, Andrew walked towards a small elevated area where he stood before the group of people that had regularly come to see him. He looked over at the people and smiled slightly, as one would to the best of their ability during a troublesome time. Andrew was delighted to see that everyone had made it to another meeting… except…

Where was Jacob?

Andrew looked to Jacob's wife, who'd stood alone, eyes swollen from what appeared to be her crying. His mind filled with the question, to which the answer had already been known, yet needed to be asked. Tears formed in his eyes as well, but he fought to keep them back as the two peered at one another. He asked about her husband's absence and she simply shook her head and muttered, "They took him." Jacob was tough and stubborn against the authorities who sought to neutralize those who'd chosen to defy the law of not publicly displaying their faith. The pastor stepped down and walked toward the woman to console her.

Trevor, standing off to the side as a witness, dropped his head. Whatever happened to Jacob was his choice, he concluded.

The pastor approached the front of the crowd once again and started the sermon, bringing forth hope and restoring faith amongst the people. He reminded them of their purpose in remaining steadfast along their journey and encouraged them to not give in to the temptation of the world by becoming imprinted and registered into the global database as ordered by Global President Dunne. The congregation showed their approval and responded to them with excitement and zeal to continue with their faith for another day.

It was a hard lifestyle, opting not to receive assistance from their government, along with having all their information stored into one database. It wasn't anything too complex, Trevor thought. People were already associated with every social media platform ever invented, yet when the government stepped in to bring forth world peace and hold a record of every citizen within the world, everyone shouted their disapproval. Sure, there had been some sacrifices, but this had been the greatest advancement by any government in world history. Trevor continued to go back and forth within himself as to the validity of their belief system, but he always stood by his father and supported his family, no matter what.

It was the next day. Several black crows squawked high within the trees above the detective as he squatted down, observing two separate footprints along the ground, both moving in the same direction. Someone else had been in these woods besides that lady. These woods had been abandoned for decades without a clean path carved out for visitors to roam around in; it'd been, virtually, a death trap. And the citizens understood this about these woods; it wasn't a place where anyone would ever make a stop to explore.

He glanced around, still squatted, rubbed some dirt from the prints between his right thumb and forefinger, and continued looking to see if anyone was around for him to ask a few questions. He was dressed in plain clothes, so had he run into anyone, there wouldn't be much cause for alarm. Unfortunately for him, however, there wasn't anyone.

After some time, he slowly traced the prints to see where they were headed. The steps remained consistent, both aligned alongside one another, leading the detective even deeper inside of the woods. As he continued further down, unfamiliar noises from unseen creatures echoed all around him, yet he never became startled. He was a veteran, so there weren't too many situations that would cause him to be rattled during this phase of his career. The detective maintained his concentration and carried on.

Up ahead, there was an old beaten up car that appeared to have been there for quite some time. He stopped and surveyed the area, noting several more footprints coming from all different directions that centered in on the area. He pulled his gun from his waist and cocked it back, fully prepared for whatever was to come. The detective noticed the cave opening behind the car, walked around it, still following the multiple prints, and entered inside. Just before stooping down and going all the way inside, he paused for a second, looking behind himself, and considered if he should come back with backup. That would probably take up too much time and besides, it would become dark soon. He turned back around and continued into the hole of total blackness.

The detective took an enormous breath as he reemerged from the cave after being hidden away for hours. The sun was setting and although it was difficult to see, he'd been skilled enough to find his way back up onto the road where he was parked, but first, there was a little more investigating in which he'd wanted to do after what he just uncovered within the cave. He continued, retracing his steps from which he'd come, almost step by step. Eventually, he reached the spot in which he originally started. For a moment he stopped, but then he continued in the opposite direction from where he'd initially chosen to begin his investigation. As he continued, the woods opened up further, swallowing up every spec of light.

Up ahead, the detective noticed, through much shrubbery and overgrowth, what appeared to be someone's home. He stopped. There didn't appear to be any motion anywhere in or around it; the home looked to be abandoned, but he wanted to be completely sure before he continued. He scanned the area and noticed off to the side that there was a massive rock that had been slightly elevated and held an excellent vantage point to view the deserted-looking home. The rock had a smooth flat surface on its top, which allowed for him to lie down across it. A pair of binoculars was pulled from his bag and he began his stakeout. The detective was resilient on settling the mystery of who'd been the owners of the religious texts and artifacts that he found within the cave and ultimately, bringing them to justice. He'd found crosses, paintings, Bibles, and hymns, all of which were severe offenses that were punishable by law.

Patiently, he waited. The temperature had dropped, and a small drizzle of rain started to fall. The elements didn't seem to faze the detective as he managed to maintain his poise. He was still, quiet, as he continued his focus on the home. Anyone else would have seen that no one had lived within this place for quite some time and would have moved along, but not him. He was set on discovering what he'd already known the answer to. Those prints, that cave, whomever they'd belonged to, had something to with this home. There weren't other homes within these woods for miles, therefore, given the distance from this place, the cave, as well as the footprints, there had to be a connection, the detective reasoned within himself.

A sudden flicker of light was seen through his binoculars, startling him and caused him to jump by surprise.

Inside of the home, Trevor and his father sat in their living area in front of a candle that Cynthia had just lit and brought before them. Noah, off to the left, played on the floor close to the kitchen while his mother prepared the food that her eldest son and her husband hunted earlier that day.

"There's something that never manages to escape me. That's the knowing of whenever something is troubling my family, even without them ever speaking a word. I've been observing you and, even more so as of late, I see that something has been weighing heavily on you," Andrew said to his eldest son.

Trevor knew his father would pick up on his frustrated mood, eventually. He was right; he was good that way. Trevor's father was a leader, therefore, a heightened sense of awareness for his flock was a necessary trait. Trevor deeply sighed.

"Our faith has kept us; it's all that we've ever known. I understand what it has done for us and the significance of what having faith in God means for this family. However, I can't help but wonder if holding onto our faith and living within the shadows will soon lead to our demise," Trevor responded.

Andrew dropped his head and sighed.

"How can we turn our backs against the God who had sustained us for so long? Why would we do such a thing?"

Andrew had long suspected that Trevor had been harboring these emotions, but he didn't understand why his son would feel that way, considering how much he'd been taught during his upbringing.

"It's not about us stopping our faith; it's now become about the survival of this family. We're living within the shadows, it's becoming increasingly more difficult to get food, and I fear it is only a matter of time before they place us within a scenario where we will have to fight for our lives. We have to think of Noah and your mother."

"Trevor, we must remain steadfast in our faith and trust and believe that all of our needs will be met. Without faith, what you have said will all be correct, but by holding on to our faith I am confident that, despite how things may seem, this family will be just fine."

"We're not fine," Trevor said as he shook his head. "You're placing our lives and the lives of others in danger. The only reason I remain is to protect mother and Noah, otherwise, I would have fled." Andrew was disappointed to hear his son speak this way, but he'd noticed something in what he'd said, which gave him hope.

"I understand, son. However, you say that had it not been for your mother and your little brother, you would have fled; if your belief against what I speak is so strong, why wouldn't you simply become imprinted, be able to have all the things in which you need, be able to help your mother and brother, and live a better life? Then, there would be any need for you to flee. That you haven't done so lends me to believe that there is some amount of belief within you. Your love for them would outweigh all."

The young man now sat alone to himself after his father patted his knee, arose, and walked away.

The detective had developed a case against Andrew Dawkins and his family and brought his findings to the attention of his Sargent, asking him for permission to seek an arrest warrant. After explaining all the details and informing him how he'd noticed Clara assisting them within the woods and how he suspected the father of conducting sermons inside of the cave that he'd found, the Sargent asked the detective if he'd questioned Clara. The detective responded that he hadn't because he didn't want her to alert them before they issued the arrest warrant, which could potentially lead to the family escaping. The Sargent understood and approved the detective's request.

Several nights later, Trevor had trouble sleeping as he lied wide awake in bed, eyes gazing directly into the ceiling of the old cabin. He wasn't sure what had been bothering him. Perhaps it was the disagreement that he and his father had a few nights prior that had gotten to him. Why hadn't his father understood where he'd been coming from; the danger that he continuously kept his family in? It was completely unnecessary, Trevor thought. They'd chosen to live poorly simply because the government wanted fairness and equality for everyone. What they'd asked hadn't been too unreasonable; surely God would understand things from their perspective, especially since they'd served Him for long. He knew where their hearts were... hadn't He?

As Trevor tossed around conflicting thoughts as he lied in bed, just outside of the front living area window, within the darkness, dark shadowy silhouettes of men in eerie gas masks crept carefully around the Dawkins' residence. It was the detective and his men gathered together, preparing for an ambush.

He wasn't completely sure if he'd heard something or not, but Trevor's thoughts became interrupted and he abruptly sat up in bed. His eyes scanned around the unlit room, trying to see what had broken his process of reasoning within himself. There was nothing, only quiet, yet his stomach was uneasy. His gut was informing him that something was happening, but he did not know what it was. Then, the bedroom door flung open and Trevor saw a tall dark figure, quickly storming towards his direction. His heart pounded as a rush of panic suddenly rose inside of him. As the figure got closer, he recognized it to be the familiar face of his father, Andrew. Andrew's eyes were bulging out of their sockets and perspiration drenched his forehead, as panic had become covered across his face.

"*Men are surrounding the house, military officers,*" he said to Trevor in a shaky and frightened whisper, "they're coming to take us. We have to leave right now."

"Wh-what do you mean?" Trevor asked while stumbling out of his bed. "How did they find us?"

Andrew responded he wasn't sure how they'd been discovered, but that they'd need to hurry if they wanted to avoid being captured.

The Dawkins' had prepared for situations such as these, conducting drills for what they would do in case of emergencies, but they never had to implement what they'd gone over. Judging by Andrew's face and the terror in his voice, Trevor knew that this had been the real thing. Outside of their home, the father and son had installed silent triggers on the grounds which would alert Andrew with an aggressive buzz from a wristwatch that he would never take off. While asleep in bed, next to Cynthia, and their son Noah in between them, the watch vibrated and jerked Andrew's left arm, causing him to jump instantly to his feet. He stealthily crawled along the floor of their home, carefully peeping outside of the windows to see what had set off the alarm. That is when he saw the shadows slowly approaching their home, holding what appeared to be military-grade assault weaponry.

Cynthia was alerted as she grabbed hold of Noah and headed into Trevor's room, where their elder son and his father had prepared a hidden door beneath the floorboards some time ago, which led to a secret passageway underground and away from the home. The family moved quickly underneath and evacuated.

One of the officer's masks came close against one of the living room windows as he peered in, standing from the side, searching for any movement or signs of life who were subject to severe punishment for their deliberate crimes against the world government. He'd stood still for a moment and from the inside looking out the window with the military officer on the other side set against the dark midnight sky, it appeared to be a terrifying painting within a movie scene.

There was quiet. Then a silent order was given by one of the men, followed by an explosive sound of the Dawkins' front door being shattered as the officers rammed through with a battering ram. The sound vibrated the ground underneath, causing the family to stop within their tracks and look back while the dirt from underground fell around them. They'd known by that sound that whatever piece of life that they had remaining was now gone. The only thing that remained was whatever lied before them.

Andrew motioned for the family to continue. Cynthia, holding their son Noah, was right behind him, followed by Trevor who couldn't help but wonder about how all of this could have been possibly avoided had they all just fallen in line with the new way of things. However, as his father had questioned him, why hadn't he gone out on his own and complied with the new order of life? These were the consequences: House raids in the middle of the night.

There was complete darkness underground except for the father and his eldest son carrying flashlights, and even with some form of light, it simply wasn't enough to eliminate the suffocating cloud of darkness engulfing the small family. The mother continued to try quieting the small child, who continued his inquiry about what was taking place.

"How much farther is it?" Cynthia questioned her husband frantically.

"Just up ahead. We should be approaching the opening shortly," he answered.

Training for officers was a strenuous and intense process, much like one would go through as an actual member of the military. The program was structured as though they were preparing for war, which caused a rift among some members in the public. Why have regular, every day officers go through such a vigorous form of training as if they were in combat if the government had proclaimed that there was no peace within the land? Naturally, the public felt as though they had been training to combat against them, the everyday citizen.

Inside of the home, six military officers turned over and destroyed any and everything around them, for pleasure, but primarily to locate the family which had supposedly lived there.

"There's nothing. No one is here," one man said in a muffled tone caused by the mask.

"Maybe they were tipped off and escaped," another answered while continuing his search. "Someone's definitely been here recently."

The *soldiers* continued their destruction of the home out of frustration at not finding what they'd come searching for. Windows were shattered, they broke furniture into pieces, and all that was left of the Dawkins's home were quiet, unspoken memories.

The detective who'd been heading the investigation began thinking to himself. *There's no way that they would have known that we were coming. It wasn't impossible, but... no way! They were here, but where could they have gone so fast? Wherever they'd escaped to, they couldn't have gone too far.*

"Men, check the floorboards. Touch every single thing in here. Tear down the walls if you have to." The lead detective, who'd also been dressed for combat, ordered. It delighted his men to do so, and they intensified their search even further. The home was now barely standing when one man from inside of Trevor's old room called out to the others that he'd found something, causing them all to scramble into where he was. The six men carrying their firearms all gazed down into a hidden door that led down to absolute darkness.

The detective pulled out a flashlight and aimed it down into the hole, revealing several steps that dropped into some sort of secret passageway. One man announced that they'd hit the jackpot. The detective stepped away and peered outside one of the shattered windows into the distance, while the rest of the men joked about who would be the first to go down into the hole. Meanwhile, the detective noticed something moving, perhaps an animal. He wasn't sure and squinted to see if he could make out what it was. It appeared to be something coming from underneath the ground.

Andrew emerged from underground on the other end, quickly scrambled onto his feet, and extended his hand towards his wife and younger child. Noah was pulled out, Cynthia, and then Trevor climbed out after them as the detective looked on from the distance. His deep breathing echoed eerily through the filter of his mask in the same way an animal does once it has set its sight on its prey. He then stormed through a busted wall frame, destroying what was left of it, to pursue the Dawkins family. One man snatched a cross down that had been barely hanging from a remaining piece of a wall as they followed behind the detective.

Aligned perfectly next to one another with their leader slightly in front, guns carried across their chest, the soldiers marched swiftly through the woods towards their target. The detective was right about everything in his investigation, as he always was, and now he was on the verge of closing yet another case. One thing led to another through a matter of connecting the dots and just up ahead, running away from the law, was his grand prize.

Trevor paused, looked behind him, and saw the soldiers pacing towards them ferociously. While there had always been the anticipation of what he might think, act, or feel if he'd ever encountered or became a target for one of the soldiers, never could Trevor have imagined feeling the level of terror that came over him at that moment. They were helpless. There was nothing they could do to escape the hands of these trained military soldiers, who portrayed themselves as everyday police officers.

"*Dad…* we have to run. We have to run!" Trevor screamed. The mother turned around, holding young Noah, and experienced the same wave of fear that had come over her firstborn.

"*Dear God,*" she whispered.

"Run, run! Give Noah to me!" Trevor demanded while pulling Noah, whose eyes were filled with tears, away from his mother.

The lead detective and general made a hand signal, and the rest of the soldiers broke off into opposite directions within the dark woods, still in pursuit of their targets. As the Dawkins family continued towards the edge of town to meet Tracy, who would help them cross over into Region One. The sound of the detective firing warning shots from his automatic weapon into the air suddenly startled them. They all flinched but continued with their pacing; knowing that if they'd slow down for a split second, it would cost them their lives.

Within the darkness, amid the woods surrounding them, the sounds of footsteps became closer, signaling that the soldiers were gaining on them. Cynthia was becoming winded and lagged behind. Trevor turned to see his mother struggling, handed Noah over to

Andrew, and told them to continue. Andrew tried to insist that they remain together, but Trevor assured him they would catch up. Clinging on to her son, Cynthia expressed she wasn't sure if she'd be able to continue.

There were more warning shots, but this time there was more cause for worry, as the shots now sounded much closer. Their doom was near. Andrew could feel it, but he ran with everything that he had with his son hanging onto his back. After some time, he noticed he didn't hear his wife and son behind him, causing him to stop in his tracks. He placed his son Noah onto his feet, as they both peered behind them into the blackness.

"Where-where is mum?" the little boy asked.

"I don't... I don't know," Andrew answered in between his breaths. For a moment they continued to gaze behind to see if they would appear, but deep down, Andrew knew they should keep running. Noises were coming towards them, and they risked standing there to see what was approaching them. As if they were spat out of a black hole, Trevor and Cynthia fell forward from out of the dark.

Trevor—on the ground with his mother—was gasping for air from the burden of trying to carry her along.

"I told you... I told you to continue, to keep going." Trevor said.

"We realized you weren't behind us; I tried to see where you were." Said Andrew.

"We'll make it. You and Noah have to get to—" Trevor never got the chance to finish his sentence.

The end of a gun collided with the side of his face, rendering him unconscious. The soldiers caught up to them and ambushed them from the sides of the woods. They emerged from the night as if they were a part of the darkness themselves and slowly, the detective came forth from behind the mother and son. Andrew's eyes bulged as his first thought was to turn around, run, and leave behind everything. As soon as the thought came, his body reacted. He turned around and fled, leaving behind everything, Trevor, his wife, who'd been left crying out to his name in the night, and Noah, who had been right there next to him when his body took off.

There was nothing I could do, he'd told himself. Trevor and Cynthia were grabbed as she continued to scream out for her husband, who'd now disappeared into the night. She screamed in anguish at her husband, who'd chosen to desert his family. *He'd chosen himself*, she thought. *Why hadn't he grabbed their son? Why?*

The officers communed among themselves, deciding whether they should continue after him, but they'd chosen not to. While the detective really wanted to get his hands on Andrew, he figured that they'd gotten enough to satisfy what he was after; at least for now. Andrew questioned himself, but he continued running. Noah was within arm's reach. He was right there, but now he was in the arms of the military officers.

Noah's father ran until he couldn't any longer. His body fell onto the ground and he simply lied there, weeping.

4
Backup Plans

There was a knock on the door. After more time had passed, a middle-aged woman answered and witnessed a man dressed in his sleepwear standing on the other side. He stood before her, head drooped down into his chest without speaking a word. The woman asked if she could help him, and through much sniffling, the man finally spoke.

"Tracy?"

The man was invited in, given tea, a blanket, and everything else to bring forth comfort. Tracy grabbed herself a cup of tea as well and sat next to him inside of her living area. Tracy asked about his well being along with that of his family. Andrew, unable to speak, simply shook his head.

"Very well then," Tracy began, "whatever has taken place, which I prefer for you to never reveal, has occurred during this evening, and since we don't know if the pursuit has concluded or not, we must get going. There's a lot that we must get done, so we have little time to waste. The police could still be after you."

Andrew looked down at his trembling hands. He tried to hold them tightly to prevent them from shaking, but the trembling simply wouldn't cease.

"Follow me," Tracy said as she grabbed hold of his hands.

Inside of a storage area, behind Tracy's home, Andrew sat on a stool as Tracy began preparing everything from her mock imprint kit. She had him come over to insert his right hand inside of a scanner to obtain the image. After a few moments, a digital image appeared on a computer monitor and a printer began printing out a clear film replicating the inside of his palm. Once it was ready, she turned, walked over towards him, and asked Andrew to hold out his hand.

"Try to be as still as possible for me, okay?" she asked with a slight grin.

With gloves and a pair of tweezers, she carefully began laying the clear film over his palm. Tracy told him to keep his hand out and to not touch anything so that the film could quickly dry. She was able to hack into the global database and temporarily register his prints into the system, which would allow him to receive all the benefits of any registered citizen.

"Now, your identity will show within the system, but it will only be visible for one month. We don't need to actually implant you with an identity device because the film will display within the database that you are imprinted with one. However, the system does conduct monthly fraud scans, and it's able to verify the authenticity of all registered citizens. It's a rather sophisticated system, so they will be able to trace it after some time.

"You will need to peel away the film after the month is up, otherwise, your location will be traced since we are using their tracking system after all. It will already be in their possession. Questions?"

All the information that Tracy gave him was going way over his head. He only needed the most important information, which was that he only had one month of being a registered citizen and that afterward, he would need to take away the film.

For a second, he considered what a life would be like if he was permanently imprinted and registered within the global database. All the obstacles, needing to hide, and worries would become erased in an instant. Then, he was reminded of his family and all that they'd stood and fought for, causing him to snap back into reality. He was back inside of the shed behind Tracy's home, nodding to show to her that he'd understood everything that she'd said.

The two arrived at the airport, and Tracy began going over everything as far as what to expect once he stepped inside. She gave him an ID and a passport, all of which matched the information on him inside of the global database. However, they served only as additional forms of verification, since the imprint displayed everything about him needed.

"The moment that you enter Region One, the most important person to you is Naomi. The Helpers are a global underground network established to assist individuals like you. I can only help you up to this point. Naomi will help you once you arrive."

"How will I be able to find her?" Andrew asked.

Tracy sighed.

"That will be a challenge for you to figure out. The only thing that we know is that she's somewhere around the New York area. This is where you're headed," she said, handing him his flight itinerary.

The two sat in silence for a time. She knew that there must have been dozens of questions circling around in his mind, so she wanted to allow him to say whatever was on his mind before his flight.

"What are the chances that I will hear from my family again?"

She thought about Andrew's question for a moment, trying to decide the best way in which she should answer him.

"We're directly in the middle of this thing now and we have to be absolutely honest with ourselves and consider the worst of possibilities to be better prepared. We have to assume that your entire family has or will become killed. Begin accepting this as a reality so that you can move forward. The sooner that this becomes real for you, the sooner you'll be able to figure out what being able to survive within the wild will look like. It's time to look towards your future."

Tracy handed him a duffel bag from her back seat that she'd brought along with them and told him that a change of clothes was inside.

"Remember, you are not to answer or respond to the name Andrew Dawkins ever again. Your name is Jared Wheeler," Tracy said.

Andrew nodded, took the bag, thanked her for everything, and headed towards the entrance.

As soon as Andrew stepped inside of the airport, he noticed cameras-too many to count-scanning the entire premise. A few of them seemed to lock in on him. Noticing this, he immediately tried to hide his face and evade being recognized by his true identity, so he searched for a restroom so that he could change out into the clothes given to him by Tracy. He didn't notice, however, the military officer eyeing him from a distance.

Once he'd found one, he entered a stall, dropped his bag, and the tears began to flow again. He covered his mouth to avoid making any noise that would cause any type of unwanted attention, as his sobbing came to the point of being unbearable.

He heard someone enter the restroom, and he quickly gathered himself as he heard footsteps slowly making their way around the enormous gentlemen's lounge. Andrew heard the creaking sounds of doors being opened, one by one, coming closer and closer to where he had been hiding. He started to panic as his paranoia took hold of him. Whoever it was, clearly weren't looking to relieve themselves. His heart slammed against the inside of his chest, knowing that they would capture him.

It must be an officer!

They must've found me!

I have to get out of here!

Creak...

Again, the officer had become even closer.

He braced himself, changed his clothing, and decided that it was now safe for him to leave the stall. Remaining heavily cautious, his head protruded from the entrance of the restroom, looking to his left and then right, before proceeding out. He didn't see anyone. Perhaps they were on the other side or had maybe given up on finding him. Andrew wondered who it was that was pressuring him on the inside of the restroom, but he couldn't dwell on it for too long; he had to get moving. He tried to settle down by telling himself that everything would be fine, but it was rather difficult to do considering the risk of attempting to enter Region One without truly being a registered citizen. Ticket and duffel bag in hand, Andrew hurriedly made his way to the ticket counter.

Once he'd reached the counter, he was pleasantly greeted by a young woman with long blonde hair, who'd seemed to have already been on her third cup of coffee for the morning, seeing how energetic she'd been. At almost a whisper, Andrew gave a basic hello which was almost an exact contrast to the greeting she'd given him. She continued saying something, but her voice faded into the background as Andrew looked around the airport for whomever it was that seemed pressed on catching up with him. He then abruptly came to himself and realized that the woman had been asking for his passport and flight itinerary. After passing them along to her, she smiled as she began studying over the information.

Built into the counter, he examined a metal contraption with an opening which appeared to be used for something to be inserted. He wasn't sure; the device had been rather foreign to him. The woman handed him back his passport and boarding pass as she smiled at the gentleman who'd clearly never seen an imprint scanner. However, it was time that he'd become introduced to it.

"Now, if you could please insert your right hand into the scanner," the blonde hair woman requested.

He stared at the scanner, not moving an inch. Then, his eyebrows raised as he looked at the woman.

"What's the purpose of this? I haven't flown in quite some time, so this is very new to me," Andrew said. He quickly tried to conceal the fact that he'd been completely away from civilization for quite some time.

"Ah, well, it's mainly for security reasons, but it also helps to ensure that the information on your flight itinerary matches the information on your imprint. It's quite convenient," she cheerfully replied.

Andrew was nervous, but he also knew that he had to move quickly as his hand carefully inched inside of the imprint scanner with its glowing green neon lights gliding smoothly upwards and downwards. Microbeads of sweat began forming across his forehead while he attempted to maintain his composure. Once his hand was fully inserted, the scanner beeped once.

"Okay, just keep your hand inserted for just a second, please," the woman said.

Andrew did not know if the film layered across his hand would properly read as him being registered within the database. *And who was Tracy, anyway; how could she be trusted*? How could she be so sure that this would work? This could've all been one massive set-up.

The machine beeped again, and the green neon lights stopped their motion and turned a dark red.

"Hmm," the woman said, scrunching up her eyebrows, "it seems like there was some type of error."

Andrew's heart pounded furiously. This was it; he was finished. This entire journey all to be captured. Perhaps he would've made it out better on his own instead of relying on Clara and her Helper buddy, Tracy. They were all connected: the military police and the Helpers; he thought. He scanned around the airport again and found the exit, thinking that maybe he could still make a quick getaway if he needed to. If he were to make a run for it, he'd have to do it now.

"These machines are so new, there's bound to be a glitch here and there," she said, smiling. "Why don't you pull out your hand and try it again."

Hesitantly, Andrew did as she said.

Again, the green lights started into their random motion, awaiting to scan Andrew's palm, expose him for who he truly was, and finally, seal his fate. There was no way around this system; the government had made sure of that.

Beep.

"See, there we are! You're all set. Have a safe flight, Mr. Wheeler."

Andrew instantly became relieved as he continued, passing through a few other checkpoints, successfully, en route to boarding his plane to Region One. In his head, he began taking back all the doubts that he had about Tracy and Clara, the hidden motives they must have had, and became incredibly grateful for all of their help, but the feeling was bittersweet. He couldn't help but wonder about whether his family had been alive or dead after he'd abandoned them in the woods.

As she began entering the train, Melanie's heart started to race, releasing a feeling that she'd been feeling more now since the announcement. The rush of the crowd, getting on and off of the train, provided little help towards her increasing anxiety. She never understood why people wouldn't allow riders to get off of the train first, so they could get on smoothly. That was one of her many brilliant ideas that she sarcastically thought about right after some fancy guy tried to aggressively maneuver his way through her.

She gave him a slight nudge, a warning, to let him know that what he was attempting wouldn't be tolerated. There was too much of a fuss taking place. Apparently, the jerk was in some sort of hurry because he attempted the move again, this time even more aggressively. However, everyone in that filthy subway was in a hurry. Perhaps, he'd felt that because it was a lady, he'd be able to get away with it, but this mindset would never pass over on Melanie and what he'd been able to get away with on so many other occasions would never be accomplished through Melanie. She accepted the challenge and delivered a mild elbow to his ribcage, causing him to stumble back slightly. He'd angrily asked what her problem was, and she responded he was, in fact, the one with the problem.

As usual around this time of the morning, the train was filled to its capacity, mainly with individuals whose jobs were downtown, which were a few blocks away from the grocery store Melanie was heading to. From the front of the train to the back, women and men were dressed in their expensive garments meant to showcase their status and prove to themselves-but mainly others-that they belong. She looked at them, both young and old, engaging in conversations with one another. Most of their dialogues were about business.

Towards the front there was a couple whom she'd seen often on this train in the past, arguing as they normally would. They were regulars and rather familiar to everyone there, and their routine was one that everyone had already seen on many occasions. It was obvious when the girl slapped the guy, and everyone continued reading the daily news from their phones and continued in their conversations without so much as lending a glance over in their direction.

It was the same old script that had replayed repeatedly, but things now had started to just feel… different. Melanie could tell that there was a shift in the atmosphere. All of what had always seemed so familiar and normal had now become strange, although all appeared to be the same as it had always been. There was a change taking place. Melanie wasn't the only person to notice it; everyone was aware of the changes that were on the horizon. How would they all be able to adjust, this was the question for them all.

Melanie's thoughts bounced around, much like the train had, on her way downtown to Flannigan's *Groceries*. Many companies had already transitioned to the Global Identity System to accept payments, but Flannigan's had been one of the few remaining stores that still accepted card payments from consumers. Even the transit systems were planning to make the switch which would make moving around nearly impossible for those unwilling to register their identity into the global database. Melanie was amongst those not on board to do so.

Flannigan's Groceries was named by the family's store owner, who had passed away, but his daughter Alicia and his son Kaleb now ran it. His name was Calvin, but he'd always wanted to create a business that held their family's last name. Calvin was known as a warm and kindhearted man who'd always been willing to help in any way that he could. His store rested in a small, secluded residential area downtown, which made it easier for everyone to get to him within the community. He was big on giving back to the community; he was all about service. In his later years, he'd brought his kids in to help him out a bit more and show them how the business was to be run. Alicia was all about the numbers and Calvin would have to often remind her that, "It's about the people; it's not about the money." He told her to never forget that, but it continued to be one of her weaker points, even after her father's passing. Kaleb, however, was able to create the perfect balance to capture the spirit and culture of what the store had always represented.

Melanie made it to her stop and headed up a few blocks to Flannigan's. As she walked in, the door chimed, alerting Kaleb, who had been looking down at his phone behind the front counter. He smiled slightly when he noticed her, but it quickly faded when she didn't look in his direction. Although Melanie, not looking his way, wasn't purposely done, Kaleb's flirtatious advances towards her were sometimes annoying. However, he was persistent, and she found that to be an intriguing quality. There wasn't anything to be made of it, as far as Melanie was concerned, because she'd just gotten out of a difficult relationship, so starting anything new was out of the question.

With Alicia being older, with every conversation and through every action, she found a way of reminding Kaleb of who was in charge of things around the store. One would think that she'd been his mother, although she was only a few years older. She watched as her little brother lit up gleefully when Melanie entered the store, causing her head to shake in disapproval.

"You look like a fool." She told him.

Kaleb gave her a scowl. Then his eyes began to quickly scan the small store to find Melanie again. His heart began beating frantically when he wasn't able to locate her as fast as he'd wanted to, but soon all was well again when he found her.

It was as if he felt himself floating away despite him knowing that his feet were planted on the ground. Blinking no longer was a priority because it meant that a second would fleet away from him not seeing Melanie; a risk he'd been unwilling to take. Her dark hair was pulled back away from her face, as it normally was, revealing her soft brown complexion across her smooth, rounded face. He was completely drawn into her piercing, dark eyes. While most people thought her appearance and demeanor to be stern and uninviting, there was something about her that drew Kaleb in. She'd just been misunderstood by people. Kaleb understood, however, and was willing to be patient enough to learn that which he didn't understand. There were times during the night when sleep eluded him, causing him to lie awake thinking about her. What was it about her? Was it the idea of pursuing her that attracted him? No, that couldn't have been it. Melanie was something more.

She was just so—

"Hey!" Alicia interrupted, slapping his arm with a folder. "Don't forget that these taxes have to be filed by Thursday. I showed you how they're done, so it's time for you to get on it."

"Yeah, yeah. I haven't forgotten," Kaleb responded. Alicia stared at her brother intensely.

"What? I said I'll handle it!" Alicia glanced out of the corner of her eye towards Melanie, then back towards Kaleb.

"Wish you'd pay attention to our business as much as you do... *other* things; you're wasting your time daydreaming about that woman. Move on."

"Relax, alright? You're out of line," her brother shot back. He looked over his shoulder to see where Melanie was so that she wouldn't hear what he was about to say next.

"Besides... I hear she's single, so it—"

"So what?" Alicia fired back.

"Whatever, Alicia. I'm done with this."

"You need to be done with her," Alicia said as she stormed away. An irritated Kaleb tried to switch gears and find his love again.

Great, there he goes, staring again. Melanie thought to herself. If he thought for one minute that she was even somewhat interested in dating him, he was wrong. Alicia's eye rolls towards her were becoming a bit much as well. If she kept it up, Melanie would have to display another side of herself. What was her problem, anyway? Surely, she didn't think anything was going on between her and her brother; he was a joke. If that was in her mind, she'd be sadly mistaken. Every time she entered the store, it would be the same reaction from those two. It just wasn't the same since their father passed. Melanie remained quiet and completely minded her own business. They were lucky if they'd received any type of greeting from her, and even then, it would be to Kaleb, who'd speak first. Alicia would pretend that she was busy so that she wouldn't have to acknowledge her; which had been fine by Melanie.

Melanie grabbed her final few items and made her way up to the front counter where her admirer awaited. She took a few deep breaths (for whatever reason, she'd been feeling more tired than usual) and walked to the front. She quickly glanced, and sure enough, Kaleb was eyeing her. At that moment, she thought of other stores she could go to next time. The problem was that Flannigan's was probably the closest, which came in handy with the fatigue that she'd been feeling.

"He-hey," Kaleb stuttered as Melanie began placing items onto the counter.

"Hi, Kaleb," she responded unenthusiastically; eyes lowered, trying not to exude warmth of any kind.

"You-uh… find everything okay?"

"Sure did."

Melanie's eyes roamed around the store as she waited for Kaleb to finish scanning her items and without surprise, there was Alicia, eyes fixated on her. At that moment, a wave of heat started rushing over Melanie's body. Her heart raced, and her mouth was watering.

"Hey, what is your problem, Alicia, huh?" Melanie exploded, she'd finally cracked.

"Problem? I have no problem," Alicia said, slowly approaching the counter.

"Yeah, well, it seems that way! You two keep eyeballing me as soon as I come into this place."

"No, Melanie, it's not like—" Kaleb started before getting cut off by his sister.

"Oh, you most certainly have a choice to go elsewhere, now don't you? But we both know the reason you don't." Alicia shot back. Melanie sighed.

"Is that what this is really about because truthfully, I feel like this might be about something else." Melanie rolled her eyes at him.

"*Please*… I'm only trying to run a business here and there are certain standards and means of doing things we try to adhere to. For instance, in case you are not aware, the world is transitioning to the Global Identity System, which will be used for all transactions. So, forgive me because I couldn't care less about your little… *crush* that you have on my brother. Now… how will you be paying on today?"

"Wow… for *starters*, there is absolutely *nothing* going on with your brother and me." Kaleb felt destroyed hearing Melanie say those words, but she was angry. She was liable to say anything at that moment. "Second," Melanie continued, "I am well aware of what the plan is, but the last time I checked, Flannigan's Groceries accepts alternative payment methods. So, sweetheart, until that day comes where you no longer do, I'll be using my card for all of my transactions with you." Melanie fired.

"That day is coming sooner than you think, dear."

"Well, it's not today, is it? Didn't think so." Melanie slammed her card down onto the counter, paid for her groceries, and stormed out of the store.

"You've got to be kidding me, Alicia! What the hell is your problem?" Kaleb asked.

"Grow up, Kaleb. You need to focus on sustaining this business. Do you realize how many mom and pop groceries have had to close? We should be lucky to still be around. Much of that is because of the changes that I convinced dad to make before his passing." Alicia said to him.

"Are you seriously taking credit for us still being in operation right now, because that would be disgusting if you were?" Kaleb sarcastically asked.

"It's the truth." Alicia began walking off until she added one more comment. "Oh, and uh… you heard what she said, right? There's nothing between you two, so you can move on now."

Melanie was so irate as she shuffled through the crowded streets and made her way to the train station, carrying her small bag of groceries. She tried her best to place her mind on something else, away from Alicia and that stupid Global Identity System, but it was impossible as every jumbo advertising screen throughout the city displayed an ad reminding everyone of the deadline to register and how simple it would make life for them.

She felt like the world was caving in all around her; life, as she'd always known it, was unraveling slowly before her very eyes. By no means had her life been perfect, but it was the life she'd chosen and had managed successfully, thus far. People's ability and will to choose for themselves was being completely eliminated from them and no one had a powerful enough voice to express their opposition. Some tried, but they became outcasts, and the narrative was portrayed as these people being the villain and, God forbid, anti-global President Dunne.

Melanie made her way back onto the overcrowded train of people who would constantly scream for freedom and individuality, which only drove them to become more and more robotic, with fewer choices despite their realizing it. She continued to breathe deeply in and out… in and out, with her heart pounding from the confrontation at the store and her rush to catch the train. She was starting to feel tired and began longing to return home so that she'd be able to rest.

Melanie stood near the center of the train, gloves on as she held onto the pole as to eliminate the contraction of getting germs. For a moment, she closed her eyes. Did she fall asleep? She wasn't sure. She looked down into her blouse at the gold cross that she'd always worn, now in secret, and all seemed to be well for a time.

Just outside of the United Nations headquarters, a large group of protestors were gathered around out front voicing their displeasure for the Global Administration's latest ruling requiring citizens to become imprinted and registered within the global database. They were heavily monitored and restrained by military officers who'd kept them to the sides, preventing them from demonstrating directly in front of the building. Protestors frequently surrounded the building, but since Hansen's announcement and Dunne's assurance that he would follow through, the crowds became drastically larger.

Jaylen, along with a few of his friends, Lisa, Cassandra, and Evan, were directly in the middle of the protestors, screaming at the top of their lungs towards the headquarters. They held signs, shouted through the bullhorn, along with anything else that they felt might get the administration's attention. There were others associated with the four as well that followed under the direction of Jaylen.

It had been more years than Jaylen could remember that he'd started voicing his displeasure with the global administration's manner of leveling things out. During the war, there was complete chaos and the right team in power was needed to bring about order and reestablish some sense of normalcy within the world. With this, Jaylen had no objection, however, it was Hansen's continued stay in power and his insistence the power would be given back to trusted elected officials. That day never came. Instead, more people were brought in under Hansen's rule to execute his global vision.

There were naysayers to Jaylen's objections to the administration, calling him ungrateful for Hansen's hard work of implementing global peace. From the very beginning, when he started protesting alone, to now, where he led his three friends and a group that continued to grow daily, there were those who showed up to show their disapproval for his demonstrations. He strived to get everyone to understand that the basic human rights that they'd been given were gradually being taken away under the guise of peace. While Hansen and Dunne's plan seemed to possess all that any citizen could ever hope for while on earth, Jaylen believed that the cost in which it came would be far greater than anyone could ever possibly imagine.

Over time, Jaylen had managed to end up on military officers' radar as a "trouble-maker" of sorts who'd been known to rouse up a crowd and cause disturbances. They arrested him and several members within his group on countless occasions, but as Jaylen began noticing things changing, along with military officers growing more strict, he scaled back their approach some out of fear as to how far the officers were willing to take things.

It wasn't a question for Jaylen, he'd once seen a protestor become a little too aggressive and more hands-on with a military officer during his demonstration than perhaps what was needed and was shot to death in the middle of the street. The crowd scattered away; terrified. Jaylen stood staring at the now dead body. Just seconds prior, the man had been moving around and protesting, just as he had been, but now he was dead. After that day, while Jaylen didn't stop protesting, his demonstrations were conducted with a little more caution.

Citizens held protests, wrote to the government, and rioted as a form of resistance to the administration's seemingly forceful manner of having everyone adhere to the new way of things. Everyone had their own reasonings for not complying. Some were worried about becoming imprinted because of health concerns, some were simply rebellious towards the government's wishes, and then others held strong religious beliefs and viewed the act of becoming imprinted as an irrevocable sin.

Jaylen and the core of his friends belonged in the latter group. Other members within their group, who protested alongside them, had various other reasons, but they all agreed that it was unlawful for them to be forced into becoming imprinted to be viewed as citizens in a world in which they'd always been a part of. After the protest was over, Jaylen headed towards the train station, jumped over the rotating metal bar that required you to pay before entering, found a seat on the train, and began making his way home.

She had finally made her way home, struggling to make it up the few steps which led to the front door of her home. Her hands fumbled through her purse as she tried to locate the keys to the front door, while still hanging onto the groceries from Flannigan's. She hadn't been one of those citizens lost in the craze of the excitement of the latest and greatest technology to get a jump on becoming imprinted. If she had, a simple scan of her forehead or right hand would've been enough to guarantee her entry.

The gold cross around her neck, which her mother had given to her, had become entangled and twisted around itself. It would be nearly impossible for her to unravel, as she would later discover. She cursed quietly to herself, out of frustration at not being able to find the keys to her home fast enough. Eventually, she reached them and, as she inserted the key, she looked up to see an envelope taped to her door with her name labeled across the front.

"*Great*," Melanie whispered.

Somehow, without her yet opening it, she had an idea of what the contents might have been.

Melanie placed the groceries onto the kitchen counter, next to the letter that she already opened and read, and she dialed a familiar, yet seldom used, number from her phone. The line rang several times while she paced back and forth inside of the small kitchen. Just as Melanie was about to end the call, a male voice answered.

"What is it?" the voice said, lacking enthusiasm. Her eyes rolled immediately once she'd heard him answer. He was the last person she wanted to reach out, but he was literally the only person who could potentially be able to help her. Her fingers fondled with the tangled-up cross as she spoke.

"I may need your help with something," Melanie said. There was a deep sigh from the other end of the line, then silence.

"Well?" She pushed.

"Help with what, Melanie?" the man asked.

"You know with ah… this whole imprint thing… they're saying that I have to register into the global identity database to keep my home." She answered.

"Okay… so what's the problem?"

"Gabe… you know that I can't do that."

"… Even if it means that you'll lose your home?"

"I can't. It's against my beliefs."

"Melanie, that makes absolutely no sense. What are you expecting me to do, huh?" Gabe asked. "I can't change these people's minds. They're making it the law. There's nothing I can do about that."

"Look, I know that, Gabe. I'm just… maybe you could allow me to stay with you for a while until I figure things out. I'll work on sorting things out before it gets to that point, but I just need to know that I can rely on you in case things don't go as planned."

"Wait… let me get this straight. The woman that kicked me out wants to come live with me. Am I hearing you right?"

"Hey! I'm not excited about this! You cheated on me, remember? Remember? That's the least that you could do. Why don't you try doing something right for a change!"

"Listen, I didn't answer your call for this! Figure it out on your own."

"Screw you!" Melanie screamed, but Gabe had already ended the call.

Melanie wasn't alone in her beliefs, her along with millions of others were conflicted with deciding to either go against all that they'd ever believed in and live "peacefully," or stand their ground and suffer through whatever was to come to them. She poured a glass of wine and then walked a few steps over into her living area, where she sat on a sofa. She took a deep breath, contemplating everything, trying to figure out what she needed to do. Once upon a time that was a beautiful idea; it was actually something that she'd dreamt of. It was a dream that had it all: the house, the white picket fence, Gabe on the grill, and kids all playing in the yard. Unfortunately, that was a dream and reality, sometimes, tends to be a nightmare. Melanie's thoughts were all over the place, and things didn't appear as though they would become easier anytime soon.

The sudden chime of her doorbell startled her slightly, causing her to jump. She wasn't expecting any visitors. The front door was only a few steps away from where she'd been sitting in the living room area. Once at the door, she peered through the peephole and noticed a familiar gentleman. But the purpose of his visit was unclear. She stepped back quietly to ensure that she didn't make a sound on the floorboards.

What was Kaleb doing here?

She was unclear why he would visit her, but she was, however, curious as to the nature of him being there. She decided to finally open the door to a half-smiling, half nervous Kaleb. He was unsure about what her reaction might be regarding him showing up to her home unannounced.

"What's up, Kaleb?" Melanie asked, leaning against the half-opened door. Although him being there was a bit odd and she'd gotten into it with Alicia earlier, she decided to remain cordial, at least initially, to hear him out.

"I just wanted to apologize, you know, about earlier today. That's not how we like to represent my father's store."

Both of Kaleb's hands were firmly tucked inside of his pockets as he nervously swayed from side-to-side speaking to her. There was something slightly boyish about his movements that derived from his not-so-subtle crush on her. Melanie was aware of it, and despite what she'd said earlier about him, it was mainly her anger towards his sister. Perhaps this was the reason Kaleb had shown up, aside from an apology; to see if Melanie had really meant what she'd said, or if it was only because she was angry at the time.

"Okay," Melanie said dryly.

"Okay," Kaleb said.

Melanie just stared at him, barely blinking, making it difficult for him to read her.

"So… ah… am I forgiven?"

"Do you feel that you're the one that should be here, *unannounced*, asking for forgiveness, or are you here on behalf of your witch of a sister as well?"

"Maybe both, but it would, personally, mean a great deal to me."

"Sure. All is forgiven." Melanie said.

Kaleb smiled. Melanie just watched. He had a pleasant smile. It wasn't the first time that she'd noticed, but she made sure that she didn't reveal that she'd appreciated it. She tried to keep it brief.

"Was there anything else?" Melanie asked.

"Well, there was one other thing. I just wanted to kind of put it out there." Kaleb said.

"What is it?" Melanie asked.

"I know that you haven't… become imprinted and everything —"

"Kaleb—" Melanie cut him off before he could finish.

"No, please hear me out. You know they're requiring homeowners to register into the global identity database and that anyone who doesn't will have to vacate their home. I know you're tough, so if you choose to continue standing your ground, I have a spot for you, just above the store that you could stay in if you like?" Kaleb offered.

"Are you kidding me?" Melanie asked.

"No. Seriously," Kaleb responded.

"Just so I can deal with the loving presence of your sister daily? No thank you, sir."

"I mean it. Look. I'll talk to her. Don't worry about her. I just want to give you another option just in case things don't work out for you as planned." Kaleb continued. "There's so much going on around here these days; everything's changing up so fast and I'll go ahead and admit it, I kinda care about what happens to you." Kaleb's stomach scrunched into a pit of nervousness as he finally unleashed the secret, in which the entire world had already known, only to be met with another eye roll from Melanie.

"Great, well, I have to get going. I have to get a few things done around this house. Thanks for stopping by." she responded. Despite not getting the ultimate response he'd hoped for, he made progress; therefore, he didn't feel totally defeated.

"You're welcome. I meant what I said; that offer stands. Take care, Melanie." Kaleb slowly stepped down from the stairs and began walking down the street. Melanie closed the door and released a deep sigh as she rested on the other side for a moment. She'd wondered about what Kaleb may have had up his sleeve and if he were actually being sincere. There weren't many other options available for her, especially with Gabe being his normal, unhelpful self. She was running out of time and resources, so she needed to make a decision soon. She looked over at the kitchen counter and thought about Kaleb's offer.

Not long after Kaleb had left, the lock to Melanie's door turned and her son, Jaylen, walked in to see his mother holding a glass of wine and seated inside of the living area. He greeted her, and she gave him a soft yet forced grin. Immediately, he was able to pick up that something was wrong.

He asked if everything had been okay, and she motioned towards the letter on the kitchen counter. She debated whether she should inform him about what was going on, and eventually decided that it would be of no use to hide it from him. Jaylen read over the letter and a knot formed inside of his stomach. He didn't allow his mother to see in his face what he was actually feeling on the inside. Although he was thrown off some, it wasn't a complete surprise to him; he could see this day coming.

"What do you think we should do?" her son asked.

She shrugged.

"Have you spoken to dad?"

Melanie scoffed before taking a sip from her glass.

"I'll take that as a yes," Jaylen said as he walked over to sit next to his mother.

"I'm thankful you got your sense of humanity and compassion from me," Melanie said.

Jaylen didn't respond.

Gabe's girlfriend walked into their bedroom and asked him what his last call was about. He told her it was Melanie, and that she was seeking a place to live because it was against her religious beliefs, and that he'd declined her request.

"Oh, I see," Gabe's girlfriend, Kristina, responded as she sat on the edge of their bed.

"What about you guys' son; what does that mean for him?" She asked.

Gabe sighed.

"I-I don't know. He's practically an adult; he does whatever Melanie says. She's got him brainwashed."

"Still, he's your son. You should always have a place for him, especially in such a scenario like this," Kristina said calmly.

Gabe turned to look at her before speaking.

"You'd be okay with that?" he asked her.

"Of course I would. He's a part of you and I accept all of you." The two looked at one another and smiled.

5
At What Cost?

Naomi had flown down from the New York City area to meet with representatives regarding civil rights matters, among other issues, for individuals who weren't registered within the global database as citizens. As a representative herself from Region One, she was seated on the side with other officials and ambassadors from both Quadrants from this Region. Representatives were all present from Region Two, from both Quadrants as well.

Across from them, seated around a partially circled wooden table, which was marvelously crafted to the likes and tastes of former President Mallory Hansen, were the four Presidents of each Quadrant, Ambassador Moreno of Region One, and Ambassador Wells from Region Two, both seated in the center. Global President Nathan Dunne, however, was not present.

The room was aligned with members of the press, who now had to go through an even more thorough screening process to gain access to the conference room. They were aligned along the walls, the rear of the conference room, as well as within the balcony. The hearing had begun, and several officials began voicing their concerns and requests to their representatives, some met with approval and consideration, while others weren't given a second thought. Wells and Moreno chimed in whenever they saw it was appropriate or if someone questioned them directly about a particular issue.

Naomi sat patiently, jotting down notes here and there until she'd been signaled that her microphone had been turned on and that they were prepared for her to speak. She wore a dark gray blazer and matching skirt that had both been well-tailored; not too loose or tight. The length of the skirt was just slightly above the knee; an inch and a quarter, just as all of her skirts that she wore to work were. Her red-framed glasses were just the right amount of color to bring her ensemble to life. Also, the frames brought forth the perfect amount of balance to match the red eagle pendant that was given to her by her mother before she'd passed away.

Naomi had come from parents who'd been financially well off but strongly believed in the value of hard work. Early on they taught a young Naomi how to balance her time between her schoolwork and play. She'd even had a calendar that instructed her on how to keep track of her progress and upcoming events that she'd scheduled. As a child, she took part in multiple sports and could play several instruments as well. However, the one thing that had always stuck with her, that her parents imparted, was the importance of helping those in need. They taught her that the sole purpose of our existence was to love and be of help to one another. This carried on with her well into adulthood and was a trait that she'd made sure was passed along to her young daughter.

"Councilwoman, proceed when you're ready," Ambassador Wells said.

Secretly, Moreno gave a quick eye roll and mumbled under her breath, expressing her displeasure towards Naomi. The two had never quite gotten along over different policies and ways of doing things. Naomi's continued efforts and challenges towards them almost came as a bother.

"Thank you, Mr. Ambassador. There's no secret as to the purpose of my being here; I believe I've made myself loud and clear as to the next phases in which I believe our world should take post-war. However, for the sake of being on the record for this hearing, I will express these needs to you all again," Naomi began.

Moreno pinched her forehead at the thought of where the councilwoman would take the conversation, yet again.

"I commend former President Mallory Hansen on his efforts in restoring our world during a time in which humanity was on the verge of becoming completely shattered. He took enormous strides in, not only restoring humanity but in ensuring that we live in better conditions than we'd ever been or could have ever imagined living in. I would also like to add that current President Dunne has done a great job of picking up where Hansen left off and that he has made sure we haven't deviated from the original vision."

Everyone listened patiently for the inevitable argument that they'd all become too familiar with during Naomi's speeches, essays, and past hearings. She'd always repeat the same things, but, as she'd stated, she'd continue to do so until they made progress.

"However," she continued, "I have such a difficult time understanding why we have taken such vigilant strides towards bringing everyone together through forcing everyone to become registered and imprinted to become classified as citizens but, in turn, we have alienated those who have chosen not to, because of personal choice and religious affiliation. This, to me, is a step backward. We have abandoned millions and millions of people, we have taken away their homes, we have starved them, and have essentially left them for dead. These people are not animals; they are human beings. And if we truly care for humanity, as Hansen and Dunne have so adamantly expressed that they do, then the very least that we can do is provide some form of assistance for them."

"Councilwoman, your request is so contradictory," Moreno chimed in.

"No, Ambassador, your policies are contradictory!" Naomi fired back.

"Okay, if you'll allow me to respond."

"Of course. Please do," the councilwoman said.

"I understand that you'd like to think that so much has been taken away from these people, but you are choosing to neglect how more opportunities have been laid before them."

"But at what cost? Why is it they no longer have a choice? Why is it this administration's way or the highway?"

"Councilwoman, please! Allow Ambassador Moreno to speak without interference! Consider this a warning," Wells interjected.

Moreno took a deep breath as she tried to maintain her composure during Naomi's interruptions. This was going precisely how she knew it would. These hearings were never any different when she had to face Naomi.

"Now, as I was saying, we have provided more opportunity to everyone on this entire planet than any administration has done before this one. No one has accomplished what this administration has done in terms of providing food, shelter, and global unity. You, however, are choosing to overlook all the good that has been done to become fixated on circumstances that have derived from a group of people's own choosing. If we are to say, 'Here is a home for you,' and they refuse this, how are we to respond?" Moreno stated.

"Ambassador, I challenge you again by asking you, at what cost do these amenities come with? If these people have to sacrifice their freedoms to have a roof over their heads, how exactly are you doing them a favor?" Naomi responded.

"Councilwoman," Ambassador Wells began, "I commend you on your intelligence and compassion in which you have for these individuals."

Again, another eye roll from Moreno.

"However, although you mentioned it briefly, you seem to forget exactly what those times of warfare were like. Do you understand the low levels in which humanity had reached? Do you truly? Every law, bill, act, that you can think of was thrown out of the window. We had become animals; we were like a wild beast inside of the jungle. So, you come in today and you toss around trigger words such as privacy, choice, and the rights of the people, questioning whether if they still exist. Sure, of course, they still exist. But to this, I say how they once existed is no longer. I believe you dream of the days before this world teetered along the lines of universal catastrophe and I wonder to myself, why is this so. Perhaps, it is because your life has always been swell; maybe there were no worries of where your next meal would come from or threats to where you may sleep the following evening. Again, I admire your courage and your passion, but our good far outweighs our bad, therefore, this administration will continue to stand firmly on this matter. No further assistance will be given."

The room had fallen completely still while the back and forth between the three had come to a halt. It'd appeared that Naomi was defeated, again. Naomi, however, felt somewhat offended by Ambassador Well's words, which bordered along the lines of her campaign coming from a selfish place, and she closed by expressing her displeasure for his remarks.

During the days of Andrew's arrival, he took full advantage of all the benefits of being imprinted. With the money that was uploaded into his account, he was able to purchase food, clothing, and even rent out a hotel all by a quick scan of his right hand. He was able to see what life was truly like to be accepted as a citizen.

Fellow citizens seemed to smile at him in public and were open to engagement; he didn't feel the need to hide from any. The feeling of strutting through the busy city streets with his chin held high gave him an indescribable rush. For the time being, Andrew could feel as though he was "one of them".

Whenever someone would hear his British accent, it would often spark a conversation about what it was like living there, if they hadn't visited before, questions about how long he'd been inside of Region One, along with other tales. Of course, much of his story was fabricated to avoid alerting people that he wasn't one of them; that he wasn't equal, and that he was classified in the absolute lowest part of society.

He was careful to ensure that he introduced himself to people as Jared Wheeler on top of creating a consistent story to make his lies believable to them as well as to himself. His story consisted of him being a business executive, not overly wealthy, but successful, out on vacation by himself, looking to take a well-deserved break from the stresses of life back home in London. Slowly, but surely, he became so engulfed in the lifestyle and the simplicity of how things were. He hung out in bars, met new friends, laughed, and indulged in living in the high life. When the night was over, he came to himself and when he was all alone; the laughter turned into tears. He knew that it would soon all come to an end and the memories of his family, while he was out living the life, just wouldn't fade away. Was this his reward for choosing his survival over there's?

Jared remembered why he was there. Somehow, he needed to locate someone by the name of Naomi, which seemed like a near impossibility, but he figured the best place to start would be to ask a few of his new friends if any of them had known anyone by that name on one occasion when they were all hanging out. Amid one of the several dirty jokes over countless beers they had, Jared managed to sneak in his inquiry to see if the name rang a bell with any of them.

They all stopped laughing and looked at Jared, puzzled. For a second, Jared thought he'd said the wrong thing and, perhaps, he'd blown his cover. He lowered his eyes to his nearly empty glass of beer, attempting to avoid eye contact with any of the men. The look in his eyes would've revealed the truth to them all.

Luckily, this wasn't the case, as they were all just strolling through their mental Rolodex to see if that name was somewhere up there. They all answered that they hadn't heard of her, but just before the conversation moved on, Erik, one of the gentlemen, chimed in.

"Well, I mean, there's the councilwoman, Naomi Alexandra Nicholson, but you're not talking about her, are ya?"

"*Ugh,* I'm sick of that lady. Why did you have to bring her up? She's so full of herself with her fake humanitarian, save the world bullshit!" Will, another one of the guys added. "Did you see her last week at the hearing? She keeps on with the same jargon whenever a camera's in front of her. She's an idiot," he continued.

"Honestly, she's on this artificial front line trying to get funding to take care of these imbeciles who've chosen to not take the imprint. How stupid can they be," Chris, the political insider of the group threw in.

They all laughed, including Jared, albeit an awkward laugh, to fit in.

"Seriously, that has to be one of the sickest forms of greed that I've ever seen. Here you are, where you have literally everything laid out for you to have a better life, finally equality for all, right? All you have to do is get a stupid invisible imprint layered into your skin; yet, you say, 'No thanks, I'd like more money for myself and my family so that we can do whatever the hell we want to do.' Screw her and them!" Chris said.

"Cheers to that!" Erik said, raising his glass. There seemed to be a pause after they toasted their glasses, as if they were waiting for some type of response to come from Jared, who'd been silent since his inquiry. Naomi Alexandra Nicholson was precisely whom he needed to speak with. However, he quickly scrambled to echo their feelings about her, to dodge whatever they might've said or done. "Thanks anyway, guys, but no way was I talking about her. She's a complete embarrassment to all citizens." Jared said.

"No, she's an embarrassment to herself," Chris said.

"You're right. Man… I really wish that I could tell her right to her face what a disgrace she is." Jared chuckled.

"She's not too hard to find. She has an office not too far from here, in the Ferguson building. Knock yourself out." Erik said.

"If you see her, do us a favor and blow her brains out," Will said in an intoxicated mumble.

Despite feeling uneasy about what they'd all exclaimed, Jared was able to pick up on all the key information in which he'd needed to locate Naomi. He knew that once he'd found Naomi, his friendship with these guys would be over-not that they were his real friends anyway-and soon enough, he would be falling off of his high horse.

The following day, Jared was able to track down the Ferguson building where the guys had said Naomi was located. It was a rather enormous building that'd looked to have been reconstructed after the wars. Jared walked inside through a security checkpoint where two guards stood, faces carved out of stone, to check everyone that should come through. Once he'd made it through, he observed the lobby area's floors, walls and limited furniture were also white. However, the walls held several large exotic paintings that provided the only splash of color within the lobby area.

He walked further towards the back, where he noticed a lady seated behind a small white counter. She'd noticed him and smiled as he walked timidly in her direction. Once he reached the counter, he requested to speak with Naomi and expressed that it was regarding an extremely urgent matter.

"Hold one moment, please." The receptionist said.

Her index finger slid across a nearly invisible panel of numbers attached to the offices of all that worked inside of the facility. The call was connected, and the receptionist spoke with Naomi's assistant through the earpiece that wasn't visible to Jared, giving off the appearance that she'd been speaking to herself. It was a common way of communicating that Jared found truly strange.

Jared finally made it upstairs into an office as he found himself sitting across from an empty desk, awaiting to see Naomi. He scanned around her office, noticing the modern details of her furniture. Her desk, however, had been covered with books and file folders. He thought to himself that she must've been an extremely busy person. Behind the desk was a stunning view of the city skyline; a view, unlike Jared, had ever recalled seeing. He found himself just staring out into the distance and after some time had passed, he heard the door to the office behind him creak open.

"Hello, you must be Jared," a female said, walking into the room to face him with her hand extended.

Jared quickly stood up to greet her.

"Yes, yes, I am."

She seemed pleasant; quite the opposite of what the guys at the bar were making her out to be.

"My name's Naomi, it's a pleasure to me you," she said as she took her seat behind the desk. She had a set smile on her face, one that, perhaps, hid some type of concern behind it. She sat forward in her chair, fingers clasped, as she studied the man in front of her momentarily. Jared hadn't said a word.

"You'll have to forgive me, but given the nature of my work, I believe in speaking direct. Is this okay with you?" Naomi stated. Jared nodded.

"Good. Now, under most circumstances, I don't take many meetings inside of my office. But, as you mentioned on the phone, we seem to have a mutual friend over in Region Two. This is where you're from?"

Jared sat up in his chair, cleared his throat, and answered yes.

"I see. Over the phone you mentioned Tracy. How do you know Tracy and how long have you known him exactly?"

For a second, Jared paused at her question. She'd referred to Tracy as him. Did this lady really know who Tracy was, or was it some kind of test? Maybe it was a test to protect herself. It made sense, given the profession she was in. At any rate, what was he to do; his temporary registration would expire soon, so he had to trust her. Naomi was his last hope.

"I really don't know Tracy very well, to be quite honest. A Helper, by the name of Clara, suggested that my family and I meet up with Tracy if we needed to suddenly evacuate." Jared said with his gaze partially lowered as the memory of his family crossed his mind once again. However, there was one more thing that he'd forgotten to add.

"Also," he began, "Tracy is female... by the way."

"I know." Naomi grinned.

"What else do you know... Andrew?"

He slowly looked up at her with his eyes now widened. She'd known of his true identity. Hopefully, this was a good thing. As of now, he wasn't completely sure.

"There isn't much else. Everything has all happened so fast. They ambushed my family and I in the middle of the night and... and..." he trailed off as he saw himself in the woods again, running away from his son, young Noah, and the rest of his family.

"*And* you escaped. Correct?" Naomi asked, picking up where he'd left off.

"Let me ask you, why haven't you become imprinted? It would certainly make things a whole lot easier for you. As a matter of fact, I think you should. You'll be saving yourself a lot of trouble. I don't need to tell you this though; you've already seen the level of harassment that you face without one."

There she was again, pushing him away through her trick line of questioning. Why would she ask him this?

"I'm not too sure, truthfully," he began. "You're probably right; things would be easier for me. I can see that, now, with the temporary imprint." He said, observing his palms. "I suppose," he said before pausing, "I suppose I'm a believer."

"Are you not sure?" she asked.

"I don't know. I was raised to believe, but the way things are now makes me doubt at times," he responded.

"Isn't that what being a believer is all about; believing through the good and the bad times, seeing things through, no matter what?"

His eyes lifted towards her. However, he concealed his disapproval of her attempting to give him what seemed like another sermon. She was beginning to sound like him when you would have these conversations with Trevor, whose whereabouts were unknown. He would've loved to say anything to him now.

"You're right, I guess. It's easier to believe when everything is going well. The true test is when the lights go out and we're surrounded by total darkness," Andrew said.

Naomi smiled softly as a sign of agreement to what he said.

"Those are the times when we find out who we really are and what we believe in-or not believe in-when the light is nowhere to be found," Andrew reflected. "I'm learning that now."

Sitting in front of Naomi and hearing her questions gave Andrew some time to think over everything. It felt as though he was inside the office of his therapist.

As he sat quietly for a moment, curiosity struck him.

"Are you imprinted?" he asked. Naomi sat back in her chair and crossed her legs.

"I am, as a matter of fact," she answered.

"Hm," he expressed. "I take it that you aren't a believer then?"

"I'm not a believer in people's rights being forced away. I am not a believer in forcing everyone to do as you say simply because someone in your position finally decided to stand up and do their job. I'm not a believer in having a dictatorship. So, I guess I'm not a believer." She said.

"Does that make you a hypocrite?" he asked. "You're taking advantage of the many benefits without subscribing to the machine. How does that work?"

"Do you, being a believer, yet struggling with if you believe, make you a hypocrite? Either you believe or you don't believe, right? How does *that* work?" she darted back.

Andrew was finally able to see the fiery side of Naomi which he's seen on the television and what his old friends found most annoying about her. However, it was somewhat good to see, in some odd way.

"Apologies, I don't mean to offend. I was just curious."

"You're not the first to challenge me on that. I face that every day from my colleagues. The thing that you have to understand is this; I believe in humanity and the rights of every individual. The idea that the times have changed and that we've given up our rights during the global war is asinine. Someone's job was done and now we're being instructed to do everything that we're told, yet no one seems to see it that way. Everyone sees the homes, cars, healthcare, and food, but they don't see that they have handed their rights and human dignity over."

She raised a good point, but it was hard to argue with all that is gained just by getting a stupid invisible imprint in your hand or your forehead. Admittedly, he played around with the idea of going through with it now and then.

"That's who I fight for," she continued, "people like you who choose not to. You may not be on the guest list, but you're still a human being with rights."

"I suppose I owe you a thank you so… thank you."

"Don't mention it. I don't do it for appreciation," she said.

"So, what happens now?" Andrew inquired.

Naomi arose from her chair and looked out into the distance of her office window behind her.

"The Helpers are an underground global network, privately funded, that assist individuals who've chosen to, for various reasons, not become imprinted. We provide shelter, food, and any other supplies that may be needed for them to survive. It's difficult but… it is necessary."

"Are you the founder?" Andrew asked.

"Not solely. There is a committee, yet for the protection of everyone else, I'm the face of the organization. Should anyone want to blame or come against us for any reason, they can come for me. I don't make it easy for them. What happens next is that we'll provide you with all the things aforementioned. You'll be connected with someone to show you how everything operates and how to maneuver. Also," she said as she walked around to his side, "you can be exactly who you are, Andrew. You're free to believe in or not believe in whatever you choose. You'll be safe."

Naomi gazed at him for a moment, awaiting a reaction from him, but he sat there in silence. After a few moments, he looked up at her, without the excitement that she'd been expecting.

"I-I don't really know what to say," Andrew said, finally. "I guess it just isn't what I was expecting. Don't get me wrong, I'm truly grateful. It's just that I didn't know what to expect coming over here. I was just trying to get away, but I don't really know what from. I never got a chance to process everything or consider what's ahead of me."

"This opportunity will give you the chance to figure all of those things out, Andrew. You're able to hold on to your identity or discover what has yet to be found. You won't be alone; there are many others just like you in search of what's next for them."

Andrew's chin dropped slightly into his chest. He didn't want to appear unappreciative, but it was all occurring so fast for him, and he wasn't exactly sure where life was heading for him.

"Do I have to decide now?" he asked.

Naomi smiled.

"Of course not." She walked around to her desk, picked up an expensive-looking pen, and scribbled something onto a small sheet of paper.

"When you're ready," she said walking back around towards him, "visit this address." She handed him the paper. "It isn't a location that we use, but you'll be pointed in the right direction."

"Thank you," he said, glancing down at the paper.

"I believe that will be everything unless you have any questions for me?"

"No, this is good," Andrew said as he stood up.

Naomi extended her hand. Andrew took it.

"It was a pleasure meeting you, Andrew. Remember to look ahead to your future now. What's done, is done. It's all about what happens next for you." She said.

He turned and began walking towards the door when she added one last thing.

"Also, when you decide to take me up on my offer, make sure that you trust them as if it were me. You and I are likely to never speak again. I wish you the best."

He walked out of Naomi's office and back into the world where, for only a few days longer, he was still a citizen that was an equal, just like everyone else.

Jaylen couldn't remember the last time in which he'd seen his father but now, there he was sitting directly across from him inside of a booth inside of a diner not far away from him and Kristina's home. Gabe and Kristina weren't married, so technically, Jaylen figured, she wasn't his stepmother. Both Gabe and Jaylen were nervous, mixed with a wide range of other emotions as well. Gabe knew it might seem a bit strange requesting to see him after so much time, but with everything occurring, he figured now was probably the best time if he were ever going to do it. He ordered food and a cup of coffee and asked his son if he'd wanted anything. Jaylen declined. Instead, he pulled out a large bottle of filtered water from a backpack in which he'd brought along with him.

"I have to say... it's great to see you," Gabe said.

Jaylen was looking down at his phone when his father had made the statement, but he raised his eyes to look at him without commenting because of the peculiar nature of the statement. He said nothing, and his eyes went back down to check messages from Evan and Lisa. He figured if it were true, he would've made arrangements to see him sooner than he had. What was it? Was it the woman he'd chosen over his mother that had been preventing him all of this time? These questions floated around in the back of Jaylen's head from time to time, but he would always quickly wash them away because he figured they'd only lead to more questions with no absolute closure. Ultimately, Jaylen decided such questions were pointless and that how things played had no impact on his life.

Gabe cleared his throat and tried to brush off the cold response from his son.

"How are things going with the protests?" Gabe asked.

"No arrests in a while, so that's a good thing, right?" Jaylen sighed.

He understood his father's approach to warming up to whatever the true intentions were for the two of them being in the overpriced bougie diner that Kristina probably introduced him to. The initial small talk, good to see you line didn't work, so now he was going for something more personal to connect with him.

Nice try dad.

"Yeah, I suppose that is." Gabe laughed awkwardly. Jaylen looked up again at him coldly. Again, things were back to being awkward.

"Maybe we should… get to it," Jaylen said after a few moments of silence. "Not trying to be rude or anything," although he had every right to be, he thought, "but I had a meeting soon with a few of my friends."

"Yeah, sure," Gabe responded disappointedly. "Listen… I understand, our relationship isn't good, but whether or not you believe me, I love you. You're my son and I care about you. I know that the only reason that I'm able to see you now is because you are grown, and your mother can't prevent you from seeing me and you can make your own decisions."

"Leave mom out of this," Jaylen said in between gulps of water from the clear bottle.

"Right," Gabe said. "The bottom line is this: If you want a place to stay, you're more than welcome to stay with Kristina and I. The door is open."

There was a missing denominator within his dad's offer that he couldn't help but notice. Why would it be okay for him to live with him and not his mother as well?

"I can live with you? No one else, just me?" Jaylen asked.

Gabe understood what he was hinting at.

"It doesn't have to be like this. It's complicated. She's taking on an unnecessary burden upon herself because of her stubbornness and her beliefs."

"I believe in the exact same thing, so what's the difference? Why should I be granted the honor of being able to live with my father after all of these years?" Jaylen asked.

Although he carried most of his father's features, who he was as a person derived from his mother. It was undeniable.

"Thanks, but no thanks," Jaylen said before taking another sip of water and exiting the diner.

6
SHELTER

"What do you think we should do?" Jaylen asked his mother.

"I don't know." Melanie sighed. They sat silently for a second before she let out an outburst, "I can't believe him; only offering to take you in when I specifically asked him to take in both of us! His new girlfriend is probably the one behind this. But I don't know, he's never had a heart," she retorted.

The two sat in a park that wasn't too far from their home as they tried to figure out where they would live within the next upcoming days. Letting go of the home was such a difficult thing for them to do. Melanie worked extremely hard to get it, and Jaylen did his part to help with the bills and fix things around the home whenever it was needed. And to lose it all over such a thing as this made it that much more of a tough pill to swallow. It had come so hard to possess, and now it was on the verge of being taken away so easily.

"Have you heard of the Helpers?" Jaylen asked.

Melanie turned to her son with a look of obvious unfamiliarity on her face.

"No, I haven't. Who are they?"

"It's an anonymous group of individuals with resources who help people like us with anything that they may need such—"

"Stop right there," Melanie cut her son off. "What do you mean 'people like us'? We're not looking for handouts from anyone. I asked your father because, technically, he's family so I thought he would be willing to help, but we don't need any special care from anyone."

"Mom, it's not like that," Jaylen responded. He knew that his mom was an extremely prideful woman, but with things going the way that they were, he felt that any type of help would provide them some type of stability.

"They are a legit group of people. Some of them even work in the government."

"And what does that supposed to mean? As far as I'm concerned, that makes them our enemy!"

Jaylen shook his head.

"Look, I get it. I know why you would feel that way. I'm always out here on the front lines, so I know firsthand how it is, but you've got to trust me on this. There's no way that I would bring this up to you if I didn't have some type of faith in them."

"Boy," Melanie said sharply as she spun to look him square in the eye, "the only thing that we have faith in is God."

It was obvious that there was no getting through to her, but time was running out. They would need to decide soon. Losing their home was inevitable, as long as they were unwilling to become imprinted.

"With all due respect, I have to ask, do you have any plans because we're running low on options?" Jaylen asked.

"I told you... I don't know."

"Well, in that case, I think you could at least hear what I have to say regarding the Helpers."

She thought about Kaleb's offer for them to live in the apartment above the store, but she didn't mention it to him. As far as she was concerned, that would never happen. What was she to do? She'd been praying day and night for something to happen or for something to change, but from what she could see, things continued to become worse for her and her son. She asked herself what it was she'd been looking for, but she wasn't sure. If what she'd been praying for manifested before her very eyes, would she know? She simply wasn't sure.

"Okay, so let's hear it." Melanie finally said.

"You know Lisa and Evan?"

"Of course, Jaylen." She was well familiar with her son's friends. They were close throughout Jaylen's entire life, so him asking whether Melanie had known who his closest friends were was ridiculous.

"Well," Jaylen continued, "they both live in this facility that is privately funded and operated by the Helpers. They 'help' those who have decided for whatever reason not to get the imprint. It's secure. Few know about it outside of the Helpers and those who live inside."

"You know about it," Melanie said.

"Again, my friends live there."

Melanie shrugged.

Melanie's first thought, once she and Jaylen entered inside of the facility where all the other non-citizens were located, was that it looked similar to a prison. An overcrowded prison, at that. Their guide was a short, friendly, gentleman wearing glasses who trotted along with somewhat of a limp with every other step that he took. They had called him to greet them in the small lobby area when the two of them initially arrived. The building was old and molded within many of its corners and had an underlying odor that the keepers of the place tried getting rid of several times before unsuccessfully.

"This place is gross," Melanie whispered under her breath, but Jaylen heard her and chuckled. Jaylen took note that he was taller than the gentleman who continued to turn around, looking up at him every few moments or so with his wide, dingy grin. The man gave them a tour of the place. The facility was on the outskirts of town, just along the border of a Red Zone. Gabe had dropped them off after a quiet and awkward ride. It was a tall, narrow, and long building made of brick, albeit crumbling brick in certain parts, without a name out front. There was only an address that Gabe concluded was the right place. He offered to help them inside, but Melanie insisted he didn't.

They were shown the many rooms where everyone lived, which included a small narrow twin-sized bed, where they would sleep. For some, more than one person would sleep on the small bed to preserve the limited amount of space that was available, so they were told. Inside most of the rooms, Melanie noticed that some people had attempted to fix them up to make them appear and feel as close to a home as they possibly could. They were taken to the kitchen area, which appeared to have been expanded to create a lunchroom type of setting. They were introduced to some of the residents there; most of them seemed kind, yet burden. Their smiles were forced. Their eyes were absent of light. They appeared much older than, perhaps, they might have actually been. It was discouraging for Melanie to see. She couldn't help but see herself and her son in their faces.

The short gentleman informed them that many of the families had been there for years and that some of the occupants were children who'd lost their parents, either during the war era or through some other unfortunate circumstance. One of their roommates was a boy named Austin, who'd lost both his mother and father a few years back. He was lively and excited to have new roommates.

He'd seemed to not be too broken, despite the loss of his parents.

Perhaps he'd gotten over it, or was simply too young when it had actually happened for him to have a strong memory of them, Jaylen thought. Austin proclaimed that he, too, had been a Christian and that he'd been led by his parents to not become imprinted despite many other children he'd known doing so. After their introduction, Austin ran off to play with the other kids that were inside of the facility.

Melanie and Jaylen looked at one another without saying anything, unsure of what to think. They sympathized with Austin, a young boy who'd chosen to carry out his parents' wishes, even in their death. He'd chosen to stick with a rather tough way of living, although he didn't have to because of what his parents taught him to believe. He was Christian, but at such a young age, how could he fully understand what that meant? These thoughts circled around Jaylen's and Melanie's minds, but they didn't discuss it. In a way, it was as though they were looking into a mirror, making flaws or errors in which they'd seen with Austin and his parents difficult to face. Seeing themselves in the shoes of Austin and his late parents placed reservations on the criticisms of what may have been right or wrong in this instance and, therefore, they went unspoken.

Jaylen told his mother that he was going to walk around to see if he could find Evan and Lisa and that he would return later.

Melanie sat on the bed and sighed as she pondered about what was to happen next for the two of them. The short host had informed them that the Helpers had many other discreet locations throughout the area, and should they run out of space, they would make necessary transfers to accommodate everyone. She had to admit to herself that she was quite impressed with the operation the Helpers ran. Just up until a few days ago, she'd never heard of the Helpers.

Inside the room, there were five beds, excluding the two that had been arranged for Melanie and her son. There were four windows aligned behind the beds that had been screened, which added to the prison-look, she thought. The concrete block walls were painted in white, matching the tile floor, and several colorful pictures hung on the wall that must have been made by other children that stayed inside of the same room, Melanie concluded. She closed her eyes and sighed as the sound of small children laughing as they played echoed in the background. This place had become the last hope for her and Jaylen.

"Hi, I'm Regina!" an energetic voice interrupted.

Melanie's eyes sprung open to see a woman around her age walking briskly towards her with her hand extended.

"I'm sorry." Regina said. "Were you praying? I didn't mean to interrupt."

"No, it's okay. I wasn't... I was just... my name's Melanie," she said, shaking Regina's hand.

"Quincy told me we had new roommates, so I wanted to stop by and introduce myself," Regina said.

Melanie was somewhat puzzled as to why Regina had been so cheerful, but figured that it was probably okay, considering the lifeless faces that she'd seen throughout their tour around the place.

"Who's Quincy?" Melanie asked.

"He's one of our neighbors here. I'll introduce you two later." Regina responded.

How had the word of our arrival traveled so fast; we've only been in this place five minutes? Melanie exaggerated to herself.

"Sounds good! I look forward to meeting him."

"If you have any questions about anything, feel free to ask. I'll be here for you. I'll give you some time to settle in." Regina said before exiting the room.

Melanie sighed again and slowly fell back onto the bed.

Inside of the gymnasium, Jaylen, Evan, and Lisa sat around catching up with one another and going over a few details of their next protest. They all seemed eager for the next demonstration, except for Jaylen, who seemed a bit quiet about the discussion.

"Um... hello?" Lisa said, waving her hands in the front of Jaylen's face to grab his attention. "Are you still with us?"

He was seated in a wooden chair, backward, with his arms folded across the back.

"Yeah, just thinking. That's all." Jaylen responded.

"You hate it here, don't you? I knew I shouldn't have invited you here. You try to do something nice for someone and they just..." Evan joked to lighten the mood.

Lisa swung at him playfully. Jaylen smirked.

"No, I'm just thinking about what's next for us; our purpose. I'm just wondering if these protests… are actually doing any good. Are we making any progress with this?" Jaylen said.

"Of course, we are. How could you think otherwise?" Lisa asked.

"Really think about it. Are you saying that simply because you don't want to feel like all the work you have done has been in vain; pointless? What have we accomplished and can look back on and say, 'this was improved because of our protests?'"

Evan, remaining silent, looked back and forth between Lisa and Jaylen; now at Lisa, awaiting her response.

"Come on, Jaylen, you know it doesn't work like that. What we do works like a chain reaction of changes taking place; it's a step-by-step process," Lisa answered.

"Okay, let's say I accept that. Can you show me the chain of events from our protests leading to change? The only thing I've seen is us being bullied, contained, and at worst, killed by military officers. I'm not pointing this out to create a negative argument; I'm just thinking."

"No… I understand." Lisa said.

"The only reason we started this was because of you," Evan began, "so where do you think we should go from here?"

"I don't know, Evan." Jaylen sighed. "That's the problem."

"Well, for now, let's just keep this amongst the three of us, maybe inform Cassandra, but whatever we do, don't let word get back to Ahmad. The guy is a ticking time bomb waiting for the chance to revolt against the establishment." Evan said.

"He's not wrong for feeling that way," Jaylen said.

"You're right, but considering we're outnumbered, outgunned, and lack power, that idea becomes suicidal, if you ask me," Evan responded. "Now that I think about it, you're kinda sounding like him; looking to 'turn things up a notch.'"

"I haven't seen him since our last protest. Have either of you?" Jaylen asked.

"Of course we have. He lives here," Lisa answered.

"Really?" asked Jaylen.

"Oh, yeah. Walks around here treating this place like it's a prison. I'm sure it's probably a flashback for him, but I told him he's gotta relax." Evan said.

The next day Regina walked Melanie slowly around to different rooms, introducing her to each one of the residents. Melanie couldn't help but notice everyone's strained smiles and lifeless eyes again, even Regina's, whenever she hadn't been putting forth her best effort to conceal it when she faced her, she had the same look as they had.

"How long have these people been here?" asked Melanie.

"Most have been here for quite some time. Once Hansen made the announcement, those who looked favorably upon us pulled together to privately fund and establish sanctions, such as these, throughout the four Quadrants." Regina said.

"The Helpers?" Melanie asked. Regina nodded.

"God bless them." She said.

Melanie's eyebrows bunched together for a second at Regina's statement without her noticing. She didn't want to offend her in any way. However, she was curious. Who were these Helpers, and why had everyone been so keen to trust them?

"I don't know a great deal about them, but I do appreciate them for taking us in; that was very kind of them," Melanie said.

"That's what they're here for. They open their doors for people with nowhere to go." Regina smiled.

"Are all of these people Christians?" Asked Melanie as the two continued to walk along.

"No," Regina answered. "There are many religions represented here. The common factor here amongst everyone here is that they don't believe in becoming imprinted or giving up all that they are into the hands of the government." Regina continued.

"But... the Helpers are imprinted?" Melanie asked.

"The founders are, yes, but many of the people who operate these establishments are not. Some are, but not everyone," the other answered.

Feeling skeptical, this was confusing to Melanie.

"How exactly do we know these people can be trusted? I mean, for all that we know, this could be some sort of side program by the government to monitor the religious people or to seclude us all in one area to do God knows what with us."

"Ahh, you're a bit of a conspirator, aren't you?" Regina alluded.

Melanie shrugged.

"Look, the bottom line is this. We don't have anyplace else to go because of the decisions we've all made. We'll be dead in a matter of days out there on our own. So, what else are we supposed to do? Where else are we supposed to go? The Helpers are our only allies in this mess. We've run out of options and the Helpers are our only hope." Regina responded, stopping them both in their tracks.

"No, listen, I get it. Things just didn't really work out like I'd hoped for them to, and I've just been pretty nervous about putting all of my trust in someone else's hands. That's all. I'm truly grateful to be here," Melanie said.

"That's good to know. If you have any plans for survival greater than this, then, by all means, explore them," Melanie's guide said before continuing to walk along with her following. "But trust me, I understand. While this place is convenient, I'd much rather things be like they once were."

7
ANIMAL HOUSE

Several months had passed, and the entire world had successfully made its conversion over to the global identity system. Stores transitioned over to the imprint system with very few minor exceptions such as Flannigan's Groceries where it still allowed some of its customers to make purchases by other means. This decision created a ton of friction between Kaleb and Alicia at the store. Kaleb pushed strongly for them to continue to allow customers to pay in other ways, mainly with Melanie in mind, but Alicia had opposed the idea. Kaleb came out with a slight edge. Unfortunately, with the success of the world's conversion, there also came the rise of more crime throughout both Regions.

One of Naomi's biggest opponents within the political arena, Patricia Sanders, had gotten off of work late one evening and decided to visit a nearby grocery. She'd put off going for about a week and a half, therefore, her list had grown longer than she'd normally like. She took her time going through the list, despite her being as tired as she was because of the daily back and forth with the likes of Naomi and others who believed that non-imprinted individuals deserved the same rights as others.

It was ridiculous to give up such freedoms when they'd voluntarily chosen not to be a part of society, she thought. When she'd finished, she simply had her items bagged and exited the store where the overhead imprint scanners identified her chip and deducted the funds from her account without her having to go through the checkout line. The option was available for her to do so, but she found it more convenient to bypass it. Being so occupied with her list, she didn't realize that the entire time she was being watched since she'd left the office.

Once she'd finished, she made her way home and parked in front of her house while one of the three inside of a suspicious-looking vehicle shut off the lights to the car only a few blocks up the street from her. Patricia walked towards her front door, scanned her right palm on a side panel of the door, and entered inside. Her security system, that she'd named Sean, greeted and welcomed her home, and she requested to hear some jazz while she put away the groceries and poured herself a glass of wine to settle in for the evening. She shut off the kitchen lights, sat inside of the living area with a glass of her favorite cabernet sauvignon red wine, and turned on the news.

Around twenty minutes passed when Sean alerted her he'd detected movement near the rear of her home. She brushed it off, telling him to disregard it and that it was probably a cat or something. After all, she'd paid a little extra to live in an upgraded community, far away from the free government homes that were given to imprinted citizens to ensure everyone had a home and where there had been high levels of crime, or so she believed.

She went upstairs to change her clothes to prepare for bed. It was Thursday and the way things were heading at work, she was sure that she would be working from home well through the weekend. Just as she'd settled into bed, Sean interrupted once again.

"Pardon me, Madame, but there seems to be unrecognizable movements coming from the inside of your home." Sean's voice was low and spoke with an urgency that she'd never heard before.

She sat up in bed, frozen, and looked towards her door.

Stillness.

She only heard her heavy breathing until there was the sound of a sudden creak of a floorboard on the opposite side of the door.

Darkness…

Then suddenly there was light showing from underneath the door!

Chills rippled across her skin.

Sean gave off a warning, demanding that whomever it was to leave before he alerted the authorities. With a disregard for Sean's order, the door to her bedroom burst open as three men barged inside, all carrying weapons and wearing animal masks.

Patricia screamed as she dove to the other side of the bed and onto the floor. What was only a matter of minutes seemed to transpire over an eternity. It was all in slow motion. One man, wearing a tiger's mask, marched towards her but was suddenly shot by a gun she'd kept on the other side of the bed. He jerked back, startled, and stumbled out of the room. Another intruder quickly jumped onto the ground, peering through the eye-holes of a wolf's mask with Patricia in its line of sight, while the other, wearing a bear's mask, stood off to the side. A single shot was fired from the one wearing the wolf's mask, striking Patricia in the leg. She yelled in agony as she witnessed a mask of a bear reaching down towards her.

They had raided her home; food and other valuables were all quickly stolen by the bear masked intruder, but more startling to Patricia was the wolf masked intruder grabbing her right hand and scanning it with some sort of black handheld device. She wasn't sure what was happening. She assumed they were stealing money from her account. All that she knew was that she was in pain. Whether she would live or die was uncertain. Without saying a word, the intruder scanning her right palm turned to the other, nodded, flung away her arm, and they left her home, carrying out their partner who'd been shot earlier.

Moments later, the police arrived on the scene to find the Patricia bleeding out onto her bedroom floor.

REGION TWO: SOMEWHERE AROUND ~~ITALY~~

Members of the press scrambled to conduct their interview with Global President Nathan Dunne, who'd been waiting patiently, sitting in a private room inside of a palace. Dunne stared, almost blankly, as the interviewer, Reynold Patterson, urged his team to hurry so that they could begin. Patterson, a lanky yet well-dressed gentleman, visibly showed his frustration and embarrassment. They were ruining an enormous moment for him, but Dunne, seemingly absent from the moment, didn't seem to mind so much as Patterson continued to apologize to him.

After some time, behind their regular scheduled appointment, Reynold sat down in front of the President. Now Reynold was composed and ready to dive into his questioning. He thanked President Dunne for joining him, and the two exchanged a few pleasantries. As anyone would exclaim, Dunne's sense of present awareness of not only the environment but of those who were around him was impeccable. Dunne seemed to know about everything and everyone around him, which, for those who weren't close to him, seemed odd. Strange even. He'd asked Patterson about his wife, as well as his two kids, and if the youngest of his two daughters still had trouble with her asthma. The President's knowledge of this slightly took Patterson back, but he maintained his composure and assured him she'd recently began seeing a new doctor who'd been extremely helpful.

As the interview began, Patterson dove right into the heart of things by inquiring about the well-being of former President Mallory Hansen. Dunne exclaimed that he'd been doing well and began going on singing his praises.

"When we really observe the history of civilization, from the very beginning of existence, there's very little doubt as to where Hansen ranks in terms of influential leaders. He won't speak of himself this way, but how can we argue against what he has done for us? Hansen has accomplished what humanity as always preached, yet has never quite accomplished. He has brought peace into a world that was once full of chaos, savagery, debauchery, and warfare. The mere words, 'world peace', had become part of gag reel of sorts before this leader stepped in and turned them into our reality. He has performed a miracle for all of us, making him the closest thing to a God that we've ever seen."

Patterson chuckled lightly as he pushed the frames of his glasses back over the bridge of his nose. When he noticed Dunne's serious demeanor, not laughing and staring directly at him as to show that what he'd spoken wasn't a joke, he halted. Patterson felt somewhat uneasy in front of the President who continued to stare at the awkward interviewer.

"There are those who've chosen to not become imprinted," Patterson began after clearing his throat, "and have continued to fight for inclusion and funding to continue their way of living without being registered into the Global Identity Database. How do you feel about this and what, if anything, has Hansen said about this issue?"

"Opponents of the Global Identity System have chosen to overlook its primary purpose of eliminating poverty, hunger, and homelessness within this planet. Cabinet members and I have a tough time justifying why funds should be given to a problem that we have already created a solution for. To be frank, we view such a request as being very selfish. These people have no reason for which any of them should face hardships currently, therefore, it is difficult for me to sympathize with them."

"As for Hansen, as you can probably imagine, he is heartbroken that people have rejected his efforts to bring us all together and finally create a fair and balanced life for us all. He's put forth so much work and we have done so much to sustain what he's done and they have thrown everything away. I will add, however, that what we will not tolerate are any acts of violence, theft, property damage, or terrorism from any of them. I realize that there has been a rise of several of them rebelling against law enforcement as well as showcasing a complete disregard for the property of those who have chosen to be citizens. This is unacceptable. You can expect this administration to come down hard on all who are not citizens. They will longer be able to dwell within the Green Zone within any Region."

"Wow," Patterson exclaimed. "When will this take place?'

"Soon. More details are to come." Dunne stated.

"Are there more questions?" Dunne asked.

"Oh… yes! Of course!" He responded with his nervous laughter before asking the President about doubters of Hansen, himself, and their overall movement.

"Those who oppose what it is in which we stand for have to take a step back and seriously ask themselves what exactly it is they're opposing. We have been very clear about what our agenda is, which is the implementation, development, and sustainability of global peace. Our track record displays that we have done and continue to do just that, therefore, I challenge you to ask them, what are they opposed to exactly? Are they against peace? Are they against unity? If so, then that places them inside of an incredibly difficult position of being our enemy."

REGION ONE: SOMEWHERE AROUND ~~WASHINGTON, D.C.~~

Cameras flashed in front of Naomi as reporters questioned her about President Dunne's recent comments during one of his rare interviews.

"We're certainly disappointed in the President's comments. I feel that for an administration who continues to present themselves as being for the people, they have shown a lack of respect for those who have chosen to be individuals and not conform to the will of society. As a person who has, along with my family, chosen to become imprinted, I do, however, admire the courage of every single one of these brave individuals for continuing to stand up for what they believe in. His vow of removing those who have not registered away from Green Zones is a clear example of what I mean regarding his complete lack of respect for humanity."

"Councilwoman, he's stated that he's planning on doing so because of the rise in crime by non-registered citizens." A reporter responded.

"The President cannot confirm that these acts have all come from those who are not registered. If it were the case, he's certainly taking the wrong approach by punishing everyone due to the acts of some. That would be completely unfair."

"Then, how do you respond to the recent shooting of one of your rival cabinet members inside of her own home?" A reporter asked. Naomi stopped to look the reporter directly into his eyes.

"Patricia Sanders and I have a long, complicated history as it pertains to how our world should be run; there's no secret there. Never in a million years would I wish that someone would enter her home; a haven, and commit such an atrocious act. However, with no intention of trying to sound insensitive, we simply do not know that this act was done by non-registered citizens. We are thankful that Sanders is still with us and once she fully recovers, I look forward to continuing our work towards creating a better and safer world for all of us. Thank you."

Within the upcoming months, council members campaigned and urged President Dunne to find alternative solutions to the rising levels of crime throughout both Regions. Eventually, President Dunne conformed to their request and decided to increase ground patrol, surveillance cameras, along with drones to monitor Green Zones throughout each Quadrant. Some members of Congress weren't completely thrilled with having officers constantly present within the streets, but it was better than having those who weren't registered evacuated. Their presence was threatening, and many feared that the officers would overlook their purpose of being there and eventually would cause them to abuse their power. Council members, such as Naomi, vowed to continue fighting to have officers removed completely.

REGION ONE: SOMEWHERE AROUND ~~NEW YORK~~

Kaleb chased the unkempt, bearded, homeless gentleman out of his father's store whom he'd spotted stealing from the produce section. He reeked of a horrible odor, causing others, whenever they were near the man, to turn their noses up at him. It was due to his smell, among other reasons. A few times, the man heard people gagging because of his stench. However, he never found himself being concerned about the reactions of others; there were simply too many other things hovering around in his mind. Seeing a homeless person was such a rare thing, with so many resources available to people. There wasn't much sympathy or empathy given to these individuals because many felt that there were simply too lazy to put forth an effort to end all of their sorrows. "Stop begging! Get yourself in order!" People would yell.

After all the time that had passed, the voices, *the voices*, were still there. Why couldn't Andrew shake the voices? Every time that he would close his eyes, he could hear his family asking him, "How could you leave us?" Over and over inside of his head, the night of his family's capture continued to play as if it were a movie reel that would start again once it finished. It would play again, right from the very beginning. All the conversations that he had with Trevor and him being instructed on the importance of watching over his mother and Noah simply wouldn't cease. He'd failed to uphold the request that he'd promised to do as the head of their household.

At times, he would attempt to justify his actions from that night by trying to convince himself that his family would've slowed him down and that they all would've eventually gotten captured. But then, he would come to himself and become face with the possibility of the alternative. What if they would've gotten away? These thoughts haunted him deep within the core of his soul and where he could not find an end to his madness, he found drugs, of various sorts, to help in alleviating his torture. His bones along with soul ached, giving him a pain in which he never thought was possible. Andrew was nothing. He was a disgrace and brought forth shame unto his family name. He was a man without honor or hope, but somewhere inside of him, a tiny flicker of faith lied dormant. Although he often ignored it, he knew it was the answer to the question of why he hadn't become imprinted, which would lead to the end of all of his physical torment. With this, he also wrestled. He didn't deserve to become rescued by the Helpers, despite this being his only reasoning for being in Region One.

Ultimately, Andrew isolated himself by venturing off into the Red Zone, into the wilderness, away from all civilization.

8
TRANSFIGURATION

It'd been quite some time since the last time Kaleb heard from Melanie and her son, and it had bothered him quite a bit. His sister noticed how differently he'd been acting around the store and inquired about it, but he knew he couldn't express what was truly troubling him to her. With all of the changes that had taken place, he felt Melanie would eventually reach out to him, although; he wasn't completely certain.

One day while at the store he'd been thinking about her heavily and abruptly decided to leave. Alicia asked him where he was taking off to, but he simply responded that he had a quick run that he'd needed to make. He ended up knocking on Gabe's front door when Kristina answered. It had been the only likely place where she could have gone to, despite Melanie and Gabe not seeing eye to eye. Since they were family, it only made sense that Gabe would take the two of them in.

"Oh, hi, Kaleb. How have you been? It's been such a long time," Kristina said.

"Hey, I've been doing well. Thank you," Kaleb answered.

As the two spoke, Gabe came from behind Kristina and invited Kaleb in. He accepted their invitation and took a seat on their couch. Kaleb didn't want to be rude, but he was rather eager to get to the point of his visit.

"I didn't want to take up too much of you guys' time, but I was wondering if Melanie was here? I haven't heard from her and I just wanted to make sure that she and Jaylen were okay." Kaleb asked.

Kristina excused herself, stating that she needed to tend to the food that she'd started preparing in the kitchen, but again expressed how good it was to see Kaleb.

"She uh… she's not here," Gabe said, clearing his throat. "She and Jaylen actually don't live here."

Kaleb's eyes squinted out of confusion.

"What do you mean? Where else could they have gone," Kaleb asked?

"I… uh… we, Kristina and I, offered for both of them to stay with us, but she declined. She said that she had already made other arrangements and decided to move to one of the shelters a ways up north just before entering the Red Zone. I drove them up myself."

The two sat without either saying a word for a moment. Kaleb sat forward, hands clasped, as he looked towards the ground trying to sort through his thoughts.

"That doesn't make any sense," Kaleb said. "It just doesn't seem like the type of move she would make. She's just so prideful. Seems like she would hate to move to a place like that." Kaleb continued.

"Being that as it may, when things go sour, you'll find yourself doing a lot of things you thought you'd never do," Gabe said.

Kaleb looked up at him, a little turned off by his comment. They were speaking about Gabe's son and his mother, not just some random person on the street.

"I suppose so," Kaleb said, piercing Gabe with his gaze.

Gabe soon broke eye contact, figuring that Kaleb was on to him and the reality of not opening up his home to the mother of his child. Technically, he felt he was only obligated to offer a place to stay to his son, who was practically an adult, by the way, so he was free from any guilt. At least, that's how he felt.

"Which one did she move to, again?" Kaleb asked, breaking the awkward silence between the two.

Gabe gave him the directions, and Kaleb made his way out of the front door. He felt relieved that he was able to get Kaleb away without having to tell him the truth about everything. Just before opening his car door, Kaleb glanced back at Gabe and Kristina's home, pondering about what really happened.

Everyone inside of the shelter became increasingly nervous behind the military officer's constant patrolling through neighborhoods. There had been an increased number of complaints of harassment by those who had the misfortune of meeting an officer. Jaylen recalled seeing Naomi on the television doing an interview and felt grateful knowing that there were people on the outside fighting for them.

Melanie's nervousness, however, became fear. She felt as though everyone's presence there made them direct targets for whatever Dunne and his patrolmen truly had in store. Melanie would always find time to escape, to be alone, to pray. She made every effort to ensure that Jaylen, or anyone else, could see her crying. Her worry continued to grow by the day, not knowing what was next to come for her and her son.

"I'm trusting You, oh God, I'm trusting You, but I fear for me and my son's life." Jaylen once heard her crying out in a designated prayer room within the shelter without her knowing he was there.

"Although we may not have been perfect, we've remained faithful to Your instructions. Please… don't forsake us to be delivered into the hands of our enemies," she continued. Jaylen's head fell as he walked away.

Drones flew high above Kaleb's car as he followed the directions which were given to him by Gabe, to where Melanie was said to be. It had been years since he'd been on this side of town. The further he drove along, there were fewer people present and fewer lights, by it being so close to the edge of a Red Zone. It was difficult, but he was finally able to find the location and parked his car near the rear of the building, which appeared as if it were vacant. He was concerned and wasn't sure if he had the right place or not as he checked the address on the paper to see if it matched the one on the building.

This must be the place, He thought to himself.

Kaleb walked around to the front and knocked on the door. He heard footsteps moving around, then there was silence. He became puzzled and looked around.

"Hello?" he yelled out.

Nothing.

Suddenly, a loud, screeching latch to the door was pulled back, causing him to jump, revealing a set of dark eyes.

"How can I help you?" an unwelcoming male voice asked.

"I-I'm here to see someone. Melanie?" Kaleb requested.

The eyes observed him without saying a word at first.

"Who's with you?"

"No one is with me. I'm alone." Kaleb sighed.

"Do you have an appointment?" the set of eyes asked.

"No. I don't have an appointment. How would one go about scheduling an appointment in this place, anyway?" Kaleb said, becoming a bit annoyed.

"By knowing the right people. People don't simply come here on their own without being sent." the eyes said sharply.

"Well, I know Melanie and her son Jaylen." Kaleb shot back. "Look, I'm an old friend and I was told that she was here. Is this some kind of prison? May I please see her?"

After a few moments of not responding, the person on the other side of the door closed the latch from where he'd been viewing out of. During this time, Kaleb wasn't sure if the gentleman was heading to get Melanie or not, but he decided to hang around for a minute.

"What type of place is this?" he mumbled to himself as he observed the facility's exterior.

Some time had passed, then he heard locks from the door beginning to open, then a voice instructing him to come in. He did as he was told, as the short gentleman told him to wait inside of the lobby area and peered at him unpleasantly as he walked away. Kaleb simply shook his head.

Shortly after, Melanie entered the lobby, and the two embraced one another. She wasn't sure why she felt the need to hug him, but it came as a natural reaction. It came as a surprise to Kaleb as well, but he wouldn't let it show. He decided to roll with it. After all, it was the response in which he'd wanted.

"I'd been wondering why I haven't heard from you. I don't know, I just sort of figured that you would've reached out to me. Listen, I know you didn't say that would take me up on my offer, but... look, I've just missed you. I just have to be honest with you." Kaleb admitted.

Melanie smiled.

"Yeah, I've been here; away from everything and everyone," Melanie said. She thought about how private the facility was and became puzzled by Kaleb being there and him seemingly being able to find her with so much ease.

"Not that I'm not happy to see you, but how did you find me?"

"I went over to Gabe's home to see you, and he said that you decided to move here instead of moving in with him. I thought it was kind of an odd choice, but I guess I understood it. He gave me the address to—"

"Wait, he said I *decided* to move here instead of with him?"

"Well... yeah, which I couldn't really understand because—"

"He told me that I couldn't live there with him and Kristina," Melanie said.

"Are you serious right now?" Kaleb asked.

"Initially, I was upset, but I got over it. He did, however, say that Jaylen could stay."

"You guys are family, Melanie; he should look out for you for however long you need the help."

"That's how I felt at first, but I sat back and thought about it. I can't be dependent on him; I just have to figure things out, somehow, for myself and Jaylen. So far, living here has been working out for us." She said, referring to the shelter.

"You don't have to figure things out for yourself; I told you, a long time ago, that I have a place for you and Jaylen. You don't have to be here. You'll be a lot more comfortable. No one knows what the government has planned for these types of places. If they're shut down, then what will you do?"

"That's not for certain," she said, attempting to avoid the possibility within her mind.

"There's been talks of them doing so, Melanie," Kaleb responded. "I'm opening my doors so that you won't have to worry about that happening."

Melanie never ruled out the possibility of staying in the space that Kaleb had above the store when he'd first invited her and Jaylen to live there. The only hurdle then, and now, was his sister finding out about it. As tensions continued to rise, however, it seemed like a better idea with each passing day.

"Maybe you're right." She said. "I just… really don't want to have to deal with Alicia."

"Just trust me on this. She won't be a problem."

Whenever it transfigured into its rare non-earthly form and outside of the flesh of Mallory Hansen, the foul, wretched stench would be far too great for human absorption. While it had been a form in which it had rarely configured to, since it had taken on the flesh, this was its natural form, one not meant for the sight of man. The physical manifestation of the darkest side of the unknown caused the living flesh, who'd borne witness to it, to become driven instantly into madness and mania. Even clothed in the heavy wool house robe, as it slowly walked out onto the patio of Hansen's secluded home, the odor caused the flies to stick closely to its leathery, scaled, burned, and unevenly layered being. Sounds from the unseen wild beast within the dark became louder as their senses became triggered at the presence of... *something else*. Some creatures were driven to rage; others were driven away by fear.

Howls and glowing eyes gathered around, yet aware and careful enough not to draw too close to the thing. The hood attached to the robe covered its head and most of its face, concealing the majority of what couldn't be witnessed in full by any man. For a time, it overlooked the view of the nearby city within the distance, basking in all that it had accomplished.

As it continued to revel in its glory, the light of the moon scaled back the dark clouds. The light beamed down directly onto the creature, to its displeasure. Slowly, its head rose, face remaining hidden, as it gazed up into the moonlight with a low rumbling growl vibrating underneath its breath. A visible and odorous steam came from its parted lips as it came into the direct sight of the moon. The eye of God. Then its retreat began, back into its hiding place, the home of Hansen, where it would, once again, disguise itself within the flesh.

9
DELIBERATING

On the rooftop of the shelter, Lisa and Evan were gazing out into the distance, deeper into the Green Zone where the lights glowed brightly, and everything seemed to appear much more alive compared to where they were located. Amid their conversation, Ahmad walked up from behind them in his usual dark and edgy demeanor to join them. He was tall, slender, yet fit, with a scar underneath his left eye in which he'd never discussed. The speculations and stories as to how it'd gotten there ran wild amongst the group of protestors. No one ever bothered to ask him about it because it just didn't seem like the thing someone should ask a person about and then on top of that, it was Ahmad. A person's guess was probably right about how it'd gotten there.

"What's up?" Ahmad greeted them.

"H-hey… Ahmad. How are you?" Lisa asked.

"Cool, just wanted to check in, see what our next move was with everything." Ahmad said.

"We're meeting up at the end of the week, at the same spot, to outline the details of the next protest," Lisa said. Ahmad shook his head.

"Another damn protest? We're still on that?" he said, gesturing with his hands while stepping closer towards them.

Evan glanced over him and Lisa's shoulders to take note of how close the two of them were to the edge of the rooftop. He didn't necessarily have any reason to suspect that anything could happen to them, but Ahmad never made Evan feel "all warm inside", as he'd once described how he felt around him.

"Yeah, Ahmad, I'm not sure if you realize it, but that's sort of what we do," Lisa said.

Her response made Evan a little uneasy. It was a little more aggressive than how he felt she should come off towards Ahmad.

"That's about all we do. March up and down the street, yelling, and holding signs, hoping that they pay attention to us. What's our plan when the government changes their mind and says we're not allowed to protest anymore, huh? The only progress being made is what they're allowing. We haven't gotten their attention as we should."

"Jesus, Ahmad, what's your big plan then, huh, since you've gotten it all figured out?" Lisa challenged.

"I think all of that marching should be over with, for starters. Next, as long as these military officers have the ability to do whatever they want with us and paint the story how they see fit, we need to be prepared for that and get just as physical with them if it comes down to it."

"This dude has lost his mind," Lisa said to Evan. Evan listened to their exchange, remaining quiet. "Do you hear yourself? They'll slaughter us in the street!"

"That's the problem! As soon as we do something that they disagree with, they're liable to do anything to us. That's the reason we have to march now. Because they hold the power and we feel that forcing us to do whatever they tell us to do isn't right. Obviously, what's right, what's wrong, democracy and all of that other good stuff for the people we used to hear and read about in books, is dead now. The only thing there is now is what's happening to us and what we plan on doing about it." Ahmad concluded, looking the two of them in the eye.

Lisa peered back; neither one of them spoke a word.

"Let's say that… maybe you're right. Simply saying we need to be prepared to fight back isn't an actual plan," Lisa finally responded.

"Being prepared to fight sounds like a better plan than not being prepared to fight," Ahmad said before turning and walking away.

As much as he wanted to not side with Ahmad, Evan felt that he'd just made a strong case for himself, but he wouldn't tell that to Lisa. She'd probably toss him over the top of that roof.

"Hey," Lisa called out to Ahmad, "where have you been the past few days, anyway? We haven't seen you around here much. Have anything to do with your big plan?"

Ahmad stopped and turned to face them.

"You could probably say that. A friend of mine ended up getting shot, I've been checking in on him." He said.

"Oh, I'm sorry to hear that," Lisa said feeling slightly guilty for sounding so snarky with her questioning his whereabouts.

"Does he protest with us?" Evan asked.

"Nah. That's not really his thing. He has more of a hands-on approach to getting affirmative action. He doesn't mind going directly to the source to get whatever he wants." Ahmad said before turning again and leaving.

"I told you, that dude and whoever he runs with when he's not with us is crazy! What in the world did he mean by that? I'm saying, he's crazy enough by himself, but a team of Ahmads running around is terrifying." Evan said to Lisa emphatically.

Lisa watched Ahmad leave and then turned around to look out into the lights, with Ahmad's words echoing within her ears.

Not far away from the shelter, Cassandra lived with her cousin, Jessica, who, despite not agreeing with everything she'd believed in, supported her reasoning behind not becoming imprinted. Jessica would side with her and her friends on occasions when it was needed. She would also allow Cassandra's friends and boyfriend, Jaylen, who was currently visiting, to come over from time to time.

Jaylen zipped up the front of his jacket as Cassandra pulled at him from her bed, encouraging him to stay a little while longer. He'd already stayed longer than he'd originally planned. The two hadn't seen one another in a while and had spent a large portion of the evening making out in the living area Cassandra lived inside of Jessica's basement.

"You know that I really want to stay… but it's so late now and I'm not trying to play around with these cops. They're serious out there." Jaylen said.

"I knoooow," Cassandra replied, rolling her eyes at him.

"Technically, we shouldn't be fooling around anyway," Jaylen said as he leaned over to kiss her on the lips.

"Oh yeah? Well, then when are we getting married?" she asked.

Jaylen pulled back with a chuckle without responding to her.

"I thought so," she said, throwing a pillow at him.

126

"No. It's not like that. You know how it is right now. No one is going to acknowledge us being legally married. As it stands now, we don't even exist in this world."

"You're right… I guess." She sighed while, again, rolling her eyes at him.

"I mean, we could have like an underground ceremony with friends and family, and just make that promise amongst ourselves."

Cassandra smiled. She appreciated the thought that he'd given to them becoming married. It showed that he took it seriously.

"That sounds cool. But I need the world to acknowledge that what we have is real!" she said playfully.

The two of them laughed. Jaylen kissed Cassandra on her forehead and headed for the door. But before he could leave, she called to him.

"Hey… you ever thought about just… doing it, getting it over with."

He stopped in the middle of his steps and turned around to face his girlfriend.

"Doing *what*? Getting what over with?" He asked.

"Imprinted. So, things can be okay. I just see my cousin, and everything seems to be fine with her, but here I am just living off of her, basically, and it doesn't have to be that way. She's sweet about it but… I don't know."

"No. We can't," he said firmly.

"But have you really just sat and thought about why we can't, though? I get it, the Bible says it and everything, but there's just so much that goes into interpreting everything that—"

"What are you saying, Cassandra?" he asked, cutting her off.

She sat quietly, thinking for a moment before answering him.

"I don't know, really. I just... I love you and I want things to feel... authentic I guess."

"What we have is already real. We don't need anyone else to tell us that who we are and what we have is real by imprinting something into our bodies. Now, I'm with you. At times, the Bible can be difficult to understand and to translate, but as it relates to this, the instructions were explicit." Jaylen responded.

"Yeah, but how do we know those times mentioned in there were talking about now?" She asked.

"You have to listen and trust what's inside you. Listen to what God is telling you. You know that what's occurring is lining up with God's word. That's why you haven't fallen for any of the enemy's tricks." Jaylen said.

"I believe in that, for the most part, you know, but some days I go back and forth with it. While everyone is living this glorious life, are God's people, meanwhile, supposed to continue living in the shadows searching through scraps for food? I just don't understand," Cassandra replied.

"Don't worry," Jaylen sighed. "We'll be fine." He said before leaving.

"I guess so," she whispered to herself.

Once on the street, Jaylen had the hood of his jacket pulled over his head and stuck deep within the shadows as he made every attempt to not become detected by officers or drones. The idea that not long ago, he was acceptable, but now that things had changed to where simply being seen by an officer could mean the end of his life, depending on the officer's mood, was something that he hadn't been able to process.

After much skillful maneuvering, Jaylen finally arrived back at the facility. He walked around to the back of the building to what appeared to be an old employee entrance and scanned a key card that all the residents were given. The door buzzed, signaling that it was open, and for a second, he paused before going in. He looked down at the card in his right hand, then at the pad to the side of the door where he'd just scanned the card. He hadn't thought about it until then, but he considered how an imprint actually worked. The only difference was that instead of physically holding the card in his hand, he would only have to scan his palm.

In theory, it was simple. Schedule one appointment and he and his mother's life would be normal again, perhaps better than it had ever been. He thought about what Cassandra had said as well, along with her doubts and her points about how the Bible could have been misinterpreted.

Could she have a point? He wondered. Soon, however, he snapped out of it and entered inside.

The next morning, Melanie told her son that she was considering moving into the apartment space above Flannigan's Groceries and that she would like for him to move in with her. Jaylen continued to lie in bed, arms folded underneath his head as he stared directly up at the ceiling.

"Oh yeah," he started, "what made you change your mind about living there?"

"Just feel like it could be safer, more secure for us. Who knows what may happen to places like these? If the government decides to shut them all down, we'll be screwed." Melanie answered, sitting up in her bed, facing her son.

"Yeah, you're probably right. I wish we had some actual family to take us in," Jaylen said.

"Don't get me started on family. It's just you, me, and God," she said.

The two were quiet for a while as Jaylen thought about what the arrangement could mean. He thought about the distance from Flannigan's Groceries to the meeting point for his group of protesters and how far it was from where Cassandra had been living with her cousin, Jessica.

Kaleb was cool, he thought. He was fine about how he felt about his mother; it didn't bother him. Jaylen respected his persistence. He wasn't a bad guy. In fact, Jaylen felt the only reason his mother brushed him off was because she was scared. She'd placed so much trust in his father and that practically ruined all of her trust in men. She dated, but the men were no good. Jaylen couldn't understand why any of them were given the light of day. He figured it was so she could have male companionship but never have to get her hopes up because she would know early on that there wouldn't be a real future with them. With Kaleb, however, it was different; he seemed like a solid dude, much different from the others. Jaylen was sure that his mother could see it, so her dodging him made sense.

"Do you like him," Jaylen asked, catching his mother off guard?

"Do I like who?" she asked emphatically in a high-pitched voice.

10
MISSING

Kaleb anxiously exited the store, locked up, and prepared to head over to pick up his new guests that would live above the store. It was early, there wasn't much traffic, and it had been before the store's opening. Alicia had taken a day off and the opening employees wouldn't be arriving until another two hours. Kaleb figured this would be the perfect time for the two of them to get settled in. His head remained on a swivel, glancing to his left and right for officers, but, hopefully, he wouldn't run into any trouble and could bring them back to the store safe and sound. It was freezing, so he continued to shift and move about as much as he could to remain warm as he made his way to his car in the back of the building. However, that plan wasn't helping so much; it was simply too cold.

As he approached the corner of the building, he heard the faint sound of footsteps as he continued on. After the visit to the shelter, he'd hoped that he had finally gotten through to Melanie and that she would take him up on his offer, but he wasn't sure if she actually would. The fact that he could express that he cared for her had been satisfying. The day that she had finally called him after his visit to take him up on his offer, he was elated.

Reaching the corner, the sound of footsteps became heavier, more aggressive, and as if numerous people were approaching as opposed to only two. The steps grew louder as they met against the pavement, each time sounding off in unison. Just before he had gotten to the corner, Kaleb jumped with his back against the adjacent wall on the outside of the store. As he did, the seemingly terrorizing larger-than-life robotic-looking military officers turned the corner, heading up the street from which Kaleb had come.

They were on a surprise early morning street patrol, seeking any suspicious activity from citizens who'd try to sneak through the law's grasp. The officers, who almost seemed to move in slow motion, at least according to Kaleb, were all perfectly aligned in a row across the street, making it impossible for a simple pass-through.

One officer was slightly more alert and noticed someone pressed against the wall of the store in which they'd been passing. He stopped for a moment, without saying a word, as his helmet scanned the gentleman and shortly thereafter, his identity appeared to the officer on the inside of the black tinted screen of the helmet.

… Registered Citizen.

…Kaleb Flannigan

… Son of deceased Calvin Flannigan.

… Mother, Denise Flannigan.

… One sibling, Alicia Flannigan…

This, along with every other detail of Kaleb, all the way down to his social security number and food allergies, was revealed. Kaleb didn't move a single inch while backed against the stone wall. The officer slowly turned away to catch up with the rest of the brigade. Kaleb was off of the hook. Once the coast was clear, Kaleb sprinted towards the back, hopped into his car, and made his way towards Melanie and Jaylen near the edge of town.

Near the side of the store, there was an alleyway which had a doorway leading into the entry to the back area of the grocery. One area led to back storage and an office, while the other had a flight of stairs that went up to a small apartment. Here is where Kaleb had planned for Melanie and Jaylen to stay for as long as they needed to. Kaleb was excited that they'd taken him up on his offer, but he tried his best to not come off as being too over-dramatic.

Melanie and Jaylen were grateful for Kaleb's generosity, yet for the most part, they'd been quiet, not quite knowing what to say besides, "Thank you." They were given a quick tour of the small, fully furnished, but cozy place. Kaleb made sure to give the place a thorough cleaning, and he'd tried his best to rid it of the damp, mildew odor, but it still lingered some. He figured, once the two moved in and given the place some form of life, it would rid itself. He thought it was interesting how lifelessness carried a smell to it.

The place had two bedrooms, one bathroom, a small kitchen, and a den area. It even had a washer and dryer. Frankly, it was a little more than Melanie had expected. The small space was stacked on top of itself, but it was perfect enough for the two of them. They each sat their bags inside of their rooms as Kaleb scrambled to help them both, but they politely let him know they could handle it.

It was odd for them both, being in a new place, but moving around from place to place without having a solid place to call home had become a theme over the last several years. Melanie and her son, while not okay with it, had become accustomed to it.

After they'd set their bags down in their rooms, they came out to see a smiling and awkwardly standing Kaleb in the center of the den. Had he been waiting for something? They weren't sure. To break the awkwardness of it all, Melanie thanked him again and gave him a hug. Kaleb thanked them for coming, reassured them that there wouldn't be any trouble, and to make themselves at home because it was their home.

However, just to be on the safe side, for the time being, he reminded them to make sure that they exited only through the side, through the alley, and not through the store. Just after another rising moment of awkwardness between the three, Kaleb said that he had a few things that he'd need to work on down in the store, so he left the keys on the table that sat in the center of the den and walked out the apartment door.

Melanie looked at her son, who'd stood gazing around the small apartment in silence. He was a little uncomfortable; not sure about what to think about the place. His mother waited to see if he had a feeling about the place that he hadn't, or was simply waiting to reveal to her. He didn't say a word. She suggested they make themselves comfortable and settle into their new home.

As the days went on, the two of them didn't bother leaving their space much; it was a complicated thing. With an increase in foot patrolmen, drones flying about, and the reports of harassment by the military officers, it could be a risky move for an unregistered citizen to meet an officer. Then, to top things off, there were the high chances of running into Kaleb's sister whenever she would stop by the store. Kaleb would check in to see how things were going and he would always ensure them he would, eventually, tell his sister about their living there whenever the time was right for them to move around more freely.

Life seemingly moved on without those who'd chosen not to become imprinted and registered within the global database; therefore, they simply did not exist within the eyes of the government. While most lived within the outskirts of every town and near Red Zones, they blamed much of the crime that continued to occur on those who weren't classified as being citizens.

Members of Congress also continued to go back and forth with one another on what they should do about those who haven't registered and if they were, in fact, the ones responsible for the crime that continued to take place. Activists, such as Naomi, stressed that it was impossible to prove that all the criminal acts had come from those who weren't registered. Even the classification of them being "non-citizens" was heavily debated. Arguments within Congress swayed the public's perception of non-registered citizens in a negative manner, causing them to look down upon them and treat them harshly whenever they were encountered throughout the streets. Mostly, it wasn't too difficult to tell who were registered citizens and who weren't.

There was a certain look and demeanor that those who were imprinted carried that the others lacked. Not to mention, imprinted citizens appeared to be slightly better groomed. Those who weren't imprinted, yet had access to resources, pooled together as much as they could to help one another with necessities such as food and personal hygiene products.

The group of protesters met together in an old abandoned warehouse, the same location in which they normally would meet, going over the latest news, and worked on what their next protest should entail. Everyone was in attendance, including a few new members who were brought along by their friends. Ahmad had also been there with his usual look of frustration at what was being said because of his disagreement with the direction in which the group had been headed. He pushed Jaylen, urging him they should do more with the number of people that they had.

"I agree with us doing more, Ahmad. It's just that I don't think arming ourselves with weapons is the answer. I just feel like that type of image on the streets from us would invite unwanted chaos against us." Jaylen said.

"They're already attacking us and getting away with it, by the way. We've all heard the news." Ahmad replied. "Let's forget the weapons for now. I know another means of making sure that none of us have to worry about lacking any essentials that we need. We wouldn't need to rely on the government or anything."

"This already sounds illegal," Cassandra whispered to Lisa.

"A few of my friends figured out a way to create an artificial imprint on our skin that actually registers within the database. It doesn't have to be imprinted or anything, but it goes over the palm like an invisible tattoo and pulls up whatever information that you input into the database. A new identity, medical records, bank information, whatever. They could also hack into other bank accounts and transfer funds into an account that you set."

"Told you," Cassandra said to Lisa.

"You're kidding us, right?" a gentleman from their group asked.

"No. I'm not kidding," Ahmad said, facing him from a distance, still in an intimidating fashion.

"That's not who we are," a soft female voice spoke from another member.

"I think that's something that we should consider." Someone else said.

The group was split and were unsure about how seriously they should take what Ahmad had just presented to them. They argued amongst themselves, then quieted down, waiting to see what Jaylen had to say on the matter.

"That sounds risky," Jaylen stated.

"Of course, it is!" Ahmad exclaimed. "Us all being at this meeting together is risky. Us going out to protest is risky. What I'm trying to say is that we are running out of options. The government is starting to close the walls in on us and I feel like they're forcing our hand. Now, I don't want that thing put inside of me. That's just not how I roll. I'm flesh and blood and I'm not up for becoming a governmental robot. That's me. So, as I said, I just think that this would be a good alternative option for us all."

"Honestly, man, that sounds solid," someone said.

Ahmad gave them a nod of appreciation.

"What happens when they catch on to us?" Jaylen challenged. "It would only be a matter of time before they do. The system is far too sophisticated. Who knows what they'll do to us."

"We can't worry about that part right now," Ahmad said.

"Why not worry about it now?" Evan chimed. "That's a big deciding factor for me."

"Well, then you're out, since you're so scared to lose what you don't already have! You're a coward anyway in my eyes!" Ahmad fired back at Evan.

"Chill," Jaylen told Ahmad, attempting to calm him. "Let's all just take some time and think about this. It's not off the table, we just need to think about it."

"I'll put it like this," Ahmad began, "I'm doing it, regardless. I just wanted to present this to you all to see if you wanted in since we've worked closely with one another."

"Why does he think he's doing us a favor by inviting us to be a part of his criminal enterprise?" Lisa said quietly to Cassandra.

"Count me in, Ahmad," someone said.

Jaylen looked at the man and the rest of the group wondering about the direction in which they'd all be heading in the upcoming months. Ahmad was right in one instance; the walls were closing in on them. Going the route that he'd offered just didn't seem like the right thing to do. He also wondered how long he'd been doing this and just how far he'd be willing to take things when things went wrong.

The next morning, Jaylen awakened to his phone vibrating due to several messages coming in from their group chat. Upon opening it, he saw that everyone was inquiring about the whereabouts of Evan. Cassandra stated she thought that Ahmad, Lisa, and Evan had all left together after the meeting since they all lived in the same shelter. Lisa replied that Evan stated he was going to visit another facility that his grandmother lived in to check on her before heading home and that Ahmad said that he was going to meet up with a few of his friends before returning.

"That's strange," Jaylen messaged. "He didn't send a text to either one of you or anything?"

Everyone replied that he hadn't.

"Have you spoken to Ahmad?" Jaylen asked Lisa.

"This morning, at breakfast, but he said that he hadn't seen or heard from him," Lisa responded.

"How did he sound when he said it?" Cassandra asked.

"In a normal, non-hostile manner. He didn't come across as if he had anything to do with it if that's what you mean." Lisa replied.

Jaylen sat up in his bed, confused. Then he got up and walked to his mother's room to ask if she'd heard from Evan.

"No. Is everything okay?" she asked.

"Not sure. He didn't make it back to the shelter after the meeting yesterday," he told her.

Melanie shook her head.

"See, this is why I don't like you going out. You never know what could happen."

Jaylen looked at his mother, then back down at his phone.

Back at the shelter, Lisa roamed around asking the other residents if they'd seen or heard from Evan, but many of them replied they had not. She went to his bed to see if he'd, for some reason, left a message letting someone know where he might have gone. That wouldn't make sense, she thought. He would've sent a text.

As she was about to leave his room, several members of the Helpers ran swiftly past the door, just missing her.

"Call the ambulance, now, *now*!" one of them shouted.

Lisa's heart began to race as she slowly followed them out towards the exit. She wasn't sure why it was beating so fast. Perhaps it was because of the frantic nature in which everyone had been carrying on.

"What's happening?" Regina asked.

"Please, go back into your rooms!" someone from the staff yelled.

"I don't have to go to my room; we're not prisoners here!" Regina protested.

"Ma'am, please... just stay inside!" the other responded.

Meanwhile, Lisa slowly continued to follow up behind them, closer and closer to the front entrance of the facility, seemingly unnoticed.

She couldn't figure out why there had been a tightness forming inside of her stomach.

What was happening outside?

Lisa's anxiety increased as the sense of not being aware of what was occurring, yet somehow knowing, elevated within her. Through the lobby area, through the entrance of the building, the Helpers ran as the door flung open, then closed again as they each flooded out one after another.

For a moment she stood back from a distance, catching a glimpse of where they rushed to, as the door continued to open and close shut. They appeared to be across the street, kneeling before something.

What was it? She couldn't clearly make out what it was. Then, a sudden glimpse of what appeared to be someone's motionless body. A lump formed inside of Lisa's throat, making it difficult for her to swallow. She slowly continued to walk to the door, pushed it open, and went across the street to where the Helpers were hovering over what she'd only caught partial glimpses of.

She couldn't understand why, but it was as if she was being drawn over to where they were. She needed to see what was there. One Helper stood with her hands covering her mouth; tears in her eyes. The dread of what she might find continued to rise as Lisa drew closer and closer. Someone mouthed and motioned for her to "go back inside" but Lisa's eyes remained fixed on what they were all tending to.

Then, Lisa's body shattered as a final look of what they had all been crouching over lent itself unto her as one of the Helpers rushed towards her to move her back inside of the shelter. She was carried back to where she'd come as her screams pierced through the cool, crisp morning air. The Helper carrying her could feel the sadness exuding through her uncontrollably trembling frame as they entered back inside.

He looked down at his phone to see Cassandra's name come across the screen. Jaylen answered and his eyes quickly turned red and welled up with tears. His hands began to shake, then the phone fell onto the floor.

11
CHOOSING SIDES

Alicia was preparing food in the kitchen as Kaleb sat in the dining area, already indulging in the breakfast that she had made for him. She was in clear view of Kaleb, and from her expression and the way she'd been behaving that morning, he knew that something was on her mind. He shook his head slightly, knowing that she would let everything all out at any given moment.

"What's bothering you?" He asked.

"What do you mean?" Alicia asked with her back turned to him as she continued to face the stove.

"You've been quiet all morning; I know that something's up. You usually get that way towards me just before you explode," Kaleb said.

"For starters," Alicia began, still tending to the food, "you don't know anything about what's going on inside of me to assume that I'm waiting for the perfect moment to go off on you. Second, if I'm quiet, that doesn't automatically mean that something's wrong with me. Perhaps, I want a moment of peace and quiet for myself, meaning no words from myself… or anyone else."

These days, Kaleb seemed to always have a sharp tongue coming at him, whether it was from Melanie or from his own sister. Alicia walked over to Kaleb with the sizzling skillet in her hands.

"More eggs?" Alicia asked.

Kaleb looked up at his sister, giving her smirk as he continued to chew.

"Sure," he responded.

Alicia scrapped the eggs onto her brother's near-empty plate, walked back into the kitchen, and placed the remaining eggs onto the plate she had previously begun preparing for herself. She came back to the table with her plate and sat down next to Kaleb. For some time, they both sat in silence until Alicia finally broke the streak in a way that only she could.

"Have you heard from Melanie?"

Here it comes. The moment Kaleb had been anticipating the entire morning. The burden that she'd been carrying was finally about to be released. Had she somehow found out that she and Jaylen were living above the store? She couldn't have!

"Um… from time to time, I see Melanie, yes," Kaleb said, trying his best to step lightly around her question.

"Please, don't play smart with me," Alicia fired back.

"Alicia, what are you getting at? Just get to it instead of acting all weird and being all nasty towards me." Kaleb's silverware clinked onto the plate as he released them from his hands.

"What am I doing that's so wrong this time, tell me?" he asked.

"I'm just curious, that's all," Alicia said in between bites of food, "at how long you tend to keep up this thing you have going on for her."

"Keep what up?" Asked Kaleb.

"You know… you thinking that you're in love while she and her civil rights activist son take advantage of you."

Kaleb delivered a sharp look at his sister and she returned an emotionless look back to him, standing firm on what she'd said.

"How dare you? Who do you think you are? You're completely out of line, Alicia!"

"Am I out of line?" she challenged.

"Yeah, you are! How exactly are they taking advantage of me? That makes no sense for you to make that type of statement," Kaleb said.

"Oh, is that so?" replied Alicia.

Kaleb couldn't tell if she'd known or suspected something, but he continued to stand firmly to maintain his bluff, despite his heart pounding inside of his chest.

"That's... *odd*," she said sarcastically. "The other day, a strange thing happened. I was working my regular scheduled shift, but I stayed an hour, maybe an hour and a half later than normal. I walked outside of the store but realized that I'd left my laptop. Careless of me, I know. So, I walked back inside, headed to the office, but just as I was about to go inside, I see, who appeared to be Jaylen walking outside of the side entryway towards the alley of our store."

Kaleb swallowed.

"Now, that just didn't make any sense to me. What business would Jaylen have coming from the upstairs living area above our store? Was he trying to steal something, had he been camping out there? I asked myself these things, but I knew that it couldn't be true. Jaylen's a good guy. I'm uncertain about his mother, but he's okay with me. I was thinking if I should call Melanie to see what she thought about all of this. Then, I thought that maybe this is a sensitive issue so, perhaps, I should go by her home to discuss this with her. But then, I remembered, she probably no longer has a home. So, I was trying to figure out where in the world she might be? I'm stumped! What do you think we should do about it, huh?" Alicia asked, staring sharply at her brother.

Kaleb took a deep breath before speaking.

"I-I was planning on telling you, but I was just looking for the right time to do so. They-they just needed—"

"Needed what, Kaleb? Another handout? They've made their choice! The government has offered to help them, yet they've refused it. We cannot help anyone unwilling to help themselves. Look I get it; they believe whatever they believe. I have my beliefs too, but I also believe that we're not supposed to live down here on earth suffering. As I've said, they're taking advantage of us."

"They're not taking advantage of us. You need to stop saying that," Kaleb replied.

"Yeah? Explain to me how they aren't? I want you to prove me wrong. What has she or her son contributed to you or the store? At the very least, they could work in the store from time to time. You somehow believe work is beneath them. You could use them as free labor; many people are doing it."

"Yeah, well, I don't do what 'many people do,'" Kaleb shot back.

"You should ration food off to them instead of giving them the whole loaf, Kaleb. All I'm saying is that you should get something in return from them because this arrangement that you currently have going on with them cannot continue."

"It's not an arrangement… it is what it is. I offered Melanie a place to stay, and she has a son."

"Well, her son is an adult. You could at least have him doing actual work instead of marching up and down every street throughout the city."

Kaleb simply could not believe the words that Alicia was saying to him. He was stunned. She had always been protective over who he'd shown interest in. Often, it would become annoying. What she was now showing was dangerously teetering along the lines of outright hatred; a side of her that wasn't aligned with how either of them was raised.

"Honestly," Kaleb began as he lowered his head in disappointment of his sister, "I really don't know what to say to you right now."

"There isn't anything needed to be said to me… only them. Times have changed, Kaleb. Soon you'll have to decide whether you want to or not. It's better to decide for yourself rather than having the decision made for you."

No longer being able to tolerate his sister's presence, Kaleb abruptly removed himself from the table. Out of the countless arguments and disagreements that the two had ever had, this one stung deeper, and somewhere inside of him, he knew that it wasn't the end.

Over the next several weeks, there were more intrusions, increased violence against registered citizens from those who weren't registered, and a rise of concern had grown even greater. The plan to correct these issues had now been placed under a matter of grave importance as the day-to-day safety of registered citizens became jeopardized.

The ideal utopia of Hansen's original plan had gone array, and it was now time for him to rise to the occasion and correct every issue that had surfaced. Was Dunne finally succumbing to all the pressure that had been put before him? Was he not able to deliver on the promises that he and Hansen had given the people? How much more blood would be placed on Dunne's hands before all trust had become lost in him?

"We need our leader, we're fearing for our safety-even when we should be in the safety of our own homes. Our global government needs to fix this." One citizen stated while being interviewed after the shooting of Congresswoman Patricia Sanders who lived only a few blocks over from his home. "I fear for my family. I'll do whatever I have to do to protect them, so if that means to take another life and increase the murder rate then-I hate to say it but I'll make sure that whoever comes for us stops breathing… you have my word on that."

Days continued to pass as Jaylen found himself unable to move from out of his bed. His phone sat on a nightstand that was next to his bed and it read twenty-seven missed calls and thirty-four text messages. Jaylen's eyes were red and swollen from crying as much as he had. A few times, Melanie came to check in on him, but she'd been unsuccessful in being able to pull him out of the room. He and Evan had grown up with one another and had been viewed as being as close as brothers their entire lives. He felt completely hollow inside and unsure about anything in life. All that they'd worked towards, all that they'd fought, had become destroyed in an instant.

Despite it all, Jaylen understood that at some point he would have to continue fighting. That was a message that Melanie had spoken to him for one evening while he remained shut off from the world.

Just inside of the living area, Kaleb revealed the news to Melanie that his sister had now been aware of their whereabouts.

"Okay, when did you tell her?" Melanie asked.

"A few days ago, but that's sort of the thing. I didn't exactly tell her; she saw Jaylen leaving out the side exit." Kaleb stated.

"That's how she found out? You didn't tell her beforehand?" questioned Melanie.

"No, it was before I could. I was looking for the right time, but I —"

"Damn, Kaleb! I thought you were gonna handle this? You were acting like everything would be under control. What did she say? Is she going to turn us in and say that we broke in and took over?"

"No. That's not going to happen. And I do have everything under control." He said. Now he was caught in the middle of two of the more passionate women that were in his life, but that wasn't anything particularly new.

"I'm going to take care of you; you don't have to worry." He said as he stepped closer and gently placed his hand on her arm.

There was something about how he'd said it that softened something on the inside of her. His words were reassuring and believable, a stark contrast to whenever Gabe spoke to her. She nodded, as she found herself slightly unable to speak as she started to melt into something that could, perhaps, become real.

Suddenly, the door to Jaylen's room sprung open, causing Kaleb and Melanie to quickly jump away from one another. Barely looking up, he didn't notice as he continued out the door without speaking a single word to either of them.

The shooting of Congresswoman Sanders was deeply troubling to Global President Dunne and even more so that they could not pinpoint exactly who had been responsible. He didn't like the message that it was sending to citizens or the unease that was setting in amongst them. He called Moreno and Wells up to his office in New York to discuss his plans for both Regions moving forward.

"You two need to explain to me how crime rates are beginning to rise despite an increase in foot patrol officers and drones," Dunne said. "How is it that I have an attack on a Congresswoman in your Region, Moreno, and there hasn't been a single suspect brought in; hm? I need answers."

Dunne was persistent, but he spoke calmly as he sat back in his Parisian handcrafted leather chair that Hansen had gifted him.

"I'm not sure if it necessarily justifies anything, but I've heard concerns from governors and Presidents within Region Two that perhaps, we have the foot patrol officers within the wrong areas," Wells stated. "They suggested that maybe we should have more of them in more central areas within the Green Zones as opposed to boarding the outskirts of Red Zones."

Dunne looked over to the Region One ambassador.

"Moreno, do you agree?" Dunne asked.

"There certainly is something to it. I've heard the same throughout my Region. While we do have enough officers on the ground, there seems to be a mismanagement as to where they are placed." Moreno replied.

"Why haven't either of you brought this to my attention? You've heard the concerns, you've seen what's been occurring, yet you've said nothing." Dunne said.

"I, personally, felt that this was a decision that you would ultimately make," Wells answered.

"We figured that you, along with the guidance of Hansen, would instruct us on what would be best," Moreno added.

"These, as with all things, are circumstances in which you have never steered us in the wrong direction," Wells said. "We trust your leadership and follow your instruction."

The two of them couldn't understand where their words and their thoughts were coming from. While they did, indeed, follow Dunne's leadership, something entrancing occurred whenever they faced him. They felt as though they became hypnotized, and all that he said to them was pure, perfect, and true. He'd been the voice of Hansen, and his voice had become that which should be worshiped.

"So, shall it be," Dunne answered. "I want every facility that shelters those who are not imprinted to become shut down. Anyone that isn't imprinted should become banished into the Red Zones within each Region. Imprinted citizens have the right to live peacefully amongst themselves without the threat of those who have chosen to isolate themselves coming to attack them," Dunne continued.

"What about resistance?" Wells asked.

"It will come. We should expect it to, but those who resist should expect that we will respond with brutal force. We have respected their wishes of not wanting to be a part of us, so they should respect our wishes in wanting them to leave. They will no longer be our responsibility or thought of in any fashion. We will give a week's notice for those who would like to become imprinted to finally do so. After the week is over, the separation will commence. This is what we shall do; make the announcement." Dunne said, concluding their meeting.

The front door opened as Jessica stood behind it, inviting Jaylen to come inside. She took his coat and told him that others were over and were in the downstairs den. As he walked down, he heard the others talking, arguing; he wasn't sure. Once he'd reached the bottom, Cassandra immediately ran to embrace him. He carried the burden of sadness within his body, and she could feel it as they held onto one another.

Jaylen didn't inform her that he was coming over truthfully; he wasn't sure where he was headed when he decided to leave. He was hoping that they could be alone, but perhaps, he reasoned, being around everyone would help with the grief he'd been harboring.

"Babe, I'm so glad that you came. I'd been calling and messaging you. I wanted to come by, but I know that you told me that it wasn't a good idea to visit you there. We all just wanted to know if you were okay." Cassandra said, fighting back tears.

"I know, I know. I'm… managing." Jaylen replied in a low voice.

Lisa and Ahmad were also there reminding him of who obviously wasn't; his lifelong brother.

The two of them came up to greet him; a hug from Lisa, followed by a handshake and embrace from Ahmad. He was offered a drink by Cassandra right after he'd taken his seat. He stared down quietly at the table they were all seated around. Lisa reached out to touch his hand, slightly startling him to get his attention.

"You okay?" Lisa asked.

"Just… just trying to make sense of it. Haven't heard much of anything; been kinda isolated away from everything for a while." He responded.

"They're saying some officers did it," Ahmad said bluntly.

Lisa rolled her eyes at Ahmad's comment despite still looking towards her friend.

"Can you… never mind." Cassandra began, but then caught herself. She regretted the fact she'd invited Ahmad over. She realized it the moment that she'd seen him standing at her door.

"Am I wrong? Is that not what's being reported?" Ahmad asked.

"Yeah, but that's not confirmed," Lisa said.

"Damn that! We know exactly what's going on. This is why we need to be on the same page with fighting back and taking back what rightfully belongs to us. They think we're supposed to sit back while they take our homes and tell us that the only way to get it back is to put some shit in my hand? Been saying it, I'm saying it again now; I'm ready to fight for this. It's not right, man. I bet you Evan would agree with me now," Ahmad said.

He knew that he would get a reaction from Jaylen by bringing up Evan's name. He was right. The two men stared at one another from across the table. Jaylen's eyes revealed his disapproval of what Ahmad had said, but he said nothing.

"Yeah, I know you feel me," Ahmad said, still peering directly at Jaylen. "See, that religion that you're holding on to so tight got you thinking that what I'm saying is the wrong thing to do. But on the other hand, the man in you is telling you that I'm right. 'You damn right, Ahmad; let's mount up tonight.' Don't worry, I can see it in your eyes; you don't have to say it. That was your boy; you want to ride for him. You know who did it. Any and everyone who became imprinted is responsible. There are only two sides to this."

"Yeah, and what happens when you run into that brick wall?" Jaylen challenged him.

"Then, they better kill me and find pleasure while they do it," Ahmad said.

"I can't stress enough how suicidal you are. You seriously need help," Lisa said.

They took a few sips from their cups, all in silence as they all tried to collect their thoughts about what had been unfolding.

"I've been thinking," Cassandra said, interrupting the momentary silence, "about this whole… imprint thing. So, like what's so bad about it again? My cousin has it, other family members have it, and they all seem to be perfectly fine. Some of them are doing a lot better than they were. Homeless people were given new homes and money. I'm just saying, it doesn't seem as bad as we're making it out to be."

"We've discussed this!" Jaylen said, sounding disappointed in his girlfriend. "If you get that imprint, you become an enemy of God."

"Aren't you still a believer?" Lisa asked Cassandra.

"Yeah, but-so if I did, so I become a bad Christian or something? I just want to take care of myself. I've never had to rely on anyone for anything," Cassandra said.

"Maybe that's the challenge; you relying on God instead of yourself or family," Jaylen said.

"I don't care how much of a believer you are; when the pressure's on you'll fold eventually," Ahmad said.

12
EVICTION DAY

Five Days Before Deadline

It was late in the evening when Ahmad stopped near a corner to light a cigarette when a man speaking to a small crowd caught his attention across the street from where he stood. He seemed frail, his clothes were ill fitting, and overall, he seemed like his better days were behind him. The man stood atop a set of steps of what appeared to have been a church once upon a time before it had become shut down and boarded up. In fact, Ahmad was sure that it used to be a church; he'd recalled his aunt taking him there when he was younger. He remembered her telling him he had a demon inside of himself and that he'd needed cleansing. When she'd told him this, he didn't understand what she'd meant or why she would say such a thing to him.

He crossed the street; becoming closer to where the man stood on the church steps, speaking. He'd gotten near, taking an occasional puff of his cigarette, but still stood back some so as to not become confused with the observers who heard the man speak. The man spoke as though he were a preacher. Perhaps he was. Maybe this used to be his church, Ahmad deduced. There had been something very off about him. He spoke as if he'd been afraid of something that he'd been told, known about, or he didn't believe the words that he was speaking himself. What he was saying did seem off, even to Ahmad, who didn't exactly share the same beliefs that these people supposedly had.

"We are God's chosen people, you see? Therefore, we are not meant to suffer." The pastor said. "What the Bible-*er*... the book says," he said, trying to catch himself from uttering the title of the forbidden book, "is that God will provide for His people a way of escape from any suffering. These have been trying times, but-but we do not have to be down any longer, people! Many of you are wondering about the imprint and what the book says about the mark, but you should know that the imprint isn't what it was referring to. The imprint is the help that has been sent to us, so we should find comfort in becoming legal citizens and receiving the many benefits arranged for us, God's people. My wife and I will be going down to become imprinted ourselves and I want you all to come along with us."

Ahmad's eyes squinted as the pastor spoke, at both the smoke getting into his eyes and what he viewed as the absurdity of what was being said. He was no expert, but he was sure that what the pastor was saying was false. He observed the crowd; some stuck around, giving him an "amen" clinging onto his every word and hoping that the pastor was right and that their days of struggling had come to an end. Ahmad thought to himself how easily the human mind could instantly transform its belief system under pressure to something that it had never once given consideration to find relief or some type of way out. Then, there were others, Ahmad witnessed, that just wasn't buying into the message and walked away, hands in their pockets, heads shaking and lowered. Ahmad tossed his cigarette and went on his way.

Naomi walked into her office with her assistant behind her and slammed her files onto her desk in anger. She expressed her outrage at Moreno's announcement that had been passed down from the President.

"They are forcing people into absolute poverty. The government not providing help is one thing, but taking away the rights of other people to help is completely over the top." Naomi said as she paced back and forth.

"What can we do?" Her young female assistant asked.

Naomi threw her hands into the air.

"I honestly don't know. They've tied my hands with this. I'm terrified as to what this could mean. This world is in trouble. Schedule an urgent video call with all the leaders from the Helpers organization throughout both Regions first thing tomorrow morning. I'm sure they'll be expecting to hear from me." She instructed her assistant. "I can't believe they're shutting us down."

Three Days Before Deadline

During the time that Melanie and Jaylen had lived above the store, Melanie and Kaleb had grown closer to one another; they'd even gone out on a few dates, despite neither one of them proclaiming that to be what it actually was. While they were obviously exclusive, they didn't want to make things awkward by placing a title on what the two of them shared, either. Melanie invited Kaleb up from his workday when he became free to discuss their arrangement and the recent events. The two sat on the sofa in the center living room area, facing one another, while Melanie appeared understandably troubled.

"You have nothing to worry about," Kaleb said, trying to reassure her. "When I made the promise to look after you, I understood all of what that entailed. There would be obstacles, but we would overcome them," Kaleb continued.

"Everything in your world is so perfect," Melanie began, "and I didn't want to interrupt things or be a burden on what may come from you being so generous to us."

Melanie had no idea of what was to come; she feared the worst for herself and her son but felt that it would be unfair to put Kaleb through any form of impending turmoil that might come. She'd learned to care for him on a more intimate level; therefore, what happened to him mattered.

"This is what we've talked about. These are the days that the scripture talks about. We've been able to survive through so much thus far, but we'll need to persevere for just a little while longer. God has sustained us, and we can't lose faith now. We must keep going. He'll take care of us no matter what will happen. He's returning to us soon." Melanie said, almost frantically. "Look, Kaleb, thank you for everything that you've done for us, but I think that this is the end," she continued, with tears forming in her eyes.

"You two don't have to leave. What are you talking about?" Kaleb replied.

"Kaleb, they won't allow us to stay here. They barely allow it now, so there's no way that they'll accept it in a few days."

"We can continue to just... be careful, just like we've always been; I'll keep looking after you. Nothing will happen to you. I promise."

"As much as you want to, you can't guarantee that. It won't be safe for us or for you. Who knows what they'll do to you if they find out that you've been hiding us?"

"I'll do whatever I have to do... even if it means my life," Kaleb said.

"We're just... we're not on the same page, Kaleb," Melanie said as she dropped her head.

"What did you say?" he asked.

"We're not on the same page." She said, now looking up at him.

"How can you say that? Haven't we grown to care for one another? Look me in my eyes and tell me you don't care for me, Melanie!"

"I can't because I do care for you… it's just that… we don't believe in the same things. Somewhere down the line, I knew that this might be a problem for us. How long can this really go on like this?"

"This has always been the case, but it has never been a problem until you made it one now. We've always believed in different things and it hasn't been a problem." Kaleb challenged.

Tears flowed down Melanie's cheeks as the two stood in front of one another in silence. Early on, as the two were becoming close, she was afraid that it might come to this. This was part of the reason she was resistant, initially. Kaleb, however, had never made her choose between him and what she'd believed in, which is why she'd grown closer to him and eventually falling for him.

"So, what happens now; where do we go from here?" Kaleb asked almost reluctantly, because of the response that he might've received. Even though he'd heard from Melanie that this might be the end for them, he still held on to a little bit of hope for their future.

"Who knows what Dunne truly has up his sleeves. Not knowing how he's planning on executing his ideas is what's frightening to me. How is he going to round up every non citizen and when he does, will he stop at simply exiling us from the Green Zones or will he go as far as to kill us?"

"No way I'm letting that happen," Kaleb said.

"How are you going to stop every army in the world from executing this maniac's plan, Kaleb? There's absolutely nothing that you can do to stop this man. He is going to do exactly what he wants and my son and I are his targets."

The two sat down on the couch, both pondering on ways to maneuver around what was in store for them. There seemed to be no way around it, and although Kaleb certainly honored Melanie and Jaylen's choice, he never fully understood the reasoning behind their decision to not become registered. After sitting in silence, Kaleb finally gave in to his curiosity.

"I have to ask you because I've never truly understood why-but why won't you become imprinted? What part of your faith goes against doing so?"

Melanie sighed as she prepared to answer Kaleb. It was a fair question, and it was good for him to know. She parted her lips, beginning to speak, but Jaylen entered the room and cut her off before she could utter a word.

"It's the final separation between God and man," Jaylen said.

Kaleb and Melanie both turned to him.

"There's no return from that point… there's nothing else that we can do to ever go back. Once a person has become imprinted, they are marked forever by our enemy; the final choice will be made. The pressure and fear that Dunne tries to apply has nothing on what will come to us should we give in to the will of man."

Melanie looked at Jaylen, both saddened that this was the world that he'd come to terms with and also proud that he understood all that was at stake. Kaleb, on the other hand, looked even more puzzled than he had earlier.

"Becoming God's enemy, that's what you're in fear of-this is what's holding you back?" Kaleb asked.

Melanie looked at him.

"Yes, it is… and the jeopardy in which we would place the fate of our spirits eternally," Melanie responded.

"Then, what must you think of me… someone who has become imprinted?" Kaleb asked. Melanie and Jaylen both glanced at one another, almost as if they suspected that the question was coming.

"We only follow what we know. You've always been an advocate of becoming imprinted and before you fully accepted us for what we believed, you even tried to encourage us to do so." Melanie answered.

"Why do I somehow suddenly feel judged, or as if you feel that you're better than me," Kaleb said as he stood up from the couch and walked away from them. "This seems exactly like what Dunne means by the separation and conflict that religion causes amongst people."

"Oh, you're on Dunne's side now?" Melanie said, jumping up from her seat in disbelief. "We have never judged you for your choices, ever!"

"And neither have I!" Kaleb responded. "Hearing you two making it sound like I've chosen sides against God himself by simply doing what I have to do to ensure that I'm able to eat and have shelter is a bit much. You know I don't agree with Dunne forcing people to become imprinted, so implying that myself, Dunne and all of 'God's enemies' are on the same side is a stretch, don't you think?"

"You're going *way* overboard with this," Melanie said. "No one has said anything regarding you being an enemy."

"Not everything needs to be said to be understood, Melanie."

Closing the discussion, Jaylen soon chimed in one last time.

"We are not your judge. For us, our love for you is evident, but what finally happens with you and your soul will be for God to decide."

Kaleb peered at them both for a moment in anger and then left the apartment without saying a word. Melanie looked at her son as if she wished he'd used a better choice of words, or perhaps nothing at all, but Jaylen glanced back at her unapologetically.

The government manufactured hundreds of thousands of new military bots to prepare for the final separation of citizens and non-citizens. Although it was Dunne's desire for all citizens to become imprinted, he understood that, for whatever reason, there would be many of them who would refuse and side against global peace and equality for all of humanity.

The military and police bots were extremely sophisticated, human-like machines built to work alongside their human counterparts. They possessed the ability to detect emotion as well as engage with humans so far as to be able to have conversations and even use force should the occasion cause for it. While there were a few already in operation, Dunne ordered for more to be created as they approached the deadline.

The use of robots was a safer solution, albeit more expensive, to combat the recent inflation of crime and what might come about during the days after the final imprint period. The robots were meant to uphold peace and with their highly advanced A.I., they were able to properly detect the escalation of danger and how to adequately deal with each situation as it came about. While they stood for peace, their presence was certainly intimidating, beginning with their towering, dark statue and glowing eyes.

The patrol bots were a dark, shiny, metallic navy blue with two eye sockets, similar to that of humans, for their glowing eyes, while the military bots were matte black with a shield-like covering over their heads parted by a glowing strip for their eyes. On both robots, their eyes glowed white, but would immediately turn a blazing red whenever they were encountering a hostile situation that needed addressing. It was common to see a few of the older models patrolling around-everyone was comfortable with them-but as the deadline approached, a few of the newer models were dispatched to increase the amount of them that were present. Dunne wanted the public to know that he was prepared to protect his citizens through any means.

One Day Before Deadline

Melanie and Kaleb sat inside of a busy café waiting for their coffee. The two had cleared things up some, but came to an agreement that Melanie would stay in the upstairs apartment above the store as long as it was possible. It would be risky, but Melanie truly cared about Kaleb and honestly didn't know what else to do once the deadline came. Jaylen wasn't too fond of the idea and contemplated moving along but leaving his mother during such a time was out of the question, nor did he know where he would go.

"With those new patrol bots being able to detect if someone is imprinted or not will make it impossible for us to go out into the streets. I don't see how we'll be able to manage," Melanie said. "We can't just stay cooped upstairs all day. We'll probably go crazy up there."

"Yeah… I understand what you mean, but it's early, you know? We'll be able to figure out better ways to maneuver around as more time goes by. Besides, at least I'll always know that you're close." Kaleb finished with a smile.

"Meanwhile, I'll be feeling like some type of prisoner," Melanie said.

Kaleb chuckled as he shook his head.

"Here's your coffee!" A server said, sitting down a cup in front of each of them.

"Thank you," Kaleb replied.

"Crazy day coming up! I hear they're taking all kinds of precautions. You just never know what those other people might have planned, the non-imprinted ones." The server added.

Great, here she goes. Melanie thought as she brushed her hair back and began peering out into the street through the window next to her. Kaleb took note of Melanie's annoyance and unsuccessfully tried to brush the server off.

"Those people should just go ahead and fall in line like the rest of us. It's for their own good after all." She continued. "I bet you two are glad that you went ahead and got it out of the way just like myself, aren't you?" Kaleb gave her a dismissive, half-hearted smile.

"Enjoy your coffee," she said, just before leaving the couple to themselves.

She didn't catch the sarcasm within the smile, but at least she left the table.

"You've got to be kidding me," Melanie said once the server had left. "I won't be able to deal with these people."

"Hey, be careful now. These are my people!" Kaleb joked. Melanie simply rolled her eyes.

Lisa called Jaylen and informed him that Cassandra, along with several other group members, had gotten imprinted a few days earlier. She told him that Cassandra had already received her new home and car as well. Jaylen took a deep sigh; however, he said that he felt little about it and that now she'd have the independence that she'd felt that she was missing so much. He told Lisa that Cassandra's decision probably explained why he hadn't been able to reach her and that their relationship was likely over. Jaylen continued to cling on to his faith that something good would come to, not only him, but to all of those who continued to have faith in God as well. The group had been parted, but a few, like Lisa, believed and trusted in Jaylen so much that they would follow in whatever decision he would make.

In those last days leading up to the deadline, many non-citizens, who were once believers in Christ and chose not to become imprinted, crumbled and gave in to the pressure. Melanie's son understood it was certainly harder to resist than to simply say that you would resist. There were tough days for him as well, when he questioned if his decisions were the correct ones and if he were leading the others down the wrong path. He'd often pray for something to change where they wouldn't have to face whatever President Dunne had in store for them, but mentally he tried to brace himself for whatever was to come.

First Day... *After* Deadline

Everyone within Region One stood watch, waiting to see what would occur, as each country within Region Two came into the day after the deadline. Anxiety and tension were built up to unprecedented levels to where the world had never witnessed before. Every television was tuned in to the world news channels listening to reports and to catch glimpses of the activity that had been occurring, hoping to know what to look forward to.

Within every home, cafe, barbershop, and airport, people were frozen at the sight of what was happening just on the other side of the world, knowing that whatever they would witness, they were about to encounter it firsthand. News channels broadcasted scenes of thousands of more military and patrol bots being placed on the grounds marching throughout the streets, scanning citizens for imprints, and requesting that those who weren't imprinted come with them. For those who refused, resisted, and fought against the bots witnessed the blazing red glowing eyes up close and the brute force that came along with it.

Human-beings who resisted were aggressively snatched off their feet and carried away as if they were slaughtered unusable cattle. Glimpses were caught of metal robotic fists fracturing facial bones as they collided against the skulls of non-imprinted citizens. Screams of horror and madness filled the streets as they were collected, gathered, and tossed into trucks to be shipped off outside of the city walls, no longer recognized or valued as humans.

"Stop resisting!" Human officers working with patrol bots yelled out from bullhorns. "We do not want to harm you! Please obey all orders and you will not be hurt!" They continued.

It was shortly after 6 A.M. Melanie's son looked down at his hands that he, for some reason, could not stop from shaking as he sat on the edge of his bed. He or his mother hadn't been able to sleep much the night before, as everyone's nerves were on edge due to not knowing what to expect. It was eviction day for all non-imprinted citizens. The thought of it actually seemed impossible to some at first and wasn't taken too seriously until the scenes of what was occurring in other parts of the world flashed across television screens.

Jaylen, however, assumed the absolute worst from the very beginning. He'd known that this day would be a possibility since he'd been a child. Melanie was able to prepare him for it mentally; it was something that they had discussed. Even then, with many discussions of what to expect, living within that very moment brought a sickening feeling to his gut.

"I can't believe what I'm seeing… this is complete chaos." He heard Kaleb say from the other room.

"All of this time… no one listened to me. People thought I was crazy, but I was right all along." Melanie's voice echoed.

"Yeah, I was one of them," Kaleb mumbled.

"Kaleb, they're coming for us. I don't think we'll be able to hide here… or anywhere. Maybe from the regular officers, but those bots…" Melanie said with her voice fading in uncertainty.

"We should be okay," Kaleb said, not sounding fully sure. "I think by them being able to read my registration it'll cause them to overlook anyone who—"

"That's not how it works. The bots are specifically designed to find anyone who isn't registered and collect them. Period," Melanie said, cutting Kaleb off.

He knew she was right, but he'd wanted to say anything to bring any form of momentary hope, even if it was false hope. Kaleb lowered his head as the two continued to stand in front of the television, watching Region Two uproot its unregistered citizens. Jaylen continued to sit in darkness, hearing the screams from the screen in the other room. It was a sound unlike he'd ever heard before, causing his stomach to twist in knots at the thought that he'd be hearing them firsthand in a short matter of time. Right outside, he heard shouting, seemingly from a massive crowd, causing him to peer through the blinds of his room.

"Bring it on; we're ready for ya! We'll take you all on." An angry assault rifle wielding man yelled, leading a mob of other gun-carrying individuals. They even fired a few shots into the air. They were ready for warfare. Seeing them made him think of Ahmad and wondered if he were somewhere amongst the crowd.

"This is just great; exactly what we needed," he whispered to himself.

A loud blaring broadcasting alert suddenly vibrated through every mobile device and television throughout the city, silencing the mob just outside. They all became quiet, everyone looking around with their guns still in the air as the snow fell upon them. Melanie's son quickly rushed into the front living area where Kaleb and his mother were. He looked at the television as the local broadcaster came onto the screen.

"This-this just in…" the newscaster began. "Sightings have just been reported of the first group of military robots being deployed and have begun to gather non-registered citizens. I repeat, sightings have just been—" the newscaster trailed off in the background as Kaleb's voice broke in.

"I can't believe this is happening," he said.

Melanie ran over to the window and the alert continued to sound off throughout the streets to almost deafening levels. She witnessed cars stopped in traffic and people standing outside of their vehicles all looking around for what was to come. It was eviction day.

Jaylen put on his boots, grabbed his coat, and headed out the door past Kaleb and Melanie, who'd tried their best to stop him. Once he'd arrived outside, he pulled the hood of his coat over his head to fend off the snow. He walked up the street and stood amongst the mob, who remained standing in silence, as the only one without a gun, a knife, or any weapon that was available. The mob stood facing in one direction.

What were they all looking at?

The steady, smooth, crisp flickering sound of propellers from behind him sliced through the screeching alarm that continued to ring into his ears. What was that sound? What was coming?

"Look... look! Here they come!" one of the mob members yelled as he pointed towards the sky behind Jaylen.

Slowly, he turned himself, stomach still in knots, tightening even more at the revelation of the world's oncoming judgment to those unwilling to comply with their President Dunne's demands. It was time. Three enormous ship-like aircraft vessels with four circular propellers towered over the city, clouding over the already gray skies, turning the vision above to near darkness. Military bots and soldiers, both prepared for eradication, stood-some dangling out with an unnerving excitement and anticipation-near the open doorway of one vessel. The other vessels appeared to be empty.

Those empty ones must be for us. Jaylen thought.

Before the vessel carrying the military bots and human soldiers could fully touch down, many of the bots leaped out and landed in the snow with a vibrating thud. The act appeared threatening, causing many to run in the opposite direction out of fear, but they would soon discover that there would be no place to hide.

The uncertainty of what these machines were capable of, even for those who were registered, was enough to raise pandemonium amongst them all. Someone quickly blazed past Jaylen, slightly brushing up against his shoulders, and nearly knocked him onto the snowy pavement. From within the herd of people, the screams began, just like the ones he'd heard on the television screen from the other cities. The screams all sounded the same, but this time, only closer.

"Let's take 'em out!" someone from the mob yelled. Jaylen noticed that some of the mob members who once stood so bravely had run off as quickly as they could upon the arrival of the military. No surprise there. Then, he noticed a military general, a human soldier, had climbed onto the roof of a car with a bullhorn and commanded everyone's attention. The site of the general caused the mob to come to an abrupt halt as some of them slid across the snowy, slippery asphalt.

"I'd advise you all to pay very close attention to what I'm about to tell you. It is in your very best interest to not engage with us or show any forms of hostility. Everyone understands why we are here, but for those of you who don't know, we are here to evacuate all unregistered citizens from within the Green Zones over into the Red Zones. We are stationed in every city, every state, city, and town throughout the entire Region, so there is nowhere for you to hide. Our robotic soldiers are designed to scan and detect all individuals who have not been imprinted and will, therefore, export them to the aircraft behind me and then help you in transitioning you into your new dwelling place. Our plan is to move quickly and with no violence, but I assure you, we are well prepared. I truly hope that you have taken heed of what I have said, as I do not plan on repeating myself. Take this as your one and only warning. We shall now begin the extraction process."

The General concluded his warning, hopped down from the vehicle and began to walk towards the vessels carrying the rest of the soldiers. It was then that a swift breeze and zipping sound whistled past the general's left ear. The General stopped immediately within his tracks. The sound finished with a clink against what sounded to be some type of metal. As the General looked ahead, his eyes met the glowing white eyes of one of his military bots, which led him to notice a piece of the robot's helmet damaged because of a forceful impact.

A shot had been fired.

The soldiers, without making a single move, all stood facing the mob-those who'd remained-and their General awaiting a signal. It was no secret as to what was about to happen as Jaylen knew that an oncoming doom was approaching. The General clenched his right fist and slowly raised it above his head. With this move, the eyes of the military bots instantly turned red, activating them into full combat mode as human military and robotic soldiers were suddenly charging towards the mob of non-imprinted citizens, including Jaylen. Their imprint detectors were activated, scanning every individual, and instantly picking up on anyone not imprinted.

Crackling sounds of more gunfire blended with screams, and outcries of distress cut through the frosty morning air. Shells whistled past Jaylen's entire body as he looked around to find his way back to the side entrance of the apartment in the store's alleyway. There was no way that he could have ever prepared for this. He wasn't a soldier.

Stay low… just stay low. He kept thinking to himself.

As he continued to edge his way through the crowd that had now turned into a live battlefield, he overstepped defeated mob members gagging on blood and some lying motionless with no signs of life remaining in them. He quickly discovered that the casualties rested on both sides, seeing the head of a robot detached from the rest of its body frame-nearly crushed-with its glowing red eyes now merely a flicker.

With rising madness, panic, fear, and violence escalating all around him, the only sound that he could hear was his heart pounding against the inside of his chest. Every other noise seemed to be muted. Throughout the warfield, he couldn't quite determine his whereabouts or which direction he should head in; everything had become spun around. He stumbled along, crouching behind cars to dodge bullets and detection from the military bots, as he tried to make his way back to Kaleb and his mother.

His eyes looked up into the sky as he prayed to be shown a way out, a way back to safety, but just as he finished, he found himself in the direct line of sight of the fiery red gaze of a military bot. He'd been discovered. The powerful steps of the robot crashed down into the snow as it quickly made strides towards him. An instant scramble to get away caused him to slip and sent him crashing face forward into the ground. The pursuit of the bot was hurried with no signs of slowing down while he rustled, unsuccessfully, through the snow to jump back to his feet. In a matter of seconds, he'd find himself inside of the vessel being shipped into the Red Zone. That is, if he was lucky enough to not be killed first.

The robot had just gotten close enough to reach down to grab him when it suddenly became blindsided by the end of a mob guy's rifle. The robot dropped into the snow as the guy continued to smash the back of his gun into its head until it flattened and electric sparks flew around it. Unsatisfied, he then unloaded several shots into the crushed helmet of the robot. It was an overkill, taking his attention away from his surroundings, which allowed the robot's fellow human soldier to sneak up behind and pierce a knife slowly through his back until he severed his spinal cord. Instantly, the snow underneath him turned red.

Jaylen finally made it to his feet and noticed, just up ahead of him, Kaleb waving for him to come to where he was. Kaleb was also yelling something at him, but he couldn't make out what he was saying as he slipped and slid past the crowd towards him. Once he made it to where Kaleb was, the two dashed into the side entrance of the store where Melanie awaited.

"Let's get going... we've got to get to the hideout." Kaleb said, trying to catch his breath.

"What were you thinking?" Melanie screamed at her son. "What were you doing? You were going to get yourself shipped out or killed. We wouldn't have known what happened to you."

"I know... I'm sorry... I-I just had to see what was happening with my own eyes. I had no idea what was going to happen." Her son said, voice quivering.

"How could you have not known what was happening out there? We just saw what they've already done in Region Two."

"Guys, let's focus. We have to move into position." Kaleb said.

Despite Melanie's anger towards Jaylen, she was still glad that her son was able to make it back safely and hugged him tighter than she'd ever had.

"It's horrible out there," Jaylen said as they embraced with his voice still trembling. "It's worse than anything we could've possibly imagined or prepared for."

"It's okay, son... we're going to make it through this. We're going to make it."

"We will as long as we move… now! Now come on!" Kaleb rushed them.

The three ran upstairs to the apartment, went inside, and headed to the bedroom, where Melanie would sleep. They walked inside of a closet and went to a wall in the rear, where Kaleb was able to press forcefully against it until it gently creaked open. They all quickly went inside to a small room where they sat quietly with only one another's breathing could be heard. Kaleb pulled a string hanging from the ceiling, which then lit up the room.

"We'll be okay here, don't worry. We just have to wait things out for a bit until they finish going through the neighborhoods." Kaleb said confidently. "I guess the view of everything from the window wasn't to your satisfaction, huh?" Kaleb said lightheartedly as he looked over at Jaylen. He simply shook his head in disbelief at what he'd just witnessed.

Close to around an hour had passed according to Kaleb's watch, and everyone had settled their nerves down a bit and mentally prepared for the days ahead. During the past month, they were able to plan for this day, much to the help of Kaleb. He'd constantly gone over different scenarios as to how'd they'd respond if certain things happened. To the best of their capabilities, they were prepared, but there were still uncertainties that lingered.

"Life will be a little different now, but we knew that. Things had already gotten out of order, but we will have to make a few more adjustments here and there. We'll have to move more—"

Bang!

Kaleb was interrupted by a noise that sounded like it came from downstairs, causing Melanie to suddenly stand up.

"*What was that?*" She whispered.

"*I'm not sure,*" Kaleb responded.

Everyone's eyes were fixed on the door of the room that opened up to the closet inside of Melanie's room. Then came the sound of footsteps, deep, heavy, thudding footsteps-the kind that nothing human could ever make. Multiple steps signified that there was more than one of whatever it was.

"*They're inside... hit the lights!*" Jaylen yelled.

Kaleb quickly pulled the string, and the room turned dark.

The steps shuffled about slowly, yet purposefully, as if they were searching for something or someone. More fear came as the steps sounded to be coming up the stairs towards the apartment. Melanie began to quietly pray to herself as the steps grew closer and closer. Suddenly, their fears became even more heightened as the front door of the apartment was broken through.

"If there's anyone inside here, you need to come out immediately. Don't make this any harder than it has to be. We're not here to hurt you." A muffled voice said it. It sounded human. Perhaps human and robot soldiers were out there.

"*What should we do?*" Melanie asked Kaleb.

"*What do you mean, 'what should we do'; we stay here. They won't find us.*" Kaleb said.

"*Keep it down before they hear us,*" Jaylen whispered.

"Where are they?" the muffled voice asked. "This better not be a waste of our time."

"I know they're here; they wouldn't be any other place, but here. We just have to check everywhere. Trust me, they're here." An undistinguishable female voice said.

"*Who in the world is that?*" Kaleb asked.

The intruders continued to move around on the other side of the walls-opening up doors, lifting beds, and looking behind everything that they came across, only to find nothing.

"This place is empty. No one's in here. We have to get moving. Thanks for wasting our time." The General said. "Pack up guys, let's move out!"

"Wait, wait, wait… I forgot. There's one other place." The female voice said. "Just check here. If they're not here, then you guys can leave, but I know for sure that they'll be here."

"*Oh, my God. What's happening; who is that?*" Melanie said as she covered her mouth in fear.

"*Just… stay calm,*" Kaleb said softly. The footsteps then sounded closer to the three of them than they had previously. They were now inside the room. A door slowly crept open; the closet door. Then more steps. They were closer.

"Lady… there's nothing here. We're leaving. Whenever you find them, let us know. You'll get your reward, okay? We're on a schedule," the General said.

"Will you just wait a second? There's another door here. They should be just on the other side." The female voice said.

This time, however, the female voice was clear, and they were all able to recognize exactly who it was. Especially Kaleb.

"*Alicia?*" He whispered in disbelief.

The hidden door slowly opened, and the sight of Alicia caused Kaleb's heart to drop. Their eyes met one another's, Kaleb's eyes revealing hurt, and Alicia's eyes revealing shock. She asked him what he was doing there, but before they could go on the soldiers pushed their way in to collect Melanie and her son, the non-registered citizens. Kaleb attempted to fight off one of the robots from grabbing Melanie but was struck, brutally knocking him to the ground nearly unconscious. Alicia quickly rushed to his aid.

It all began to slow down. Melanie and Jaylen were separated. The fight of freeing themselves was unsuccessful because of the strength of the bots; it was far too much. Melanie's cries for her son rose to a deafening, high-pitched screech. Jaylen could barely hear anything while the army of human and robotic soldiers dragged them both through the apartment, down the stairs, and onto the snowy streets.

Alicia pleaded with the General to release Kaleb, who'd been tossed inside of a large van that was going to transport prisoners and others that were attempting to hide non-citizens. With his vision almost in a glaze, Jaylen looked around and noticed the streets looking slightly more different than they had earlier. It looked more like the end of a war, no longer active like it once had. It was quieter; the snow had become even redder, and held more dead bodies of non-registered citizens who had put up too much of a fight. The soldiers had won.

"Jaylen... my son?" Melanie beckoned for his attention. He looked over to acknowledge her. "Don't f-forget..." Melanie paused because of her shivering from terror and the freezing cold. "Remember... who you are. God chose you. You won't die here today... you have a purpose," Melanie said to her son.

He heard his mother's words-every one-but he only wanted to be near her. He needed to touch her. Slowly, he pulled himself up to his feet as he staggered towards her. As he got closer to her, he heard brisk steps coming towards him, even faster now-through the snow; then he was struck on the right side of his temple, causing him to collapse into the snow. Jaylen's eyes remained fixed on his mother. Seeing the sight of her son in pain was unbearable.

Melanie, angered at the unnecessary punishment that was given to her son, charged towards the military bot who'd struck him. The military bot had his back turned towards her, but quickly sensed an enemy had been approaching it and spun around, firing a single shot that echoed up into the frigid air.

Melanie instantly stopped within her tracks. She looked down at her chest that was slowly turning red and a pain in which she hadn't been accustomed to started to overtake her. Jaylen looked up towards his mother, unable to clearly process what had been unfolding in front of him.

Melanie grabbed at her chest; her hands were now covered in her own blood. She slowly fell to her knees, turned her head to look at her son, and reached out to him. Jaylen's eyes were quivering; still trying to comprehend what was happening to his mother. His hand reached out towards hers; her hand reached out towards his, but they were unable to connect. Kaleb, hands tied behind his back, peering through a window, witnessed the entire scene. He began to go berserk; stomping and screaming inside the back of the van. He'd even slammed the back of his head against the inside of the van, but he could not feel the pain from it.

Two firm grips came down over Jaylen's weakened body; one at his legs, the other around his shoulders. His mind was in disarray, in utter shock at what they'd just done to his mother. They chained him inside the back of one of the enormous vessels alongside many of the others that were lucky enough to not have been killed. There was a mixture of cries, groans, and stunned silence. Jaylen's head slowly lowered; feeling numb.

The vessel flew off, far into the distance, and eventually began its descent into a Red Zone within that area where everyone became released. Everyone ventured off, most of the large group sticking together, while others, refusing to accept their fate, attempted to put up a fight and were killed.

For Jaylen, there was nothing left to live for within the Green Zone; it had become a dead place. His mother was gone, Kaleb had been arrested, and he wasn't sure where Lisa or the others whom he'd marched alongside might have been. While everyone walked off together to figure out what life meant for them moving forward, a woman who had been part of the group noticed Jaylen walking off into the distance, creating a single trail of snowy footprints in another direction by himself. She wondered about where he was heading. Jaylen walked until it had become too cold for him to continue on; he was shivering uncontrollably then he collapsed.

Time had passed. It was dark when his eyes opened. He hadn't been sure about how many hours had passed or whether it had been the same day. He felt warmer; a jacket had been placed on him and he'd noticed that he'd been moving inside the back of a car.

How did I get here? Where is here? Jaylen thought to himself.

He was laid across the back seat and although he wanted to quickly jump up to see what was happening, his body wouldn't allow him to just yet. From an angle, he could only catch glimpses of some strange figure driving the vehicle.

The bottom of his face was masked with some type of cloth, and a hood was pulled over his head, which only allowed for his eyes to show. He didn't speak or acknowledge Jaylen once. The stranger's eyes seemingly didn't blink the entire time, Jaylen observed; they remained fixed on the path that lay ahead of them.

13
GROCERY SHOPPING

There was a sudden jolt that nearly sent Jaylen falling onto the floor of the backseat as the car came to a stop. He quickly caught himself by throwing his left hand up against the passenger seat in front of him. The driver's side door opened, and the stranger exited the vehicle. He then swung open the side door behind him and stared inside. Jaylen's and the stranger's eyes locked in on one another as dozens of questions circled around Jaylen's mind.

"Who are you?" he blurted out. He could feel the cold air drifting inside of the car from the passenger door being opened where the stranger stood looking in at him.

"Come," the stranger said. Then he walked off.

The young man lied across the backseat as he watched the stranger walk off towards some enormous structure, which he wasn't quite able to determine what it was, given his vantage point. Where was he asking him to come? He didn't know where he was or who this man was, for that matter.

With all that had transpired, it was becoming increasingly difficult to trust anyone; he hadn't had an opportunity to fully grasp the loss of his mother. Yet, what else was there to life; where else was he to go. Nothing made sense to him. Jaylen was taught to never blame God, but after all that had happened, he couldn't help but ask God "why".

He began to cautiously edge his way out of the backseat of the car and out of the opened door, placing his boots into the frozen ground. He stood looking to his left, then to his right. It was pitch black in each direction, making it impossible to clearly see either way. He looked up towards a streetlamp that hadn't been working. It had probably been years longer than he could imagine since the last time it had been in operation.

He looked to now see that the enormous structure was an old, abandoned church. Once upon a time, it was probably quite the spectacle but now, it had been boarded up in some spots, a few windows appeared to have been broken, and chunks of the church itself seemed to had broken off. Despite its obvious aging and deterioration due to lack of use, he could still tell that it was an immaculate and well-crafted structure.

He witnessed the stranger enter a dark purplish, perhaps mahogany, door of the abandoned church. For a few moments, he stood there, contemplating whether he should follow him. Eventually, he decided that he would at least keep out of the cold. Inside of the holy place, there was a faint odor that lingered within the air, which Jaylen couldn't quite determine the cause of.

Many of the pews were overturned, broken in half, and some had huge chunks missing from them. Crows flew in through the broken windows and observed him from elevated vantage points; one sat atop of the podium in the pulpit in the front of the church. To the right, Jaylen noticed the man standing near a door as if he were waiting for Jaylen to see him before he vanished through the doorway. Then he was gone.

"H-hey… who are you?" Jaylen yelled out to him but the man continued walking. Jaylen reluctantly followed suit.

He followed the random guy, who picked him up from out of the snow, down a dark hallway, and then down a flight of stairs. He didn't see him, but he continued along in the direction in which he'd headed. Once Jaylen had reached the bottom, he could tell that he was inside of some open area yet he was unable to fully make out where he was due to the complete darkness which surrounded him.

"Hello?" Jaylen called out to the man. Shortly after, he heard what sounded like the flickering of a lighter. Then the stranger emerged from a room holding a torch that he'd made to give them light.

"That's better," the masked man said.

"Listen, I appreciate what you did for me and everything, but I have to—"

"This way; I have food," the stranger said.

Jaylen sighed in frustration. However, he followed along. He was curious as to who the guy was, but he'd been just as equally hungry, which was just enough motivation to continue forward after the man.

Ahead, he found him inside of what appeared to be a kitchen that had seen better days. It was a large kitchen that could hold multiple people at once, but there was something that caught Jaylen's attention. There was a decent amount of food that had been stored inside that piqued his curiosity as to how it'd gotten there. The questions were stacked on top of one another; it was time for the man to answer some of them.

"Look, I'm not taking another step after you or accepting anything from you until you tell me who you are," Jaylen bargained.

The two had a brief stare-down competition before the stranger finally complied with Jaylen's demands.

"Fine," the stranger said as he slid down his mask. "My name is Andrew."

The man's face was heavily bearded and appeared as if it hadn't been cared for in quite some time. Andrew removed his hood as well, revealing his long, locked hair. He didn't quite appear as Jaylen had imagined him to be underneath all of the layers. Nonetheless, progression had been made and for that, Jaylen was grateful.

"Finally, we're getting somewhere," Jaylen said before introducing himself. He asked Andrew why'd he picked him up, but Andrew replied that they could discuss everything over food to which Jaylen obliged.

The two men sat at a table inside of a room next to the kitchen over food that Andrew had prepared. Several lit candles were the only lights that were given off inside of the room as they sat in silence for a time while they ate their food. They both ate some type of soup with all sorts of mixed vegetables from a can. The freshness of it was questionable, Jaylen thought, but he wasn't complaining. He couldn't remember the last time he'd had anything to eat.

He didn't realize that he was hungry until he'd actually started eating. Losing everything had completely ruined his appetite. Still, he couldn't understand why or how he'd now found himself sitting inside the basement of some abandoned church within the Red Zone eating expired soup from a can.

"Why?" Jaylen asked before a slow sip from his spoon.

Andrew's eyes slowly looked over at him. For a moment, the scene of them being seated there together, glancing over to Jaylen, Andrew could see the face of his son, Trevor.

"I-I don't know. I felt… compelled to. You looked like you needed help so I—"

"There were others. You chose me; why?" Jaylen asked, cutting him off as he peered down into his bowl. He wasn't sure if he'd seen something crawling inside of it or if he'd simply been seeing things that weren't there.

"Again, I'm not sure. Some time ago I was a pastor and I haven't been around anyone for quite some time and I guess I wanted to get back to being able to help people; I suppose. I saw you there; you weren't moving. I figured that if I didn't help you that you would be dead soon." Andrew said.

Eventually, Jaylen told him, "Thank you."

"Are there others?"

"Only you… for now. I hope to bring in others. I have rooms set aside; with beds, food, and other supplies that they could use. I've collected several items over time that may be of use."

"'Over time'? How long have you been here?"

"I'm… not really sure. Quite a while, I guess." Andrew answered. "I've seen the seasons come and go; harsh winters, scorching summers. Being away from civilization, sometimes I wonder if I've gone mad in my thinking."

"You could have become imprinted and chosen a better life for yourself," Jaylen said.

"Yes, perhaps I could have, but the same goes for you. Why live this way?" Andrew asked him.

"I have my beliefs." Jaylen shrugged.

"I heard that pastors were becoming imprinted. What do you think of that?" Jaylen asked.

Andrew mumbled something underneath his breath. A prayer.

"May God have mercy upon their souls," he said.

Jaylen looked over to Andrew out of the corners of his eyes, wondering more about the estranged pastor's past.

That night, the men went into two of the many rooms beneath the sanctuary of the church that Andrew had prepared. Inside of his room, Jaylen had trouble sleeping; he lied on his side, crying because of the many losses he'd taken, trying his best not to cause attention to himself. He felt gut-wrenching anguish, unlike he'd ever felt before, as his mind questioned repeatedly *why*.

He and his mother had always tried their absolute best in trying to do things and conduct themselves in the right manner yet, his mother's fate hadn't turned out the right way. Jaylen had become overwhelmed with grief but his only form of comfort came from holding on to his mother's words and all that had been taught to him by her.

In another room, Kaleb fell asleep feeling filled with hope that, with the addition of Jaylen, this was a sign of a new beginning.

A few days later, the two men rode around the Red Zone in search of others that they could help, Andrew explained. Out of the many things to cross his mind, Jaylen asked Andrew how he was able to get gas to continue traveling throughout the Red Zone. Andrew responded that he'd figured out how to boost it from old gas stations or that he would simply get another abandoned car that could still run properly if he needed it.

They continued to roll along for quite some time, finding no one, but they were convinced that there had been others. Jaylen had been dumped off with hundreds of them and Andrew mentioned that he would stumble across a person now and then "before the whole eviction had taken place." There had been a small level of obligation that had come over Jaylen where he'd felt the need to tag along, but he didn't quite understand the point of the mission.

"Why search for anybody? Why not just... look after yourself? Eventually, they'll all turn on you and do whatever they feel is best for themselves anyway. They'll neglect all that you've done for them; all that you've taught them, just to do the opposite." Jaylen said, slightly trailing off into thoughts of his crew.

Andrew was quiet for a moment, feeling somewhat guilty for his past mistakes because of what Jaylen had said. He thought about how he'd preach to his family and congregation and ultimately wound up abandoning them.

"Perhaps," he finally began, "this is a way of making things right for them... as well as for myself."

Further, they traveled along into what was once a lively city area but was now only a shell of what it once was. Tall skyscrapers with shattered windows that were destroyed by rioting and warfare barely stood alongside vacant streets that were decorated by emptied, burned, and rusted vehicles.

One building caught Jaylen's attention, as a man had been hanging from one of the windows. However, he didn't appear recognizable due to the group of birds that had fed off of the now mutilated corpse. This somehow didn't bother him; he noticed, as the sight of his mother being killed in front of him had hardened something inside of him, and there could never, perhaps, be an image more devastating than that… ever.

The sun had begun to set, eliminating the limited amount of natural light they had remaining. Still, they hadn't come across anyone, and Jaylen became convinced that no one had ventured out as far as they had traveled.

"Maybe no one's out this far," Jaylen said leaning against the window seal of the passenger side window as he gazed out hoping to find someone.

"Maybe," Andrew said, "but you never know. We just have to keep going. Finding one is plenty."

Jaylen sighed as he started to become somewhat restless because of the lack of sleep from the night before. His eyelids fluttered as their headlights beamed through the dark, unlit streets, and orange cast sky. There wasn't a single sound to be heard except for the humming vibrations that came from the engine of the car.

As his thoughts faded and became less and lee comprehensible, he noticed a flickering light within the distance of a store that they were quickly approaching.

"W—wait. Wait!" Jaylen suddenly became alert.

Andrew slammed on the brakes and asked Jaylen what he had seen.

"Go back some; I think I saw a light inside of that old grocery store. Maybe a flashlight. Someone might be inside." Jaylen wasn't sure why he'd become so invested in Andrew's hunt for people but, he reasoned, that since they'd spent so much time out there already, they might as well return with something to show for it.

The car slowly rolled back as Andrew shut off the lights and the two men peered over their shoulders inside of the old ramshackle grocery store. It had been nearly obliterated from what they could see. The front windows, doors, and shelving were broken and overturned.

"What would anyone find in this place?" Jaylen said, thinking aloud.

"You'd be surprised; there's always something you could use. Leave no stone unturned," Andrew said before shutting off the engine. "Let's go."

As Andrew exited the car, Jaylen noticed a large knife inside of a sheath on Andrew's right side. He considered for a second why he might need a weapon and before jumping out of the car behind him, he remembered what happened on his last day inside of the Green Zone and wondered if he should have a weapon of some kind as well.

They stepped right through the broken glass that once formed the front door of the store; neither one of them saw anything as they continued. As they stepped over broken and destroyed grocery items, Jaylen imagined what the store must have once looked like. Despite the store that they were currently in being larger, it brought to mind Flannigan's Groceries, where he and his mom once both shopped and lived.

Andrew led as he scanned the store. They flashed their light in every direction, only to discover nothing.

"Are you sure you saw someone?" Andrew asked Jaylen.

"No, I'm not sure. I thought I did but, I'm not certain," Jaylen answered.

"I suppose it's worth a look anyway," Andrew said.

They continued walking up and down each one of the aisles, where each shelf carried less than the last one. They came to the end of the aisle that they were currently on, turned to the next one when a flashlight suddenly turned on towards them, placing the two of them in the line of sight of whoever was on the other end. The two men froze instantly, then the blasting sound of a shotgun echoed into the air.

Andrew and Jaylen stumbled backward behind one of the shelves in the aisle from whence they'd just come from. Both men frantically checked themselves to see if they'd been hit; luckily, they hadn't. They looked at one another, eyes widened, trying to figure out what had just happened, but neither one of them had the faintest idea of who had just fired at them.

"*Get to the car*!" Andrew instructed Jaylen. "We've got to get out of here."

The two of them quickly scrambled in fear towards their car parked outside, trying their best to keep their heads low. The move was risky; had the shooter caught them in their line of sight, they both could have easily been blown into pieces right in front of the store near the checkout lane. Upon making their way through the shattered glass in the front of the store and back to their car, they met their worst fear: a double-barrel shotgun aimed directly at them both.

"Toss over those keys," a male voice said behind a gas mask.

Jaylen's and Andrew's hands were in the air, showing the man behind the gun that they weren't a threat.

"That isn't necessary," Andrew said.

"Do you know me? How are you to decide what's necessary for me? Keys!" the man commanded once again.

"You're not a killer," Jaylen said, stepping forward slowly with his hands still in the air.

The man quickly removed his mask and cocked the shotgun. Jaylen stopped.

"You sure about that?" the man challenged.

"Oh, I don't doubt that you've killed, especially during these times but, you're not a *killer*. There's a difference between having killed someone and actually *being* a killer. Had you been a killer, my friend and I would have both been laid out in the front of this store and you would have been halfway up the road by now in that car next to you. If you were a killer, I wouldn't have been able to go into so much detail about who you are and who you aren't." Jaylen said.

"Or maybe I was deciding on whether or not I should let you live and at this very moment, I just decided against it. Either way, in both scenarios, the common denominator is that I get the job done." The man contested.

"To be honest, you'd be doing me a favor." As Jaylen finished, he turned his back to the gunman and was now facing Andrew's terrified face.

"Guys, no one has to die!" Andrew tried to intervene. "Sir, whatever you were searching for within this store, I assure you we can provide it for you. I have a place and I am searching for people to help throughout the Red Zones. Please, just come with us; we are stronger and better together." Andrew reasoned.

The man looked at Jaylen, whose back was still turned towards him and his shotgun, which he finally decided to lower.

"You're searching for people to help?" the man asked, trying to confirm what Andrew had just said.

"Yes, we are," Andrew confirmed.

The man lowered and shook his head.

"I'll tell you one thing, you keep searching long enough, you'll find people except, it'll be the wrong kind of people. Now, I'm ashamed to mention some of the things that I've done to survive but, there are people a lot more dangerous than I am out here. Consider yourself lucky that you met me first instead of them."

Jaylen turned back around to face the gunman.

"So, the man who greeted us by almost blowing us into pieces is the good guy?" Jaylen asked.

The gunman lifted the shotgun over his right shoulder, barrels now pointing into the air.

"That's right," the gunman smirked.

14
NOTHING AND EVERYTHING

Out of the corner of her eye, Cassandra thought she'd seen someone that she knew; someone that was once close to her but, perhaps, had always been apart from her. Jessica continued in conversation without realizing that her cousin's attention had drifted away. They were out shopping in the busy downtown area near Cassandra's new place when Cassandra saw a guy that looked eerily like Jaylen. But it can't be, she thought. She hadn't been able to think clearly or get a good night's rest since the removal of the non-imprinted citizens several months ago.

She hadn't heard from anyone within the group since it occurred. After catching glimpses of what had taken place on social media and news outlets, she couldn't help but fear the absolute worst, and that constantly kept her awake at night.

"Hey, what is it? I feel like I'm talking to myself suddenly," Jessica said, stopping Cassandra in her dazed tracks.

"Oh… I'm sorry. I just thought… I thought I saw someone that I knew." Cassandra answered.

Jessica looked at her cousin for a moment, somehow with a good idea as to who she might have been referring to. She tried her best in helping Cassandra make the transition over into the life of an imprinted citizen go smoothly but; it hadn't always been easy. Cassandra held on to a lot of guilt in some odd version of survivor's remorse as if she'd made it out and the others didn't. She would always try to ration within herself that they'd all had a choice, and that she had chosen what she'd felt was best for her. *How could I be at fault for looking out for myself,* she thought.

Then there was the loss of what she and Jaylen had once shared. She would imagine the disappointment that he must have had for her, that is, if he were still alive. He did all that he could to prevent her from becoming imprinted but, during the last hours, she went through with it. She couldn't bear to continue living the way that she'd been living.

"Things have just been a little difficult for me, you know? So many of my friends, Jaylen, they're gone! We believed in many of the same things and despite things being easier for me now, I can't help but wonder if I made the wrong decisions." Cassandra expressed to her cousin.

"You can't beat yourself up over this; you made the right choice. Just look at how fast things turned around for you! You can't possibly feel bad for taking care of yourself, especially when it didn't involve harming anyone. You'll meet new friends, so just focus on moving forward, okay?" Jessica responded.

Two military bots on their way out of the police station gave Alicia a quick scan as she made her way past them without slowing. She frantically rushed towards the front desk where she saw the officer who'd prevented her from seeing her brother on many occasions already due to minor technicalities. Nearly out of breath, Alicia requested to speak with Kaleb.

The officer, who could stand to lose a few pounds, maybe forty, as far as Alicia was concerned, sat behind the bulletproof window and turned away from her despite her speaking to him. He seemed occupied with his cell phone, reading the latest gossip around the world to keep himself entertained during his shift.

"Excuse… *me!*" Alicia pushed.

The officer, still facing away from her, simply looked at her from the corner of his eye as if she'd been interrupting him from something of valued importance.

"Yes; how can I help you?" he asked.

She felt annoyed because out of the many times that she'd been down to the station to get things arranged so that she could see Kaleb or attempt to get him released; she knew the officer was aware of who she was and why she was there. It was obvious that he was trying to give her a tough time.

"I'm here, *once again*, trying to see my brother. His name is Kaleb Flannigan." She sighed.

The officer slowly sat up, causing the chair to creak from the amount of pressure he'd placed on it, and began typing on the computer in front of him.

"Let me check to see if he's in our system," he said.

Alicia's eyes closed as she shook her head.

Of course, he's in there, dammit; you know he is; she thought. However, she tried to remain calm, so that she didn't jeopardize her chance of seeing her brother.

"Let's see here—you say his name is Kaleb Fl—"

"Kaleb Flannigan. Kaleb, with a *K*." Alicia said with her frustration leaking through.

The officer glanced over at a fidgeting Alicia standing with her arms crossed. For a moment, he wondered if she was on any drugs but;

she seemed to take care of herself. He'd seen addicts of all kinds, however, so he still didn't put it past her. He turned back to the screen.

Finally, she made it past *officer* lard and through a series of security scans and now sat, nervously, in a visiting room waiting for her brother to enter. The room wasn't big; there was one door, to which Alicia's back was towards, white walls, a few tables with a couple of chairs around them, and no windows.

Two guards stood on opposite ends of the room as well, to ensure that everyone complied with the visitation rules of the prison. Two other families were there visiting their incarcerated family members. Although she tried not to stare, now and then, she would glance over at the prisoners who sat with their families and tried to guess what they'd done to become locked up. Whatever she came up with, she knew she was probably wrong in her guess.

She heard the door open behind her, and she spun around to see two guards bringing Kaleb in. As they uncuffed him, he gave her the coldest stare that she'd ever seen from anyone that was so close to her. Alicia's quivering smile towards him quickly vanished, and her head slowly dropped to her chest in shame. Once he'd been unchained, Kaleb stood there for a moment, not moving.

"What's the call, Flannigan, you going or not?" A guard asked.

The way that he stared at her, Alicia hadn't been so sure if he'd be willing to speak with her; it'd been clear that he was angry with her. Eventually, he made his way to the seat in front of her. She cleared her throat.

"It's good to see you." Alicia said.

"Can't say the same." Kaleb sharply replied.

"Kaleb, I'm sorry. I'm so very sorry; I can't express that enough. You have to believe me; I had no idea what was going to happen. Had I known—"

"Yet, you made the call anyway." He cut in.

"I didn't think that they would… kill her. I didn't like her for you, but I didn't want her dead; you have to believe me. You know that's not who I am, Kaleb." Alicia stated, trying to keep her voice down. "When I saw you inside of that closet with them… my heart dropped."

"What part of the world have you been hiding in, huh? Haven't you heard the stories about how non-imprinted citizens have mysteriously been found dead? How do you think they wound up dead, huh, Alicia? Who's killing them? Why aren't these cases being looked at? Don't come in here, sit in front of me, and play ignorant. You better start saying something to me that makes sense." Kaleb said.

"I—I wish I could take everything back. I can't explain to you how I feel inside; but please know that I feel absolutely horrible about everything." Alicia said.

"You had someone I loved killed. You deserve every ounce of pain that you feel, every single ounce." Kaleb fought back the tears that had begun to well up in his eyes. "Have you heard from Jaylen?"

"No," Alicia said regretfully. "I haven't."

"Sheesh, so he could very well be dead, too," Kaleb said.

"Yes, Kaleb, that's a strong possibility, okay? Is that the response that you want to hear from me? Or maybe you'd like to hear that I plan on killing myself once I leave here, huh?"

"Whatever is best for you. That's what you always strive for right," Kaleb said, "even if it means ending your own life, that's what was best for Alicia, even if it brought everyone else around your misery?"

Alicia, sensing that she was becoming upset and wanting to push back against how he'd been responding to her, took a deep breath before speaking another word.

"Okay, look, Kaleb, I came here to apologize from the bottom of my heart. I truly wish that it hadn't happened, and I am absolutely sorry for hurting you. Also, I came to let you know that I'm working on getting you out of here. I've spoken to a few lawyers and they feel that they have a really strong case. Despite the charge of hiding a non-registered citizen, by you already doing a few months, and you not having a criminal record, we think we can have you home soon."

"You're working on getting me out of here, to go back out there?" Kaleb asked, leaning forward. "What's out there? A world that kills you for thinking differently, *being* different or Lord forbid, having a difference of opinion. I'm not sure if I want to live within a world that doesn't accept someone because of what they believe in. What, are we the lucky ones who get to live because we believe in nothing? Maybe believing in nothing is believing in the wrong thing. To be quite honest, sis, despite carrying the burden of a lost loved one, I think that I'm doing better than you are being on the inside of here. Somehow being caged has me feeling freer than I've ever been."

The three men arrived back at the church, which was now Jaylen's home, at least for the time being. They showed the gunman, who stated that his name was Daniel, around the place cautiously, not knowing if they could fully trust him or not. Although it wasn't in his plans,

Andrew was prepared if the man had any tricks up his sleeve. Daniel observed the place, every corner, as if he were an inspector looking for any flaws with the construction of the place. Clearly, there were many, which made his detailed look into the place all the more puzzling to the other two men.

"Is it not up to your liking, my friend," asked Andrew?

"No, this will do just fine actually," Daniel replied, peering at the crumbling stone in the sanctuary's basement where Andrew had prepared several rooms for other people and families to dwell. "Not quite the five-star hotel experience that I'm normally used to but, this will work." Daniel smiled and patted Jaylen on the arm as he walked past him. Jaylen stared at the spot on his arm where the new guy had touched him.

Later that evening, they all settled in, prepared dinner, and sat at the dining table where they all ate together. Andrew inquired about their new guest, asking where he'd come from, and how long he'd been out in the Red Zone.

"Honestly, I've lost all track of time," Daniel said. "I guess the answer to that is that I've been out here long enough to figure out how to survive on my own."

Daniel noticed Jaylen staring at him between bites of his food.

"I've also learned how to determine whether or not someone is an enemy... as well as how to deal with it," Daniel said. Jaylen wondered if it had been some type of threat, him saying that and looking at him. Andrew noticed the underlying tension between the two men and attempted to subdue it as quickly as possible.

"I think that we've all been through quite a bit but, the key thing to remember is that, on this side, we aren't one another's enemy and that we need to do everything that we can in working together for us to survive as long as we can," Andrew said.

"Very well said, my new friend; I agree!" Daniel said, shifting his attention away from Jaylen.

"You mentioned that you've lost track of time and that you don't remember how long you've been out here?" Andrew inquired.

"Yes, that's right." The man replied.

"Are you able to tell whether it has been days, weeks, months; do you know?"

"Not exactly, only that it has been a long time. Seasons have changed; I've had to learn how to adapt but, I must say, it has become more and more difficult. I may not appear to be so but, I'm very close to my end; this is no way for a human to live. Digging through dumpsters and abandoned stores for expired food, and that's if you're lucky, finding anything that tastes fresh is the new gold." Daniel said. "To tell you men the truth, I've prayed many nights, as I doze off to sleep, to never wake up again. That would be the best thing to find out here; to open your eyes one morning and discover that you're no longer living in this world, all while never having to compromise who you were or what you believed in. Yeah, that's the dream." Daniel sighed softly.

Andrew and Jaylen looked at one another; neither one of them said a word.

"What do you believe in?" asked Andrew.

"Nothing… and everything. There's nothing left for me to believe in out here; only God, and that's everything."

"Same here," Jaylen said, chiming into the conversation.

"Were you brought here from the air carrier?" Andrew asked.

"God, no," Daniel responded. "I was here well before then. Had I been inside of the Green Zone on that day, they would have probably had to murder me. No offense, if that was you guys' experience."

"Back at the store, you said something. You said that there were dangerous people out here; who were you talking about?" Jaylen asked curiously.

Daniel paused, looked at them both.

"Some bad dudes, man," Daniel said, looking over at Jaylen. "I don't know where they originate from but, I know they were here before me. To be out here, you've made a serious decision and commitment regarding your life. See, there are two groups of people out here: those who believe in something and those who don't. Those who are out here and don't believe in anything are the most dangerous people you'll ever come across. They're down to do anything for anything to anyone at any time. That's who those guys are; they're Barbarians. Whatever you do, stay clear of them."

15
JUST LIKE OLD TIMES

A fire burned inside of a barrel within the center of a warehouse as Lisa and a small group of other non-imprinted citizens all sat around it, trying to keep warm. The glow from the flame revealed a dazed look of disbelief that had settled onto her face and her eyes appeared to be hollow and as if nothing were behind them.

Her thoughts were on her friends, whom she'd now had no idea as to their whereabouts, except for Cassandra, who'd been living comfortably within the Green Zone. Lisa would now always become angered whenever thoughts of Cassandra would enter her mind. Her weakness was repulsive, and any resemblance or reminder of her would create instant nausea inside of Lisa.

Despite many of the non-imprinted sticking together when they'd been first released into the Red Zones, over time, the number of them dwindled down as some believed that they would be better able to survive on their own. Also, there had been petty disagreements among them as well, which caused the number to shrink down even further. Lisa had said little since the day that they had all arrived and just tended to follow along with a small group within the larger group of them that spoke and reasoned with one another as if they had sense.

Every abandoned store for miles had become ravaged through for anything that could be of some use: clothing, firearms, knives, blankets, and food. As days went on and the desperation grew, even the expired food became an option for some. Old homes became dwelling places, along with anything else that had a roof and could keep them warm. On every turn, each street was a skeletal remain of an old world that held remnants of a life no more. Dreams, hopes, wishes, and embedded traces of warfare held onto every fiber of that which was left standing, serving as leftovers for those who'd been viewed as castaways by those living inside of the new world.

As Lisa sat there, she tried understanding how a life that had already been so difficult had now taken a turn for the absolute worst. Lisa's faith remained intact, but she couldn't help but have questions to which the answers seemed to be so far away. After some time, however, there had been something that had broken her dazed state. She noticed a mother holding the hand of her young daughter walking past her. She wasn't sure if she'd seen any children since she had been there; maybe she'd seen others, she couldn't remember. They were here, she thought, mother and child, together inside of this hell within hell. The decision was made on behalf of the mother to not have her child imprinted and now this was their life, scrambling for food and shelter when the option was available for all their needs to be met. As the two scrummed along, Lisa became conflicted; she didn't know what to think of it. And then she thought about Cassandra once again.

Months after the non-imprinted citizens became removed from Green Zones, there was a strong objection by a small number of citizens and a few members of Congress, led by Naomi, on how things were handled. Naomi's outcry was loud, and she was determined to fight against what she believed to be unfair treatment against citizens within both Regions. She wrote articles, did interviews, spoke on social media, and voiced her displeasure in front of Congress only to get nowhere.

It was shocking to see the high number of protesters who'd once fought for the inclusion of non-imprinted citizens, now down to only a few hundred at a time. This signified that the protesters were mainly made up of those that hadn't been imprinted. The visual of seeing those marching throughout the streets in a limited capacity pleased President Dunne and his administration, as well as Hansen, who'd continued to monitor things from afar. However, there had been uncomfortable rumblings of fear, a lot of which had been created by Naomi, as to the power that the people's government had over them. Seeing all that had been going on, Hansen decided to deliver a public message for the first time since his assassination attempt.

He spoke from his secluded home, where his message was broadcasted across the world for everyone to see. The timing of Hansen's appearance couldn't have been more perfect, due to not only his message but also serving as a distraction as to what had been occurring. His speech was eloquent and profound, just as his global citizens had always remembered.

The assurance and relief that all would be well was widespread, as the trust of their former leader had become renewed. Former President Hansen sat behind his desk within his office, appearing more poised, healthy, and more certain about the future than he'd ever been. Being able to hear him, actually, see him, strengthened the people and once again they felt empowered to stand with their government.

"The trust that you have instilled within your leaders has not been taken for granted, which can be traced back to every promise made to you being kept as evidence. We were explicitly clear as to who our enemies were, and we were even gracious enough to extend our hand in an attempt to show mercy; they spat into our faces and waged war against us. You were able to see for yourselves, out of your own front door, the mayhem and warfare declared against those who hold an obligation to shield you from any harm. It was them, who chose not to be a part of us, that attacked us and while we are not bullies, we will most certainly not be bullied. Outright acts of brutality and destruction are not within our nature. Our mercies permitted them to live amongst us for a time, yet, they revolted against their neighbors and congressional representatives. From the very beginning, my calling was to restore order through any measure deemed necessary and this calling has been dutifully continued through the vigilant efforts of President Dunne and his administration. I implore you, that just as you have trusted in me, continue to lend this same trust unto your President. Thank you."

Andrew and the other two men managed to find others within the Red Zone to help in providing them with food and shelter. They filled the rooms within the basement of the abandoned church with those who'd been cast away by their government for not following the new standards of living inside of the Green areas. The people were grateful and always made sure to express their gratitude, Jaylen and Daniel as well, and despite all things shaping up, Andrew knew that there would be darker storms coming upon the horizon.

These were the times that the believers had always spoken about; it was written within their Bibles and other similar texts; it had been preached inside of churches and synagogues, and the prophecy of these days had been carried down from days well before any of them had ever walked the face of the earth. Whether these were indeed those times that had been spoken about was a mystery for the unaware.

There was confusion amongst believers and nonbelievers alike due to the disconnection from their source over time. Some had become dismissive as to whether or not the prophecies were real and as the days of trouble became longer and more extended, their faith began to diminish causing even some of the most respected advocates of the faith to turn away from where they once were. The drop off was subtle, yet noticeable to those who kept watch.

Century after century, year after year, day after day, the coming of the present time came near. During the last days before churches became abolished, the believers, during every meeting spoke with great worry and wonder among themselves as to how these times of tribulation had "snuck up on them" when, in fact, they were given advanced warnings, repeatedly, throughout time.

Some believers questioned how they were to truly know that these were the days spoken about in prophecy. They challenged that the warnings that were given from centuries ago couldn't have possibly been speaking about the present day. With their uncertainty and blinding confusion, they made their choice to continue living on with the shred of hope that they hung on to or they decided that the end of their struggle had ended and that the global identity system was the divine change that they'd all prayed for during the trying times.

A few times during the week, Andrew would speak to the group of believers that they had brought in. It was a revival of the church, of sorts, within the Red Zone. He spoke with a fire that ignited everyone, bringing forth a renewed sense of hope and faith that had gone missing inside of them a very long time ago. They had all been away from the church setting for a long time, so the days when Andrew would stand before them inside of the muddy, molding, and deteriorating basement of the church, something inside of them would become rekindled each time.

It was important to not be seen by anyone, like the Barbarians, who had been looking for an opportunity to steal from them or do greater harm, so they would congregate on another level beneath where their rooms and kitchen had been. When he'd first seen the open space, that had been two floors beneath the actual sanctuary of the church, he couldn't help but think of the cave that he used to preach to his small congregation in and the underground passageway that he and his family passed through, leading to his unheroic escape into Region One.

The days when he had an actual church had started to fade from his memory. He couldn't remember what the building had looked like. Each time that he would try to picture it and couldn't, it frightened him. He couldn't understand how he could forget something like that, and when he would begin to wonder if he would forget the faces of his family, he would quickly try to brush off those thoughts.

Everyone gathered around Andrew, who stood within the open space so that they all could see him. He never asked them to but, after a while, they would sometimes sit on the ground with their legs crossed. His face would glow from the lights of the burning torches that Daniel and Jaylen had made and hung in the corners of the room. The people would all look on, all with the same look inside of their eyes. They each possessed a look of hope, a look as if they were searching for a specific answer; the correct answer. Neither of them was sure what that answer was exactly, but they all just knew that they would recognize it once they'd heard it from him.

Andrew recognized this and had well prepared during his time dwelling in the Red Zones before any of them had been there. The entirety of his days was spent praying alone in his room. Although the people couldn't see how this was possible, they all understood, especially given his position. Two guys whom Andrew put trust in, Steven and Nigel, would keep watch and answer questions by the people while he prayed. Although Andrew trusted these two, he remained closer to Jaylen. He was special to Andrew and Jaylen respected him for having a vision and most importantly, for saving his life.

For reasons Jaylen couldn't fully understand, he would pick up traces of jealousy sent towards him from Steven and Nigel. He would usually brush it off as nonsense and a waste of time, considering the larger issues that were at hand. To him, they were a couple of old privileged former pastors hanging on to their heyday that no longer meant anything to anyone.

After Andrew had finished speaking, Daniel and Jaylen sat outside on the front steps of the church, looking out into the distance of the night sky.

"It almost seems like the stars no longer give off their light nowadays," Daniel said.

Jaylen looked up into the sky; he'd only found a few stars. They were dim.

"Yeah," Jaylen said quietly.

"We're just down here all alone... trying to feel our way through the dark. I'm pretty sure we're heading in the wrong direction." Daniel added.

Jaylen didn't respond, he just kept staring out as far as he could. After a while, Terrance, one of the new guys, came out front to join the two men.

"What's up gentlemen?" Terrance sighed as he sat down next to Jaylen.

Jaylen simply nodded his head, acknowledging him.

"Hey, man," Daniel replied. They were all quiet for a moment until Terrance broke in with a question.

"So, what's the story with this Andrew guy; he just goes around trying to help people in the Red Zone?" Terrance asked.

"I'd say that pretty much sums him up," Daniel answered. "Does he have to have a story?"

"I mean, I guess not. I was just wondering if I should really trust him or not, that's all."

"You've already eaten the man's food and slept in a bed he's provided for you, for several nights, might I add. I'd say you've made yourself pretty comfortable and that you're past the point of trying to figure out if the man has a trick up his sleeve for you or not."

"Yeah, maybe, but you never know. It could come later down the line. These preacher guys are tricky, you can trust me on that."

"Look, he's cool alright?" Jaylen said sharply without looking at Terrance.

"Whoa, alright, man, I'll take your word for it!" Terrance said, lifting his hands into the air playfully as a signal of giving up on the conversation.

"Personally, I don't care what the man's title is or used to be; he offered his help, and I obliged. Not too much worried about a con artist at this point. I did well out here on my own beforehand. After a while, I now know who the real enemy is out here and he ain't one of 'em. I'd advise you to recognize who the real enemy is as well before it's too late for ya." Daniel concluded.

"Oh yeah; and who might that be?" Terrance asked.

16
BARBARIANS

It waited.

Just outside of the mansion, he stood wearing the skull of an unlucky victim painted in black that had been rigged and attached to a dark-colored gas mask. Its gloved hands, covering the many cuts, scars, and bruises, were to its side as it positioned itself directly in front of a handcrafted marble fountain that must have cost a fortune once upon a time. The luxury and fine craftsmanship, of course, meant nothing outside of the Green Zone. Nothing held any value. Underneath the mask and the being itself, there was nothing birthed from the light, only the spawn of the deepest and darkest parts of the abyss. The skull of death displayed outwardly exemplified what was beneath.

From the outside of the mansion, flickering candle light flashes were shown as the sounds of talking and laughter every now and then could be heard. Inside of his ear, a dried, empty voice crackled over an unseen earpiece, asking him if everything had been in place. In the same tone, the being responded to the voice with a simple, "Yes."

One of the non-imprinted groups that had been moved from inside of the Green Zone was able to find a safe haven inside of the mansion. It was large enough to house the fifteen to twenty-something members comfortably as well as all their food and supply needs. It had been an unusual adjustment, but they were able to find strength in their belief system, pull together, and somehow make the best of what they were facing. They found a rhythm to their living that they all meshed well with, which allowed them to work reasonably through most situations, no matter how challenging. The strength of their unity, however, was on the brink of its most threatening test yet.

It was a normal evening for them all, one that had been filled with wine and stories from their past. Mark, one of the mansion's occupants, made his way towards a restroom down the hall from the main living area where the others had been gathered. The restroom was next to one of the many enormous rooms replenished with windows inside of the home. He let out a strong steady stream with a grin on his face thinking of how he'd never been able to afford such expensive bottles of wine in his past life that he and the other residents were enjoying, but were now available to them all for free.

He figured that there had been some good that came from the government uprooting him from his life simply because of what he believed in. He gave himself a shake, ran some water over his hands, wiped his hands on a hand towel that was still hanging on a rack, and proceeded to exit the restroom.

Mark froze.

He noticed a shadowy male-looking figure standing in the corner near an opened window. It was dark, with something covering its face. A mask? A skull? He'd been unable to clearly make out who or what exactly it was.

It just… *stood* there, staring directly at Mark.

"H-hello; can I… help you," Mark asked with his voice trembling? "Are you in need of some kind of help? W-we may be able to help you if… there's something that you might need."

It didn't answer.

Not knowing what to say, think, or do next, Mark began to slowly move towards the exit of the room which was across from where the figure was standing. He started with a normal walk, peering out of the side of his eyes at the black shadow.

It watched him.

The mask of the figure gently moved along with Mark as he moved across the large, open room. He got closer and closer to the door, picked up his pacing some... then all-out terror fell over Mark as the shadow rushed full speed towards him. Mark's scream for help was cut short.

Sara thought she'd heard something amid everyone's laughter, but she couldn't be too sure, so she continued on with everyone else. They all stood around holding expensive glasses and cups of some sort to drink some of the finest spirits they'd ever had. They'd collected some of the nicest attire that they could all find to really look the part. Gradually, as time went on, they'd become the part of those they'd been portraying.

"God sure has taken care of us; we're living better than we'd ever lived. He's kept His promise to us," one resident said. They gave forth cheers and shouts of "Amen," and "Hallelujah," as they toasted one another with their glasses.

Then, quietly, from down every hall, from down both sides of stairs, from the back of the mansion... they came. More of the shadow figures, all wearing gas masks and either an animal skull or a human skull painted in black, flooded in and circled the group in the center of the room.

"What's happening; what's going on?" a resident asked.

Silently, the skulls all stood there with a piercing gaze directly at the residents. Trying to see through to the eyes of the intruders, the residents could only see absolute darkness.

"What do you want?" another asked.

The front door carefully creaked open and suddenly, the skulls formed two lines, in unison, to provide a pathway for someone or… *something* to join them.

There was a shriek from one of the women occupants at the sight of the one that had entered. It had been different from the others; this one was without a gas mask, instead; it wore the skull of a lion, also painted in black. Like the others, it wore all black, but the clothing differed from the combat gear the others wore. The towering lion skull wearing figure was wrapped from its shoulders to the floor in a black cape covering of some kind.

The men held on to the women as they all gradually edged to the back of the home while the lion skull slowly moved in closer to them all. Before any of them could break free through the rear of the home, parts of the line of skulls from both sides pulled together to prevent the residents from escaping. They were outnumbered, with nowhere for them to go.

"We don't want any trouble," Frederick, one man, said, stepping forward to the lion skull. Frederick was solid in stature; by no means a small man, but he'd still been an inch or two shorter than the figure in front of him. "Let's just talk things out and figure out what needs to be arranged, okay?"

After a few moments of silence, a long, deep sigh came from the skull of the dead lion.

"We are not here to bargain," a heavy, monotone voice from the being stated.

"We are not here to speak at great length. We seek to claim all of your supplies, food, as well as this residence. Either you will comply…

or you will not. This I will say to you and yours only once. You may now leave peacefully."

The skulls opened up their barrier in the back of the room, and a few of the men and women quickly escaped. Frederick turned to see the backs of them as they ran away and the worried eyes of those who stayed and watched in horror, not knowing what to do. Frederick slowly turned back to the being with uncertainty, with a feeling in his gut that who, or whatever these things were, was serious. However, there must have been something that could be worked out; the place was enormous. Surely, they would all be able to live there and the more of them that there were, being able to accumulate more supplies would be easier, as they could cover more search ground.

"I'm not sure how much of the place you've seen already," Frederick said, releasing a nervous chuckle, "but it's extremely big; I think we'd all be able to—"

Frederick gagged on his own blood caused by the blade the size of his forearm being jammed into the right side of his neck all the way through to the other side by the being. The dark empty sockets of the lion skull peered into the widened, terrified eyes of the man who'd now been reduced before him. Frederick reached for his neck. But whatever attempt he had in mind to save himself was futile as blood gushed in every direction, even onto the lion skull. The being's gloved right hand tightened the grip of the handle, with the blade still protruding through the left side of Frederick's neck, when, with one full thrust and spin of the blade into a clockwise motion, the head became severed.

The remaining residents all screamed in hysteria and scrambled to escape. It had been too late; the skull creatures were everywhere. Their blood spewed across the floor and walls, becoming part of the new décor of the mansion. Their cries, begging, and pleas for their life became muted to the ears of those who hadn't been invited and drowned out by the sounds of tearing flesh and the snapping of bones. This was the cost.

The leader turned to the front door and two of the skull beings opened it and escorted a man in with his hands bound with rope in front of him, wearing a black bag over his head. He was brought in front of the lion skull and the black bag was removed.

It was Ahmad.

His eyes scanned the room back and forth, observing the scene of a massacre. He couldn't believe his eyes. He wanted to be a part of a team where he could survive no matter what, but this seemed to be more than what he'd been expecting. This had been the organization that he told Jaylen and the others about within the Green Zone, however, he did not know about the levels they were truly willing to take things.

Ahmad's hands were untied, and the leader handed him the blade he'd used to decapitate the man earlier. What did he want him to do with it?

"Your initiation," the lion skull said.

The being stepped to the side and extended his hand to the head lying on the floor by itself, that hadn't been too far away from the rest of Frederick's body.

"Claim your skull!"

Ahmad swallowed as the feeling of him no longer having the option of turning back came over him. This was it; he had to do this or else he would risk having his own skull worn on someone else's head as if it were some type of helmet. The others stopped, stood up, and watched. They formed a line on either side of the head as Ahmad slowly crept towards it. It had already been explained to him; he knew exactly what he needed to do. Seeing the lifeless, shocked eyes of the decapitated head staring up at him sent chills through his spine as he knelt down beside it with the blade in his hands. Ahmad looked over his shoulder and up at their leader and saw the black lion skull towering over him, watching his every move.

His fingertips became slippery with blood and other unknown fluids from him attempting to get a good grip on the skull. In his left hand, he held the skull, and in his right hand was the long blade. They were all silent. Ahmad slowly and carefully began to cut around the shredded flesh from where the blade had sliced through. He grimaced with each clearing of skin being removed away from the bone. The noises it made while he separated the flesh from Frederick's face from the skull underneath caused him to gag every so often, but he managed to successfully hold it in. Soon he was complete, and he was able to remove the skin completely away from the skull.

The being motioned for Ahmad to stand to his feet and he did, blade in one hand and his newly acquired skull in the other. Ahmad was now an official member. He looked around at the others all donning their handy work-half skull, half gas mask. He couldn't help but wonder about what he'd gotten himself into; now he was one of these guys! Ahmad was terrified, but it was too late to remove himself from them.

For the first time, he thought that his disbelief in anything had perhaps been a trap and had led him down a path that he could not retreat from. They, too, didn't believe in anything. These beings didn't worship Gods or devils; they simply believed in survival at any cost. They classified themselves as survivalists but being up close to them and seeing how they operated, Ahmad could see why others referred to them, now including himself, as Barbarians.

17
FAMILY BONDING

There was an unusual feeling and energy within the air inside of the Red Zone that those who hadn't been imprinted learned to notice. When night came, the atmosphere became even eerier. Instead of there being quiet, things were... still. Nothing seemed to move; not even an inch. The flatlands lied dormant and lifeless as well as the buildings that stood tall with overgrown shrubbery overtaking them to the point where it would be best that they became demolished.

The non-citizens disbanded over time and had they not been shipped over into the Red Zones together, they may not have known that anyone else lived within those areas besides themselves. Some branched out into buildings to find their domain, while others found homes in residential areas for shelter. Homes were good for not only shelter but also for discovering non-perishable food items if a non-citizen was lucky enough.

After the seasons changed and the snow had melted away, it became easier to see and travel for Red Zone residents. This was important because living outside of the Green Zone was a matter of survival of the fittest and being able to find food and supplies first gave those individuals a significant advantage.

Naomi sat inside of Global President Dunne's conference room along with the ambassadors for both Regions. Dunne sat at the head of the table and to Naomi's left, while Lucinda Moreno and Vincent Wells sat across from her. She'd been trying to meet with the President for weeks, but he'd been booked with prior appointments with Presidents from the four Quadrants and other government officials.

"Thank you for understanding," Dunne began, "how busy my schedule has been, councilwoman; there have been quite a few last-minute aspects of our world's final transition that I've been trying to tend to, but things appear to be aligning well, I should say."

"No, thank you, Mr. President." Naomi couldn't help but notice a slight touch of nervousness in her voice. She observed Lucinda with a smug look upon her face towards her; perhaps she'd picked up on her shakiness too and had gotten some type of satisfaction from it.

"I understand that you've had some... concerns, for quite some time." Dunne sat relaxed in his chair, legs crossed, hands loosely clasped, as he tried to get to the root of their meeting.

Naomi had never met with the President one-on-one in any formal capacity before and she quickly realized that the opportunity to do so again, if granted, would be far down the line, so she knew she needed to make this time count.

"Yes, yes, I have." Naomi sat up in her chair. "Our treatment of non-imprinted citizens has been absolutely horrendous," Naomi said, looking at Dunne square in his eyes.

In a discomforting gesture, Wells slowly lowered and squeezed his forehead. Lucinda quickly looked off towards the bookcases to the right of her, trying her best to suppress her displeasure with Naomi's beliefs. Dunne glanced over to Lucinda, saying nothing, then back to Naomi.

"Continue," Dunne said.

"Well, it's just that, how this administration went about handling those citizens who were against becoming imprinted was poorly done. I feel that you three somehow had forgotten that you were dealing with human beings; those people were treated like animals and they continue to be viewed and treated as such to this very day. There was… so much that could have been done where they could have not been obligated to receive Hansen's imprint and still been able to live inside of the Green Zone. It didn't have to result in bloodshed and forcing these people to be placed in the position of forfeiting their beliefs just for the sake of having a roof over their heads."

For the duration of time that Naomi spoke, Dunne gave her his undivided attention; he barely blinked. Naomi wasn't sure where the conversation would lead but she knew the President needed to hear what was said.

Dunne shook his head and chuckled lightly. Suddenly, Naomi became thrown off as to what he could have possibly found funny about what she'd just said to him.

"You have to forgive me," President Dunne began. "I've seemed to have lost my manners. Would you like a glass of water or perhaps a cup of coffee?" The timing of his offer confused Naomi. Was he not listening, after all?

"No, that's okay. I don't need anything. I just—"

"I believe I'll have a glass of water," Dunne said.

"Shall I bring in Erickson?" Wells asked, speaking of Dunne's office butler.

"No, Wells, I'm more than capable of pouring my own glass of water. No need to hunt down Erickson, wait for him to come in, then wait for him to pour it. I would have already quenched my thirst by fixing my own glass by the time he arrives," said Dunne.

"I'm sure he's just outside of the door, or at least he should be," Wells reasoned. Moreno then quickly turned to Wells.

"Give it a rest, will you?" she said sternly to him.

By then, Dunne had already walked to the bar area, poured a glass of water, and was headed back to the table with the rest of them. Naomi's eyes widened and shifted back and forth between the three world leaders, feeling even more confused. What was happening at that moment? Was this some form of distraction they were attempting to pull off? Whatever the case, Naomi kept her poise and remained focused on her purpose for being there.

"You were saying, councilwoman?" Dunne said, taking his seat again.

"I think I've pretty much… said all that I've intended to say. I don't think that it has been expressed to you how those people feel; you had your agenda, and you made sure that it was carried out to the end."

"You're wrong, councilwoman," Dunne said after taking a sip from his glass.

"How so?" Naomi asked.

"Countless times, councilwoman, this administration has extended its hand to establish peace and civility amongst all people. And in exchange, what have we gotten in return? We have been slapped in the face and these… rebels have plagued Quadrants within every Region with absolute destruction wherever they stand."

"No… no there's no proof that these acts were at the hands of non-imprinted citizens." Naomi said, shaking her head in disagreement.

"Oh, but there is, councilwoman. You should know that we have cameras, drones, and scanners everywhere, monitoring everything at any given time. There is endless proof verifying that these heinous acts of crime have occurred because of them. Their exile is a result of their own doing, you understand this?" Dunne continued.

"How can you say this… Mr. President? These people gave you no reason to do what you've done to them."

They all sat for a moment, silently.

"From my very first day, my stance has always been to protect the citizens of this great world. I have delivered peace to all of us, that includes you, councilwoman, through the direction of our first prominent leader, Mallory Hansen and it has been my obligation to uphold his vision to the very end." Dunne stated. "Have I not made this clear? Those who have gone against this cause have strong objections to our society being a place of order. How can anyone say, with clear consciousness, that we are not better today than we were before Hansen came to restore order?"

"Are things better? Certainly," Naomi replied. "But you have to acknowledge, Mr. President, that there were aspects of the old world that worked but have now been neglected within this new world, such as civil rights and the freedom for an individual to choose to live however they feel is best for them without their basic means of living becoming jeopardized."

President Dunne slowly leaned forward in his chair, now resting both of his forearms on the wooden table with his hands clasped together. "Okay… what are you asking for, hm? What is the purpose of this meeting? What are you hoping to accomplish here today?"

There was silence as they all peered at Naomi. A lump formed in her throat as she tried to quickly gather her thoughts and figure out the right words to say to them. She felt as if she was speaking for the millions around the world who'd become ostracized and cut off from places that they'd always known to be their home. What could she say to them; were they truly asking to listen, or were they simply allowing her to speak, serving as a pacifier, to soothe her temporarily and then continue on in a manner that had been already decided until the world's end?

"I... plainly... I want these people to not be discriminated against. I want them to still have access to food and housing without having to become imprinted. We should not cast them away because of their beliefs or affiliation with any religious institution."

"I'm afraid... your request is unreasonable." answered Dunne. "Your ask has already been budgeted and made available to everyone under minor circumstances and those people said, 'no' to their government. Okay, I understand. Well, then, you must leave; this land is for those who have chosen to be here. Then, upon this request, they became violent. How are we to respond, councilwoman? I ask you. I will not permit this empire to fall as all those before me have."

The meeting concluded and the two Regional Ambassadors stood, as did Naomi, as President Dunne escorted her to the door. Naomi wasn't sure what she'd hoped to accomplish in the meeting, but she just knew that she needed to say everything that she could to the President's face. Now that she had said everything, she felt she hadn't gotten anywhere, and she left feeling defeated. President Dunne smiled, shook her hand, and thanked her for her hard work and "speaking on behalf of those who may feel voiceless." He told her that the door for them isn't closed and that they still had an opportunity to become imprinted should they choose to. Dunne then shut the door behind her.

"She's smart; very tough," Dunne said. Moreno rolled her eyes at Dunne's sentiments. Wells, however, nodded his head in agreement.

"Such a shame... she could've been special," Dunne concluded.

The Regional Ambassadors knew their President well enough to understand exactly what he meant by that statement.

Every now and then, Jaylen, Daniel, and a few other men, including Terrance, Matt, and James, would make a run deeper out into the Red Zone to find food, water, and any other supplies that they thought would be of use for the rest of the people back at the church hideout. During one of their runs, they got lucky enough to find weapons; this was a rare thing, as Daniel would explain to them. Initially, Jaylen had been hesitant to take them, but Daniel had explained to him to "look at it as a gift from God" because the day would come when they would need them.

The men loaded up two of the trucks around the back of the church with a few weapons and rations of food and water as they prepared for their journey. As they prepared themselves, Andrew overlooked them and said a prayer before they ventured out into the wilderness.

"Does he ever come along," Matt, one the men, once asked before they drove away.

"No; he doesn't have to," Jaylen said. "He's the one that brought this place together in the first place. All of the food, beds, and water that were here from the very beginning were put here by him alone. Andrew's done the work already, now he just watches over us like a spiritual leader."

Matt didn't respond; he just looked back at Andrew from the back of the truck as he became smaller while they drove further out into the distance.

Today, it was much of the same as any other time before they headed out; everyone would thank them, James' wife would kiss him, teary-eyed, telling him to be safe and that she loved him, Matt would ask a dozen questions, nervously, Terrance would have this serious, focused look on his face that Jaylen felt was over the top, Daniel would be fueled with anxious excitement, and Jaylen would simply be quietly to himself concentrating on what was at hand.

They drove out for miles down old abandoned highways. During some stretches, they had to maneuver through vacated cars that were stopped in the middle of the road. The humming sound of the engines was the only sound to be heard from the lead truck which Daniel drove, and the truck that followed, driven by Terrance.

Daniel stuck his head out of the driver's side window with his eyes closed as he inhaled a deep breath while his foot was still on the gas and right hand on the steering wheel.

"Ahh, gotta love that fresh, sweet, poisoned, air hitting your face!" Daniel said.

Jaylen looked over at him and then back out of his own window, which was rolled up without saying anything.

"Hey, man, can you keep your eyes on the road?" Matt requested.

Daniel pulled his head back inside of the truck and turned around to look directly at Matt with a wide grin on his face, who'd been sitting behind Jaylen while still zooming full speed ahead.

"You scared, Matt?" Daniel asked.

"No, I just don't want you to kill us… there's a difference."

Daniel laughed.

"Let's stay focused," Jaylen eventually said.

The Red Zone, even during the daytime, held an engulfing feeling of decay that they all noticed. There were dead animal carcasses that lied alongside the road, along with decayed human flesh that they would sometimes run across. They'd become accustomed to seeing these things, so it no longer bothered them whenever they'd unintentionally step on an animal or human skull. They would look down at the shattered, crumbled bone pieces stuck beneath their boots and continue on.

Daniel had driven for about an hour and a half when he'd gotten off of an exit into a town that they hadn't explored before. Many of the grocery stores, marts, and neighborhoods that were close to the Green Zone had already been dug through by non-citizens who'd been looking for anything to survive with, so the strategy now was for them to explore other areas. The farther out the better; there were smaller chances that anyone had been through those areas.

However, they would come to realize that because they'd waited too long to explore other areas, by the time they had, many of the food items had become expired. For some items, if it had only been one or two months past the expiration date, they would still bring it back with them, hoping it could still somehow be used. No matter what part of the world they were, non-citizens faced the same issues within the Red Zone.

Jaylen and his men searched through each home, recklessly tossing aside whatever they didn't feel was useful. They ravaged through cabinets, closets, sheds, secret rooms, and flipped over mattresses, hoping to find anything useful. They also grabbed any medicines that they could find. Early on during their outings, they hadn't thought of this, but some of the members at the hideout had requested that they bring back anything that they could find.

Their supply runs would last hours at a time, including the time driving out and the time driving back to the hideout, so instead of driving back the same day, they would often find a place to rest up overnight, continue searching the next day, and drive back when they felt they had gathered enough items.

They loaded up the trucks, but it had gotten late, so they stayed the night in one of the homes they'd gone through. They pulled mattresses from the bedrooms and all laid out in the living room area. These homes had been abandoned since the days of war and many of them, being unkempt, were molded, infested, and rotten. As they all lay there, a huge rodent scudded across the floor, startling Matt.

"Jesus Christ!" Matt jumped off the mattress as everyone laughed at him.

"Did you see how big that thing was?" Matt asked.

"C'mon, it's just the house pet," Terrance said jokingly.

"Where's a cat when you need one?" Matt asked.

"That thing probably ate it," James said.

Jaylen smirked and nodded in agreement with James.

"We live in New York; you act like you're not used to it," Daniel said.

"I don't care where we live! I'm not used to that; no one should be used to a dog-sized rat running around all over the place. Who's comfortable with that?" Matt asked.

"Look at this guy! He's all high-class now, talking about comfort and being too good for a little pet rat," Terrance teased.

"Not sure how things have been for you, bud, but I haven't been comfortable in only God knows when," James replied.

"No way I'll be able to sleep in here," said Matt.

They all laughed.

None of the men could get any rest; they all lied down or sat up deep in thought. Their minds all wandered around thinking about all kinds of things, ideas, and places that allowed them to escape from where they currently were.

"I find it kind of hard these days… to remember what life was like before the wars broke out," James said. He hadn't been talking to any of the men in particular, but his foggy memory of the days before chaos broke out seemed to escape him.

"That sounds about right," Daniel agreed. "Seems like the days of war outnumber the days we actually lived in peace. Not much I remember before then."

"Yeah… same here." Terrance was able to relate.

Jaylen sat upright on his mattress, looking at the flickering flame of the candle resting on top of a mantle in front of him.

"I remember… I remember my mother," Jaylen said. "That's it. We had a home, everything was normal, but then… I don't know what happened. Now I'm here; she's not."

The room fell even more silent than it already had been. It was as if all the men were grasping at some type of memory within their minds, no matter how small, that they could recall which would somehow transport them back to a better time when all things were well with them.

"My wife and I were… normal, I guess," James said. "We had a home, like this one. She and I both worked, we traveled the world. From what I can piece together, we were happy."

"Sounds like a solid life you had there," Terrance said. "Mine wasn't anything special, I don't suppose. I mean-I worked… a *lot*, hung out with a few women from time to time, that's about it. I wanted to find something special with one of them; never really seemed to work out. I made good money, you know? It was hard to find someone that was really open to getting closer to me for who I was as a person. Then again, I was probably too paranoid and closed off. Who knows what happened? Then, when the wars broke out, everything shifted. My job folded, and I didn't know which way was up. The only thing that kept me sane was my faith and even that wavered at times. But I made a commitment, you know? I was committed to die for what I believed in," Terrance said.

"You still feel that way now?" asked Jaylen.

Terrance thought about it for a second before answering.

"I suppose so. Things have gotten ten times worse since then and here I am in the middle of nowhere with you guys. I could've easily thrown in the towel for a better life, we all could have. So, yeah, I'd say I'm still committed."

"Good call, buddy," Daniel affirmed as he got up from his mattress.

"Hey, where are you headed?" James asked.

"To take a leak, man. Is that alright, buddy?"

"Hey, what are you guys' vices?" asked Matt.

"Vices? I don't know... I like to gamble every now then if that counts; I used to anyway," James answered. "If anything, that was the only thing that haunted my wife and me."

"For me, it's definitely women," Terrance said, shaking his head. "I love the idea of settling, but I somehow find every excuse not to. Meanwhile, I line them all up for tryouts... one... by... one."

"I don't mind taking a pill or two every now and then," Matt said. "It's not like... to the point where I'm concerned or where it could possibly kill me or anything, but it probably is best that I don't have them constantly on hand. I'd probably always be high. I don't think I have a problem, do you," he asked, looking at Terrance?

"Yeah, man, sounds like you do have a problem," Terrance joked with a straight face. "Probably should stay away from the medicine cabinet."

Then they all got quiet, as if they were waiting for Jaylen to give up the one thing that plagued him.

"I don't know if there's a... vice that I have," Jaylen finally responded.

"We have Mr. Perfect over here, gentlemen," James teased. The guys chuckled.

"No, it's just that… there's not anything that I pursue for pleasure that may be harmful to me versus something that I tend to struggle with. Well, I guess they could also be the same; it depends."

"Oh yeah, and what might that be," Daniel asked as he returned to the room holding an opened bottle of whiskey?

"Forgiveness," Jaylen answered, thinking of his father.

They became quiet, except for Daniel.

"That's a good one," he said. "Whatever your vices are, keep 'em low and to a minimum. This is the end; the last thing you'd want out here is to get derailed by your demons."

Afterwards, Daniel took a long swig from the bottle of whiskey he'd found and wiped his mouth with the forearm sleeve of his shirt.

18
LOST RELATIVES

It had been over a year and a half when Kaleb had been released from prison. Alicia had gotten him out, but he never thanked her; he felt she didn't deserve it since she'd been behind him being in there in the first place. The gate buzzed and slid open, revealing Alicia waiting for him on the other side with an awkward, uncertain smile on her face.

She wanted to hug him, but she wasn't sure if that would've been the best move for her to make at the time. She was right. He didn't even acknowledge her; he simply walked right past her and headed to her car parked off in the distance. She sighed, dropped her head, and walked to her car.

While he was inside, she saw to it that Melanie was able to have a proper burial, and she got lucky enough to allow them to release Kaleb so that he could attend. That had been a near-impossible task, but she continued on with the thought that it had been the last card she had available to redeem herself for what she'd done. Of course, however, Kaleb continued to let her have it, even at the funeral.

When he first arrived at the grave site, he asked Alicia if having Melanie killed hadn't been enough for her and if seeing her finally being put into the ground would bring her the satisfaction she'd been longing for all of this time. Despite the sharp comments that he continued to spew towards his sister, Alicia remained silent each time, although sometimes she wanted to explode.

The car ride back to the inside of the city was long, silent, and extremely tense. Alicia figured she'd stop trying to get her brother to speak and that whenever he was ready to talk, he would come around in doing so, hopefully.

"How's mom?" he eventually asked.

"Oh, she's great, actually. She's been asking why haven't you written her back or taken any of her calls," Alicia answered.

More silence.

"The store is doing well, surprisingly; I even had to hire two people. I haven't been there as much lately and with you being—" she stopped herself.

Kaleb looked at her from the corners of his eyes.

"I just needed a few more extra hands around the store to help out a bit."

"Let's just get this out of the way," Kaleb said. "It is going to take me a *very* long time to move on from what you did."

"I know, I get it," Alicia said while keeping her eyes on the road. "I don't know if I could ever forgive you in the sense of what that word actually means, but you're my sister and I think that there's something in that. There's no way I'll ever forget this, and I can't lie to you and say that every time that I see you now I won't be thinking of Melanie."

Alicia took a deep sigh as her eyes welled up with tears.

"I-I know, Kaleb. I understand; it was a horrible mistake that I have to live with forever… I regret everything about the part I played in the relationship between her and I. Seriously, I messed up… I really screwed up."

"Look, um, I know that Jaylen is out there somewhere in the Red Zone. Hopefully, he's still alive. I want to find him and help him in any way that I can." said Kaleb.

"You're not thinking of… trying to bring him back into the Green Zone, are you?"

"No. I don't think that would be the wisest thing to do; the police would kill him on site. There just has to be a way where I could make sure he doesn't starve out there at least. Living out there, it just seems like there's an expiration date being out there after a while. I was the one in prison, but somehow, I couldn't help but think, even being out in all of that open space, that he had it worse than I did. For him and all of those others, the entire world is their prison. And we made it that way; we suffocated them. We blocked off every corner, squeezed every block, and made it uncomfortable for them at every turn. I just have to find him, gotta make this right." His head slowly turned to Alicia, who had both of her hands firmly on the steering wheel. "You could help me with that, right?"

"Sure, absolutely! I definitely can," Alicia quickly responded.

"Good," he said.

The elevator door opened as a pair of all black Italian handcrafted leather shoes gracefully stepped out and echoed down the corridor towards a security checkpoint. Two military bots were overseeing the identification scan. They both noticed that the gentleman had been holstering a weapon. However, there was no cause for alarm. During the scan, they identified him as being a high-ranking government official. The man gave a nod to the two bots and passed through with his shoes, once again echoing down the hallway. He made his way to the front, where a young woman had her head down, focused on her work at the computer.

"*Ahem!*" The gentleman respectfully gestured, attempting to get the woman's attention.

"I'm so sorry, Sir," she said. "Didn't see you standing there. They have backed me up with so much work I—"

"It's fine," the man said.

"What can I do for you?" the woman chuckled.

"I'm on the board of advisors for the President of Quadrant Three, and I also happen to be a friend of councilwoman Naomi Nicholson. Well, she and I share a couple of mutual friends, rather I should say. I was in town for a couple of days, I had a few meetings, and was hoping to speak with her. She helped my family and I out quite some time ago and I really wanted to thank her for all that she'd done for us. I was hoping that I could be somewhat of a pleasant surprise for her."

"That certainly sounds like the councilwoman," the woman said. "She's always extending her hands to help someone in need. God, she's an angel. Okay, so I believe that she's scheduled to be in and out of a few meetings today, but maybe you could catch her if I send you up. I'm sure she'll be... *thrilled* to see *you*." The woman threw on a little extra to show the gentleman that she'd been fond of his appearance. "Now, I'll just need you to place your right hand inside of the scanner in front of you, you know the procedure, and I can buzz you in."

A small scanner box slowly arose from out of the desk where the gentleman would be allowed to scan. He placed his right hand inside of the machine, palm facing downward, and awaited confirmation from the clerk. His name, photo, occupation, and other information displayed across her screen. The name read:

Trevor Dawkins…

"Thank you, Mr. Dawkins. I'll buzz you through." Trevor smiled, thanked the woman, and proceeded through a side door as he headed up to find Naomi. Naomi was one of the final links to him finding his father, who'd abandoned him and his family all of those years ago.

Naomi's secretary greeted him and offered him a seat and coffee, but he declined the latter. He sat inside of her office, legs crossed, awaiting her arrival in a chair that was positioned across from her desk. As he sat there, he began to wonder if his father had sat in that same exact chair once upon a time. Perhaps he had. He looked at all the photos, awards, and accolades that decorated the office and became thoroughly impressed.

"You will have to forgive me for keeping you waiting for as long as I did; I've been in and out of meetings all day. How are you?" Naomi briskly entered her office, announcing her apologies as she extended her hand to the gentleman who'd come from Region Two to visit her. Trevor stood, buttoned the top button of his suit jacket, and shook Naomi's hand with a charming smile upon his face.

"It's quite alright. Pleasure to meet you."

"I understand that you're on the board of advisors for the President of Quadrant Three," Naomi said as she walked around to the back of her desk. As she did, not once did her eyes move away from him; there was something familiar about him. She opened her hand towards his chair as an offering and he, once again, took his seat. As he began taking his seat, she noticed the gun attached to his hip. Although he held a high government job, she thought it to be a little odd that an advisor would have a weapon in public.

"That is correct. I've worked on the board for a few years now. I've worked incredibly hard to come into this position and I appreciate this career more and more every day. It was… a second chance at life for me," Trevor stated.

"I see," Naomi responded, still unable to remove her eyes away from him. "Forgive me if it seems that I'm staring, but… you look awfully familiar to me. Are you sure this is the first time that you and I have met?"

"I'm quite sure that we haven't met, but we do, however, share a couple of mutual friends. This is the purpose of my visit today, actually," Trevor said.

"Right, my clerk mentioned that you said that. And who might our friends be, exactly?"

"I understand that you are, or were, rather, one of the leaders for the underground organization known as the Helpers, correct?"

"Go on," Naomi said, neither confirming nor denying Trevor's statement.

"Well, several years ago, your organization provided a way of escape for me and my family. We were a stubborn family, so we went about things the difficult way, but there were members of your organization that continued to look after us. One member was someone by the name of Tracy. Do you remember her?"

This stranger knowing about the Helpers and bringing up Tracy's name made her uneasy, but she wasn't quite sure why. He did say that she provided help for his family. However, there was just something strange about him that she couldn't quite place her finger on. Why did he ask if she *remembered* Tracy as if she were no longer alive? Maybe she'd been reading too much into everything, so she tried to keep her cool so that she could find out more.

"Yes, I do; she's an old friend of mine. How is she doing?"

"She's doing well, I presume. I'd only seen her once before, and she'd seemed to be doing well. I actually first met her during a time well after I was originally supposed to meet her. That's a funny story." Trevor chuckled.

"Please, do tell." Naomi was becoming anxious and hoping that he might disclose information on if she was indeed doing well.

"As I mentioned, my family and I lived somewhat of a recluse lifestyle, away from any type of civilization. You see, we were not imprinted. My father was a pastor, a stubborn one, and he was unwilling to discontinue his practices. This had been extremely problematic for us, as you could probably imagine, since all religious practices were banned. We lived on the outskirts of town, near the edge of the Red Zone there, but through my father's congregation, a family member of one of his members had been associated with the Helpers and this woman was willing to help us. Should anything go wrong, she arranged a way for us to escape into Region One and eventually, connect with you. Well, things did go wrong, horribly wrong, and military officers discovered us within the night, forcing us to leave our home. The plan was to make it to Tracy's house, but some of us never made it. My father, however, did somehow manage to make it there. I suppose he'd gotten lucky. Isn't that something?"

Trevor peered at Naomi with a blank stare, waiting for her to comment.

"Wow, that is… unfortunate that all of you weren't able to make it over here… together. I'm sure we would have been able to help you all. So, what happened; were you captured or—"

"Yes, because my father had been, and as far as I'm concerned, still is, to this day, a coward," Trevor responded.

"I understand," Naomi said, clearing her throat.

"I'm almost certain that he was able to make it over safe and sound; do you recall meeting him?" Trevor asked abruptly, trying to speed up to his point of being there.

Naomi paused. Over the years, she'd helped thousands of individuals find a place to live inside of the shelters. Ordinarily, she rarely remembered them, but somehow, she'd known who Trevor had been speaking of. At that moment, she was faced with the dilemma of whether she should tell him that she had, in fact, met his father. Again, she looked down at his waist where his gun had been still visible.

"You know, over the years, my organization has helped so many people and—"

"He would have gone by the name, Sebastian. Does that ring a bell? Tracy was able to provide me with that bit of information."

As he disclosed that information, Naomi had been certain that the meeting between Trevor and Tracy wasn't a pleasant visit. She wondered about what type of force he used to get Tracy to reveal such sensitive information. Had Tracy still been alive?

"Are you imprinted?" Naomi asked. She hadn't been necessarily attempting to change subjects, she'd only wanted a clearer understanding of who Trevor was today before divulging too much information to him.

"Well, of course. How else could I hold such a position?"

"What about the rest of your family, where are they? Are they imprinted as well?"

Trevor rolled his eyes and sighed deeply, clearly becoming more and more frustrated.

"They are safe and sound inside of Region Two."

"And they're... imprinted," Naomi asked again?

"That's not important," Trevor said quickly without batting an eye. "Where is he?"

"I—I don't know. I do remember meeting him, I do, but he seemed... bothered by whatever had just happened, and he decided not to accept my help. It was as if he wanted to punish himself or something, so he just left and that was the last time that I'd ever seen or heard from him."

Trevor didn't say a word as his gaze remained fixed on her. Naomi wasn't an easy one to intimidate, but there was something eerie with this guy. He was set on accomplishing a certain *thing* and wasn't planning on letting anyone or anything prevent him from accomplishing whatever that thing was.

19
New Assignment

After prayer, Andrew stepped outside and requested to speak with Jaylen on the backside of the church. This wasn't an unusual request, as far as Jaylen had been concerned, yet it was odd that Andrew had wanted to speak with him outside and away from where anyone could hear them.

When he opened the back door of the church, he saw Andrew standing in the middle of the neglected and abandoned parking lot with his back turned as he stared out into the distance. He looked around first, checking his surroundings out of habit, and then headed down the steps to connect with Andrew. Jaylen slowly approached him from behind and cleared his throat. Hearing him, Andrew turned with a look of concern upon his face, which caused some worry to arise within the pit of Jaylen's stomach.

"They said that you wanted to see me?"

"Yeah," Andrew replied in a low voice.

In the back of Andrew's mind, he'd already known the reasoning behind the problem that they faced, but it had been the means of going about the solution that was troubling him.

"The last couple of runs, they've been a little light," Andrew stated.

"Yeah, I know. We've been—"

"No, no, please. There's no need to explain. I'm not coming down on you and the guys, you've done just fine. It's just something that I've noticed."

Andrew paused for a moment and looked out into the dark night, once again, that displayed only the silhouettes of what had once been a lively city.

"The timing of your trips has taken longer, which means you've been traveling farther out. The farther you continue to venture, eventually, you'll run into others from different Red Zones, which would indicate their scarcity as well. Running into others could also potentially increase the likelihood of more conflict. It could turn into a war. Also, a larger percentage of the food that you've brought back has been spoiled or unusable."

Jaylen sighed quietly to himself, trying to see where Andrew was getting at. All of what he'd been saying was true, and it had been something that he and the rest of the crew were well aware of. The thought of running into others who were searching for food and supplies had always lived in the back of their minds, which is why they always brought weapons. It wasn't something that they were looking forward to, but it was something that they had been prepared for.

"We've got to make changes." Andrew said.

"What… kind of changes?" Jaylen asked. "What can we do about it?"

"It's clear that sourcing from the Red Zone is coming to an end; I suppose it was inevitable. I mean, how long could anyone survive from whatever remained out here, anyway? We were plucking through scraps in search of more scraps. It was only a matter of time." Andrew said.

"What did you have in mind?" the other asked.

"It's risky, but it may be our only remaining solution. Somehow, someway, we have to begin sourcing our supplies from inside of the

Green Zone in order for us to survive as long as we can out here. It's the only way."

"How in the world are we going to do that without getting slaughtered?" Jaylen was puzzled.

"I'm not so sure," Andrew replied.

Jaylen thought to himself how easy it must've been for Andrew to get supplies in the Red Zone when he'd been out there all by himself. He provided a place for them and asked them to find more supplies, but that had always been within the Red Zone. Now he'd been asking them to search for goods in a territory where they could become killed immediately once it was discovered that they were not imprinted. It was a suicide mission that Andrew, himself, wouldn't be taking part in, yet he'd been asking them to. The request took Jaylen back.

"Wait, do you understand what you're asking?"

"Of course, I do. I wish there were other options, but for our survival, in the long run, this is it."

"Just to confirm, you won't be joining us, correct?" Jaylen questioned sarcastically.

Andrew slowly walked towards him, sight set to a fixed gaze into Jaylen's eyes, and stopped once he'd gotten face to face with him. For a moment, Andrew saw Trevor's face as he looked at Jaylen. His question triggered something in Andrew's past that he'd been unable to escape and still haunted him. He thought for a second whether the request had been unfair to them, as he contemplated if this had been just another notch upon his belt of cowardice.

"Inside, there's someone there. Someone is willing to help, and it seems that… you may already know them. They will give you food, medicine, anything that you need. You know them; you have a complicated past with them, but it will become placed behind you. This is the way."

"Who is it? How do you know any of this?"

"It will become clear once you are inside of the Green Zone. For now, this idea will be too foggy for you to understand. Have faith that every step will be guided. I've seen it; it is true. You must trust me, Jaylen."

Jaylen stepped back, shaking his head.

"That sounds insane. Maybe... maybe we're supposed to max out our resources out here and that's the end. Maybe we're supposed to die out here! Did you ever think of that? What if doing all of this to stay alive is against the will of God?"

"He would've shown me if that had been true," Andrew responded.

"Funny how you didn't see yourself being a part of this excursion, don't you think?"

"Jaylen! All of this, all of this was shown to me! He told me to establish this place. Had I not listened His sheep might have been scattered!"

"Oh yeah, what about the others in different areas that aren't here? Shouldn't it be, 'no sheep left behind'?"

"There's time for us to find others and for those that I cannot reach, perhaps He has called someone else, like me, to do the same as I have done here. He will never neglect His flock, especially in the darkest of days when all seems to be lost. We *are* His flock, Jaylen. We must listen to His voice during these times; it truly is a matter of life and death. We must think and move with intelligence; there is a way for us to survive. And no, it is not His will for us to die out here. Think of Elijah when he went out east of Jordan by the brook because of the drought in the land. God sent ravens to bring him food, and he was able to drink from the brook. He will come for us, just as He promised, but until then, resources have been made available to us and we have to trust that our needs will be supplied."

Jaylen listened to Andrew, understood, and he believed him.

As time had gone on and food had become even more scarce, the faith in the believers had begun to waver and their kindness, compassion, and patience for one another had grown thin. Inside of Lisa's group, she witnessed two men get into a heated argument over food.

One had accused the other of stealing a portion of food from his plate while he'd stepped away for a moment, but the guy insisted he hadn't. They argued for quite some time until they began shoving one another, and then they came to throwing punches. Others were too drained to stop them. It was as if they hadn't noticed them at all, it seemed. Both faces of the men were bloodied and swollen, but eventually, the man who'd been accused of stealing the food had gotten the upper hand as he pierced a long piece of broken glass through the chest of the other, slicing his own hand in the process. Visceral screams and animalistic grunts were heard from the other side of the abandoned building. Then there was quiet just before the crunching sounds of gravel beneath someone's feet came back towards the group.

The accused sat back down in front of his food, reached over to grab the rest of the dead man's meal, and continued eating. No one looked at him. No one said a word. As it turns out, he had stolen from the man's plate earlier, just as he'd been accused of. Lisa had seen the entire event unfold.

Situations like that had become a common thing. This wasn't unusual now, and people just carried on about their lives. It was simply a matter of survival of the fittest; it was human nature. In some ways, it was as if humanity had regressed. For some of them, they'd forgotten who they were and why they were there and had become a forgotten people. It was as if they'd ceased to be human beings, but beasts within the wild.

Wearily, Lisa rose to her feet and walked out to where the deceased man's body lay. His eyes were open and stared directly up into the air, blankly, until Lisa stood over him into his line of sight. She looked down at the piece of glass protruding out of his chest. Tears welled in her eyes as she knelt down next to him, whispered a prayer, and closed his eyes for the last time. Afterwards, she walked away, leaving the rest of the group behind.

There was so much uncertainty about everything; she did not know where she would go. She was tired, hungry, thirsty, and her breathing had become increasingly difficult as she walked along. Her only thoughts and hopes were that she would simply die in her tracks. This had been her prayer.

Back at Flannigan's, Kaleb had set aside several items inside of the back entryway near the office. He carried boxes that didn't need to be refrigerated and stacked them alongside the office door. Alicia saw his work, rolled up her sleeves, and pitched in. Although they'd been packing items aside to assist Jaylen, neither one of them had a clue about how to go about getting the supplies to him.

"I considered maybe taking a few things out there, seeing if I could find him," Kaleb said.

"No way," Alicia responded. "That'll be way too dangerous. Traveling out there alone with an enormous amount of food on you is bound to make you a target. You have to remember, those people out there are probably starving and, more than likely, willing to do anything for their next meal."

"Yeah, you're probably right," her brother replied. "Knowing that he's out there with people like that, living under those conditions, just makes me want to find him even more. What if I could find him and bring him back here?"

"To do what, Kaleb? If he gets caught, he'll be killed or if he's lucky, tossed into prison until he's forced to become imprinted. If you have him live above the store again, once again, it'll be like him being inside of a prison. He could never leave this store ever again."

"I have to figure something out somehow. There's gotta be a way for us to make sure he's taken care of," Kaleb said.

"We will, Kaleb. We will."

The area was nearly a ghost town. No one, willingly, lived on the edge of a Red Zone. The only one there that day was Trevor, on top of what had once been a tire shop during its better days, and two military bots on the ground that had been given to him for the rest of the time he would be in town. Trevor squinted through a pair of binoculars to look out into the distance for what he might find. Nothing appeared to be alive. As he surveyed the land, in some parts, he noticed what appeared to be human remains. He sucked at his teeth as he continued to examine the terrain.

"Don't you worry, I'll find you," he said to himself.

"Hey what do you guys really think, huh; do you still believe in the whole rapture thing," Matt asked? "I mean, honestly."

Out on the front side of the church, Matt, Terrance, James, and Daniel all hung around talking and passing the time.

"I guess," said James. "That's the only reason my wife and I haven't given up and gone ahead and gotten that imprint."

They were all quiet for a moment, thinking about what they'd been asked. All they had were memories of the religious text and what it stated on such topics, and their memories were fading. This was their fear that the memories and words from the religious manuscripts would fade away as well.

"To tell you the truth, I'm not sure. It's not that I don't believe, it's just that we haven't seen any type of sign or anything since this world has gone to hell," Terrance stated.

Daniel stood listening.

"Yeah, I know what you mean. Just something to show that we're on the right track would be helpful to us out here. People are still believing, but many of us are only hanging on by a thread," Matt said.

Finally, Daniel chimed in.

"What type of sign are you people looking for, exactly? This is the sign! Everything that is happening right now has already been foretold. You think because you're living in it presently, that this is something new? Uh-uh. This is all old stuff being dug up and finally getting its time under the sun. You all seem to have forgotten a few things since they burned your Bible. Everything inside of it should have been written in your hearts. Do you know why that verse was written there?" Daniel asked, pointing at Matt?

Matt stared at Daniel with a blank look, without answering.

"It's because this day was always coming. Now that it's here, what do you fall back on? You all sit here now, wavering in your faith, questioning the skies, hoping, and praying for some sort of sign because you didn't prepare. Now that you're in the wilderness and it's time to harvest, there's nothing there because you're empty," Daniel said.

Feeling somewhat chastised and belittled, Terrance jumped in.

"Hey, you need to pull that back a little, don't you think? You don't get to pass judgment on us," Terrance challenged. "None of us are perfect. Reading about life from a book is a little different from actually living it. All we're saying is that things have been extremely tough on top of how hard things had already gotten and we've been hanging on for as tight as we can, but we're just asking for a little something, anything, to encourage us to keep going. Now, I'm not rushing His timing. If we have to stay down here longer, that's fine. Just give me something, a boost, that just helps me to keep going! Some days it feels like we're losing down here." Terrance was passionate about what he'd said as he stood face to face, addressing what Daniel had stated.

Both men looked at one another, each with fire in their eyes, as the other two men watched them quietly. Daniel could feel Terrance's emotions exuding from him and his longing for a sign from God, and he empathized for him.

"Look, I understand," Daniel simply said as he placed his hand upon Terrance's shoulder. Daniel then walked back towards the front door of the church and stopped.

"You know, I agree with what you said; some days it does feel like we're losing out here," Daniel said, glancing over his right shoulder before walking inside of the church and leaving the rest of the men to themselves.

Neither one of the men said anything for a while until James noticed something approaching their direction in the distance. It looked as if it were a person.

"Hey, check it out," James said, pointing to someone.

"Who's that?" Matt asked.

"Looks like a lady," James concluded. "We should probably bring her in. She looks half dead from here."

20
SUPPLY RUN

Lisa sat up in her new bed with a blanket around her, drinking water from the cup that Jaylen had given her. He sat in a chair across from her as the two reconnected from the last time they'd seen one another. She'd traveled a longer distance, farther than she'd realized, and had been extremely tired from the journey, but she was thankful for Andrew and his people taking her in. Not to mention, it had been refreshing to see a familiar face in Jaylen.

"I thought everyone was dead; I'd given up hope in thinking that I'd ever find anyone from our group, alive, at least," Lisa stated between taking sips from the cup. "There hasn't been a day that's gone by where I see a corpse lying on the side of the road or in an old home. People are revolting against one another, the believers I'm talking about, and they are killing the other if they feel it's necessary. I'm not so sure anymore if we're the good guys, I mean… I think we are," Lisa went on, "but I'm not entirely sure. We're on the outskirts of civilization, but somehow, we seem just as bad as the ones we view as animals on that other side."

Jaylen had been just as confused and lost as anyone else within the Red Zone who'd chosen not to become imprinted.

"Yeah… I know what you mean," Jaylen tossed in. "I don't know who's who or what's what anymore; everything all comes down to simply being able to survive at this point. Every day, I'm still praying, you know? But… I'm not so sure if anyone's prayers are being answered these days. It seems like every day we discover a new bottom of hell."

"Wow," Lisa whispered. "I don't think I've ever heard you speak with any type of pessimism in your voice since I've known you."

Jaylen smiled.

"I don't blame you. I'm not judging you; you're right after all. We're just going about this thing one day at a time until… I don't know," Lisa said.

"I wonder what happened to Ahmad? He was trying to get us to connect with some group of people he'd met," Jaylen said, trying to shift the subject.

"I don't know, honestly. I never trusted that guy and I'm sure that whoever he vouches for doesn't mean any good for anyone. Do you ever think about Cassandra," she asked?

"I'd be lying if I said I didn't." Jaylen sighed. "Guess I saw it coming though; wasn't really surprised. I just wish… it could've gone differently."

"Hmm, I see. What about your mom, is she here with you too?" Jaylen fought to hold back his tears unsuccessfully as a few tears streamed down his cheeks.

"No. No, she's not." He took a huge breath in and exhaled. "I really wish she was, though. She uh… she… she was killed, right there in front of me. And I couldn't do a single thing about it. I was so helpless. After all the things that she'd done for me, provided for me, fought for me, and I couldn't help her when she needed me the most. It was literally life or death and I could not save her."

Lisa rose from the bed and came over to hug her longtime friend, trying her best to console him. She attempted to consume as much of the hurt, pain, heartbreak, and anguish as she could. Those feelings flowed through him and into Lisa's body as she inhaled and tried releasing his burdens through herself as best as she possibly could.

The black SUV sped down the highway inside of the Red Zone as Trevor sat in the back seat with his trim black suit and dark sunglasses peering out of the window. He'd been told that the air might be contaminated due to chemicals that had been used during the many wars that'd transpired, so they had given him a gas mask to bring along with him. It sat next to him, but truthfully, by him once living within the Red Zone with his family, he'd gotten used to the air. If there had been anything in the air, he'd already had it, as far as he was concerned. Every Quadrant was different, however, but he'd been too focused on other things to wreck his brain worrying about something such as polluted air. His mission was to find his father.

"Wait, wait. Go back. I think I saw someone walking along that property back there."

Something had caught Trevor's attention while they were traveling. It looks as though a man dressed in black was walking across the yard of the lot they'd just passed. The SUV slowly drove down the long driveway leading up to the front of the property and parked in front of the fountain that hadn't worked in years. Trevor hopped out, buttoned the top button of his two-button jacket, and started towards the front door.

"Sir... sir," the driver called out to Trevor, "your mask." The driver sloppily scurried around to the backside of the SUV, grabbed Trevor's mask, and ran it over to him.

Trevor smirked as he took it from his driver, turned back, and walked towards the front door of the mansion. He put on the mask and looked around to see if the person he'd seen had still been around. He didn't see anyone, so he knocked on the door, whose paint had chipped and faded away. His eyes showed through the large clear eye sockets of the mask as the muffled Darth Vader sound of his breathing continued. At first, there was quiet, and it'd seemed as if no one had actually lived there. Trevor turned around, remaining on the porch, and looked out into the front of the home with its high grass and overgrown weeds before turning back around to face the door. He was about to knock again, but the door suddenly opened.

A man of average height dressed in a black long-sleeved t-shirt and black pants stood on the other side. His face looked as though he'd been angry that someone would dare knock on his door. He didn't even bother to greet Trevor.

"Hello, my—" Trevor stopped mid-sentence to remove his gas mask. "Hello, my name is Trevor Dawkins. I work on the advisory panel with the government within Region Two," he said with his hand extended.

The man in black didn't acknowledge that his hand had been there at all. He simply peered at Trevor square in his eyes without uttering a single word.

"Very well then. I'm here because I'm looking for an individual and I simply wanted to know if, by any chance, you'd seen him." Trevor reached inside of the jacket of his suit and as he did, the man at the door looked over his shoulder at the driver who'd been leaning forward over the steering wheel to monitor them from the inside of the SUV. Finally, Trevor pulled out a picture of Andrew and held it up so that the doorman could see it. The man's attention came back to Trevor, then slowly to the picture.

"Do you recognize him?" asked Trevor. The doorman studied the picture briefly, then slowly shook his head.

"Well then, thank you for your help. I'll be on my way." Trevor then noticed two other men, also in all black, approaching from behind the doorman.

They all held the same sort of lifeless look in their eyes, Trevor observed.

"Would you and your friend like to come inside? You've traveled a very long way," the doorman offered, as Trevor had been turning around to return to the SUV.

"That… that's very kind of you, but I have to get going. But if you do see or hear from this man, please let the Global Identity Center know for me please." Trevor jumped into the back seat, and his driver quickly sped off. By then the other two men had come out and the three of them watched them drive off into the distance.

They prepared the two pickup trucks to leave, and the men were all saying their goodbyes to their friends and loved ones. The men were granted well wishes and given lists filled with items to bring back if they happened to come across them while they were out on their run. Everything had been normal, just how it'd always been before they went out except, this time, there was one difference. Jaylen hadn't told the rest of the men that this particular trip might be a little on the riskier side because they would be going into the Green Zone for supplies. Their trips were now taking longer because they'd been traveling farther out to find useful items. In their minds, this journey was to be no different.

"How did the others react when you told them," Andrew asked Jaylen as the two stood in the center of the main basement room where Andrew would have everyone gather for his teachings?

"Uh, they, uh… I didn't exactly tell them. Not yet, at least."

"Jaylen, it's important that they know right away. If they want to back out, you have to leave them with that option."

261

"Yeah, I know. You're right. I'll tell them."

"Just remember, nothing is more important than your lives; you sense danger, you get out of there. And stick together under every circumstance. If one of you becomes captured, there's not much…"

Andrew paused for a moment as he thought about what he was saying, how his family had become captured, and how he responded. Jaylen stared at him strangely for stopping in the middle of his sentence.

"If either of you gets caught, there's not much any of you can do; you'll have to keep going," Andrew stated, picking up where he'd left off.

"Yeah, we'll see. That all depends. I've been itching for some get back, so if they lay a hand on us, we might have to take our chances out there. Just send up a prayer for us that we'll return." Jaylen then headed outside to the back of the church to connect with the rest of the men.

Andrew's head dropped as he couldn't help but think of how Jaylen had been better than him in ensuring that he wouldn't leave anyone behind. No matter how long and often he'd prayed, despite finding a new group of people to teach God's word to, that gut-wrenching feeling of guilt would never disappear. It continued to haunt him.

At the back of the church, Jaylen approached the men, who were all standing around and joking with one another before they'd left. There wasn't an easy way for him to say it, so he figured the best way was for him to be as direct as possible.

"Listen, guys… we're going into the Green Zone for supplies this time." He stood with his hands resting upon his hips, waiting for one of them to respond, when Daniel stepped forward.

"I don't know, maybe I've been waiting out here in the sun too long and, perhaps I've started to hallucinate and start to hear things, but it kinda sounded like you said that we're going into the Green Zone… for supplies," Daniel said.

"Hey Jaylen, man, that's insane," James said.

"What's that about; why there? Why are we going there," Matt asked?

The men bickered amongst one another, and they all threw out more questions.

"We're running out of places to get food. More and more of the loads that we've been bringing back haven't been good enough to eat and we are continuing to run low, faster than we normally would. You guys know this. We have to do what we have to do if we're going to survive."

"Yeah, I kinda saw this coming somewhere down the line," Terrance said. "Definitely thought this would come much later, though. Much later!"

"Wh—what about us just going out farther, like we've been doing lately?" Matt nervously asked. "There's less of a chance that those spots have been picked through by anyone."

"Yeah, but think about how long that stuff has probably already been out there. Then we have to get to it, then we have to bring it back. Just think, it was already there before there was a Red Zone. It's been out here since life was actually considered normal," Terrance said.

"You've got a point," James said. "This just sounds a little suicidal. We're not just passing through for a quick visit to see a few relatives, which would be dangerous enough on its own, but we'll be stealing from there as well, and we have to make it back here."

Daniel gazed at Jaylen while everyone talked, trying to get a read on him to see if this was something he really stood behind. He looked for anything that would betray him and possibly reveal that he hadn't been for them going out there, however; he seemed to stand firmly on the decision. There was a tell in his face, suggesting otherwise.

"So, what's your plan?" Daniel asked with his left forearm leaning over the side mirror of one truck.

Everyone became silent to listen to what Jaylen had to say in response.

"Well, according to my calculations, we should arrive a little after sunset, which will work in our favor. We'll be able to blend in a bit and work within the shadows when it's necessary. The key thing is to get inside and avoid detection from the military bots at all costs since they have the scanners. The regular officers, we can work around them. Just avoid any form of engagements with them," Jaylen said.

"That's fine, but what about the reason we're there? Where are we going to get supplies, and how are we going to get 'em?" James asked.

Jaylen sighed.

"That part, I'm not fully sure about."

Matt groaned in his displeasure.

"So, we're just running in there like cowboys hoping for the best!" Matt's heart was pounding inside of his chest. They all were nervous, but this is what it had come down to.

"Whatever happens… we'll be right there with you," Daniel said to Jaylen.

The two trucks traveled down the empty roadway with only the sound of their engines purring along. They drove past the wide-open ghost world, which was filled with empty homes and skyscrapers. During most of their journey, there wasn't much said by any of the men, as they had all been too terrified about what lay ahead of them, except for Jaylen.

He'd been focused and prepared for whatever would come. If it meant that it would turn into a shootout in the middle of the city streets with the military police and their robots, then he was ready. In his mind, being killed in the middle of the streets to avenge his mother's death was a death worth dying. While some of the others may have felt differently, for Jaylen, there was nothing left to lose.

They approached the outer border that separated the Red Zone and Green Zone, and almost immediately, everyone began to tense up. It was obvious when they had reached the inside of the Green Zone, everything instantly became alive. The closer they'd gotten towards the center of the Green Zone, the livelier things became. This was the case in every Quadrant. The lights became brighter; the laughter became louder, and it appeared that life was easier.

They parked their trucks near the outskirts of town and remained inside to observe the scene and come up with a game-plan now that they were inside. The idea was for them to see how the area functioned now so that they would know how to maneuver around. In the meantime, they waited.

"At some point, we're going to have to go deeper inside; there's hardly much of anything on this side of town," Daniel said.

"Yeah, you're right. I'm just trying to scope everything out first," Jaylen stated as he scanned the scene.

"Well, there's not much to scope out here, that's for sure," Daniel replied.

They were partnered the way they usually were, with Daniel behind the wheel, Jaylen in the passenger, and James seated behind them in the first truck. Parked behind them was Terrance, who'd been driving, and Matt seated next to him.

"What are these guys waiting on?" Matt asked.

"Oh, you're in some type of hurry now? A few hours ago, you were on the verge of tears when Jaylen mentioned we'd be coming out here," Terrance said.

"That's a lie," Matt challenged. "I'm saying since we're here now, we might as well get to it."

"Listen, be cool, alright? They're probably just trying to figure out how to go about this thing," Terrance suggested.

Night fell and Jaylen and the others sat silent, but now and then they'd toss out an idea. They kept the more absurd ones to themselves. Jaylen thought about Andrew's words, promising him that he would find someone to help him, but he didn't know how or when that was supposed to happen. But then—

"Wait… head west, near the subway. I have an idea," Jaylen said.

"Finally, an idea in motion," Daniel said as he started the engine.

Neon and fluorescent lights glowed across the city streets as they traveled along, and while they weren't the only ones on the road, their pickup trucks looked like foreign objects to the flying vehicles hovering next to them and some above them. The men gazed out of their windows and up into the air to see them.

"Well, that's new!" James said in amazement.

There had also been drones hovering above the city as well to monitor and keep track of everything that transpired throughout each Region. The men took notice of this and tried to remain as careful and stealth as possible.

They drove past and noticed the registered citizens out laughing, drinking, partying, and enjoying themselves with their loved ones. Jaylen looked at them, seemingly without a care in the world, and then he thought about his mother and Austin, the little boy that they'd shared a room with at the shelter.

They both deserved to still be alive, to enjoy themselves as well, just like everyone else. But not this way. Not under these conditions. For the first time, he had an eerie thought to himself that, maybe, his mother had been better off dead. He figured she was finally able to escape the chaos that they had to live through.

"They got us out of here and things really took off, huh," Daniel observed.

"Sure, appears that way," responded James.

Another thing that Jaylen noticed was how everyone looked to *have it together*. They looked... polished. He couldn't explain it, but one thing that he knew for sure was that he and his men didn't look like them. He was sure that these people were completely unaware of what was going on just on the other side of this place.

"We're going to stick out like a sore thumb out here. We'll have to be extremely careful," he said.

They arrived in front of a small store that looked familiar, yet somehow different to Jaylen. The vibrant yellow sign with blue lettering flashed the name FLANNIGAN'S in cursive. That sign hadn't always been there.

"There's an alley off to the side; park there," Jaylen directed Daniel.

As they were just about to pull in, a military officer in his dark black combat gear walked across the alley entrance. He stopped in his tracks, and they all made eye contact with one another. Everyone's heart within the trucks raced uncontrollably. This was it; coming out here had been a huge mistake! They never should've come inside of the Green Zone.

Without taking their eyes off of the officer, as discreetly as they could, Jaylen and James began reaching for their guns.

"*Shit! We're dead*," Terrance said softly to himself, as he witnessed everything from the truck behind them.

"*On my word*," Jaylen whispered.

"*Hand me my gun*," Terrance told Matt. "*If this is how it's gotta go… that's just how it is.*"

"*Damn right*," Matt said as he reached behind the seat for Terrance's handgun.

What was this cop's next move; what was he going to do? Did he have a scanner on him? Did he pick up that they weren't registered?

"Are we striking first?" James asked.

"Just… wait," Jaylen mumbled. *"We'll see how he plays it. He makes any dumb move, we blaze him."*

Jaylen cocked back his gun. James did the same, as well as the others behind them.

Then the officer gave them a subtle salute with his hand and continued along his way.

Everyone sighed with relief inside both vehicles.

"Jesu—*s Christ!*" Matt exclaimed.

"Close call," Daniel said.

"Yeah, it was, but let's stay alert," Jaylen said, watching the officer turn the corner.

The two trucks then slowly pulled inside of the alleyway next to Flannigan's Groceries.

Jaylen noticed when they walked in that everything appeared to look much like he'd remembered, only a little smaller than he'd recalled. There was a gentleman who'd just finished purchasing his groceries and headed out towards them near the exit. The cashier was someone Jaylen had known very well. It was Alicia. The two of them looked at one another first, without saying a word. There was a wrenching feeling of anger inside the pit of Jaylen's stomach that he tried his best to fight back. She was behind his mother's death.

For a moment, he thought about killing her right there on the spot. However, he reconsidered, she wasn't the one that had, in fact, actually killed her. Judging by the look in her eyes, he could tell that she knew exactly who he was. Alicia slowly walked away from behind the counter and in his direction. She wasn't sure about what he'd been thinking or how he would react, but she figured she couldn't simply avoid him, even if she'd wanted to. She stopped a few steps in front of him.

"H-hi." It was the only thing Alicia could say. It was also the measuring stick to see where his temper had been. If he spoke back, that would be a good sign, she concluded.

He gave her a simple head nod. That was enough for her.

"Hey, Alicia we have to get ready to—" a male voice said then stopped once the man came out onto the floor.

It was Kaleb.

He saw his sister standing in front of a group of men, and he noticed one of them had a face that he would never forget. Kaleb ran to Jaylen and hugged him as hard as he could. He couldn't hold back his tears; it was as if seeing Jaylen was like him somehow being able to see Melanie again. While Jaylen had felt emotional as well, he'd been successful at holding back his tears. Seeing Kaleb and Alicia forced his feelings to become scattered all over the place.

"I knew I would see you again. I just knew it," Kaleb said as he stepped back to get a better look at him. To Kaleb, Jaylen looked as if he'd aged quite a bit, but he figured he had to have been younger than how he actually appeared. It was to be expected, he assumed; he'd been through a lot.

Kaleb and Alicia looked just like everyone else he'd seen in the Green Zone: polished.

"It's good to see you," Jaylen said. Kaleb, teary-eyed, smiled.

"I need your help, Kaleb. And before you agree to it, I want you to know that we will probably need your help for an extended amount of time."

"Anything, Jaylen; I'm here for you."

"Out in the Red Zone, there's a group of us gathered and us guys go out into various areas to bring back food and supplies for everyone. Well, food and supplies are running low and they're becoming harder and harder to come by. Seriously, anything that you can do, you'll be doing all of us an enormous favor."

"Follow me," Kaleb said after looking at Jaylen and his men for a second. "Alicia, lock the front door and pull down the security gate."

They all followed Kaleb towards the back, near his and Alicia's office, and saw stacks of boxes filled with food and other supplies piled on top of one another.

"As I said, I knew I would see you again; I wanted to make sure that I was prepared. This is all yours," Kaleb informed him.

"*All*?" Jaylen couldn't believe that Kaleb had done all of this for him. How could he have even known that he was still alive, let alone figure that they would see one another again?

"Yes, all of it! And don't worry about running out; just like this time, I'll restock more supplies so that when you're ready, you'll have something for the next trip as well. Whenever you need it."

Jaylen and the rest of the men all thanked him and they began loading the trucks by using the side entrance that Jaylen and his mother used to use when going up to their upstairs apartment.

During one of the trips back in to grab more supplies, Alicia stopped Jaylen.

"Listen, this has haunted me since… the last time that I saw you. I just wanted to say that I'm… I'm sorry about everything, Jaylen. Sorry for how I treated you two and I'm sorry for turning you in. I'm sorry that I got your mother killed." Tears poured down Alicia's face as she covered them with the insides of both of her palms.

Jaylen released a deep, shaky sigh as he tried to hold back his anger and resentment towards her.

"I… I've learned to," he hesitated, "I've learned to forgive you. Before you ever said it, I'd already forgiven you. My mother, on this day, is in a much better place." Afterward, the two of them embraced.

After the trucks were loaded, Jaylen and his guys set up a game-plan to schedule recurring visits for more supplies. Again, they expressed their gratitude and headed off back into the Red Zone.

They were excited and well pleased with the number of supplies that they were able to gather. It had been the most that they'd ever collected during one of their runs. They all sung praises for Jaylen as they traveled back, but Jaylen remained caught up on how Andrew knew they would find someone and that things would work out.

However, as they got back closer to the church, they hadn't noticed that, off to the side of the road, they'd driven past a member of the Barbarians, who'd been standing out in the night, in his human skull and gas mask, making careful observations of this group of men in their trucks full of supplies, the direction in which they'd come from, and the direction in which they were headed.

21
PRIVATE DINNER PARTY

Over time, several more runs were made, but they hadn't noticed that someone had been on to them. They continued their trips successfully into the Green Zone and back to their hideout. During one of their trips, they were trailed, and they were traced to Flannigan's all the way back to the church. They were exposed without their knowing and it was only a matter of time before they came to realize that their routine of bringing back goods to their secret fortress was no longer a secret.

"You said that there are five of them; are you sure?" Inside of the mansion, one of the leaders of the Barbarians spoke with three of the members who'd been spying on Jaylen and his men. One member who he'd been speaking to was Ahmad.

"Yes, we're sure," another member answered.

"Did you recognize them?" the leader asked.

"No, we haven't," the third replied. "Usually we're at a distance from them so it's a little difficult to see their faces."

As they always were, they were dressed in all black, but without their masks revealing their lifeless and soulless expressions to one another. If they weren't leaving the mansion, their masks usually remained off.

"A few times, when they've arrived back at their spot, I've seen others come out to help them unload. I'm not sure how many of them there are, but there's definitely more than the five that travel into the Green Zone."

"So, you'll need more men?" the leader asked.

"Yeah, well, more would probably come in handy." the other answered.

Ahmad only listened. He'd made a few of these ambushes with the others and had become familiar and numb to the routine. Frankly, he'd been surprised that there had been people still within the area. He'd figured that the word might've spread by now about their presence and that everyone would have been smart enough to vanish. Apparently, they hadn't, and these guys were in line to be their latest victims.

The meeting ended and Ahmad and another one of the members who'd been there went outside, got into one of their cars, and drove off. They headed deeper into the Red Zone to see if they could find a few things of use that they could bring back to the mansion, mainly food. Ahmad sat in the passenger seat while the other drove. Their masks were carefully laid on the backseat.

"Man, I really miss the good old days," the driver said.

"What do you mean?" Ahmad asked, looking over at him.

"Before you came in, we used to go into the Green Zone and would steal from anyone who had what you needed. And it was different back then. We had the devices where we could transfer people's funds directly into a fake account that we had set up and everything would read as being legit. We had the artificial imprints then, but the government improved their system and ruined that whole thing."

"Yeah, I remember those times. That's originally what made me want to join you guys, to be able to get the fake imprint. One of my guys told me about it. He was part of that hit against that Congress lady," Ahmad said.

"Oh yeah," the other one questioned? "So, you're tight with Anthony? I led that hit, me and another guy. That went smoothly. Didn't expect her to have the gun, though. She almost blew our asses out of there."

Ahmad chuckled.

"Now… here we are, stuck in this dump, digging around for scraps. At first, we were here because we wanted to be. We couldn't get down with how they were forcing everyone to live the way they said. It was their way or the highway!" The driver banged his hand on the dashboard of the car. "What type of way is that to live? We got it; the world was in shambles, but Hansen came in as a dictator and pretended like he was doing everyone a favor. 'It's better than it was. You don't want to go back to that, do you?' What is that for a leader to say to the people?"

"Hansen, Dunne, all of them are insane," Ahmad agreed. "This whole thing of them giving everyone whatever they could ever want or need is just this giant cover-up of whatever they've really got going on. I'm not sure what it is, but I'm going to avoid the trap, that's for sure."

The two men continued, traveling through different abandoned towns, with their masks on, going through old homes and stores for supplies. They didn't find much of anything, as expected. It was just the way things were now.

"I don't know who those guys are, or who's been looking out for them in the Green Zone, but we'll definitely be paying them a visit soon because this is ridiculous!" Ahmad's mentor threw the handful of items that they'd found in a house onto the backseat, jumped back into the driver's seat, slammed the door, and they sped off.

"Does it ever get to you… the violence?" Ahmad asked.

"You mean, against the people out here?" the driver asked.

"Yeah," Ahmad answered.

"No way, man. Not anymore, it doesn't. I know that it gets to you early on, but then you understand why it goes that way. All of us, citizens, non-citizens, we're all products of our government from over time. We are as good or as bad as our government. They're animals and they've turned us into exactly what they are. I know what I've become; it is what it is. The entire world is one big jungle and the Red Zone is the jungle floor. Don't be fooled into thinking that what we do is something heinous because those motherfuckers in the Green Zone, with their fancy lifestyles and the holier than thou saints out here in the Red Zone who feel like they've made this grand sacrifice that will get them into this imaginary land in the sky, hands are just as filthy. We're all in this hell-sphere together, just as evil as the next man."

"What we do is survive. We give everyone the choice first of leaving with their lives, anything otherwise, then we have to make an example. We can't take chances with people, you know? Because remember, they're just like us; we're all animals. You show an ounce of weakness and you'll be bleeding all over the floor because they struck first and because you wanted to listen to them reason with you while they figured out how to get the upper hand on you. We don't play around with them and we up the ante. They can be believers in God and everything, but they'll kill you and ask for forgiveness. We go the extra mile to send a message, letting them and anyone else know not to try us. So, to answer your question, no. It doesn't bother me, doing what we do. I don't lose sleep at night knowing that I survived another day."

Special arrangements were made ahead of time to notify the restaurant that former President Mallory Hansen and current President Nathan

Dunne would dine with them that evening. Given the rare circumstances, the restaurant closed its doors to the rest of the public. The owner herself tended to their table, and she ensured them that the best team and chef were working that night. Behind the scenes, everyone worked up a frantic sweat as they nervously tried to put forth their best efforts. Both men entered through the back of the restaurant and greeted everyone before being seated.

The tablecloth was a pristine white that was examined by the owner beforehand to make sure that it had been completely flawless. Hansen ordered an incredibly rare Cabernet Sauvignon whose vintage had been nearly three decades old. It wasn't on the menu, but he'd requested something rather unique and the owner pulled from her secret collection of wines that she'd saved for special circumstances such as these. After a few swirls, inhaling its aroma, taking a sip, then inhaling again, Hansen smiled at the owner.

"Excellent," he replied.

After a few very brief exchanges of small talk and placing their orders for food, the two men got down to business.

"How is our... *project* coming along?" Hansen inquired.

"Gradually." Dunne peered down at the table and responded as if he'd already known that Hansen would be disappointed in his progress.

"Mm. That's unfortunate, now isn't it?"

"I'll say," Dunne said.

"We're up, for now, but we must exert ourselves more, showcase the strength that we are capable of. I shouldn't have to explain this to you, again," Hansen said softly as he leaned forward towards Dunne. "Our time is restricted... we must break their will and do it now. Our army, here on Earth, combined with that in the spirit realm, is far too powerful for Him to maintain a covering over them. He's lost hope in them before, it will happen again. And you," he said now pointing at Dunne, "have to make sure that it happens."

Their food had arrived, and they now had several dishes laid out before them as they continued their private conversation.

"We have those in each Quadrant, inside of the Red Zones, who've been doing their part, but progress has been slow. As circumstances continue to become increasingly difficult for them, I foresee them exerting their will even more on the others surrounding them. They're well known throughout each Quadrant in terms of how they operate and what lengths they will go. In due time, the believers in all Quadrants will be eliminated or converted over into the imprint system. It will happen sooner than later," Dunne said to bring reassurance to Hansen.

"How confident are you in that?" Hansen asked in between a bite from his steak. "Are you relying on your wildcards to take care of it, because that's all that they are?"

"Not solely," Dunne answered. "They've done a good job of getting rid of themselves as well. Everything that the wildcards have been doing has been a bonus. I have faith in the spirits that I've put in place that they will continue to apply and increase the necessary amount of pressure that is needed to complete our agenda, seeing as that there are no... interferences. Did you know that they've given them a name in some areas? One of my personal favorites that I've heard was the *Barbarians*."

The two shared a laugh.

"Well, you finally have all of those who are not imprinted in one place; it's time to take advantage of this opportunity and fulfill the prophecy," Hansen ordered. "My only point is that your…Barbarians will not be enough to complete this."

"Then, we'll have to do an invasion within all Regions. And if we do so, we'll need a viable reason for doing it," Dunne responded.

"Yes, I've thought about that," Hansen said before taking a sip from his glass. "I have an idea in mind for that; it should give us probable cause. We have to make sure that people continue to have faith in us. Don't worry, it'll all play out perfectly."

Upstairs, inside of the old and run-down sanctuary, Andrew sat alone on one of the few pieces of what remained of a church pew. Lately, he'd been distant from the rest of the group of people that he'd brought in, but he wasn't exactly sure why that had been so. He noticed he started to distance himself around the time he first had the vision. Although he told Jaylen, as well as Nigel and Steven, about the vision, there had been something that he'd been holding back.

"There you are. I'd been looking all over for you," Jaylen said as he came up the stairs into the sanctuary. "How are things here?"

"All things seem to be well for now," Andrew replied with a strained smile across his face. "How are things downstairs?"

"Everything is perfect! I doubt things could be any better. I mean, considering our circumstances," Jaylen said as he took a seat next to Andrew. Andrew noticed that Jaylen seemed to be in one of his rare cheerful moods. It was refreshing to see, but there were troubling things on his mind that prevented him from matching his energy.

"Hey, we never really discussed the vision you had and how you knew we would find someone in the Green Zone to help us. Obviously, I know Kaleb, but he'd already been prepared for us and you knew he would be. And ever since then, he's had supplies ready and waiting for us. It just amazes me; how did you know?"

"Like I said, I just had a feeling, a vision, I just… knew," Andrew answered.

"Wow! I know you always bring everyone together to speak, but it's like you're a prophet or something too, like the stories I remember from the Bibles we used to read. I don't know, but you may carry the spirit of Christ," Jaylen stated.

"No, Jaylen, please," Andrew started, "I'm deeply flawed in ways you couldn't imagine, much to my shame, that I'm sure Christ would find no place within me."

"You're kidding me. Until I met you, I've never seen such a gift held by anyone. Those stories that I remember reading, I didn't think existed in our time, but seeing the gift used through you gave me a renewed hope that Christ, not only lives but, that He hasn't forgotten about us."

"Jaylen, *stop!*"

Andrew had never shown an ounce of anger towards anyone within the group. It was startling for Jaylen to witness it from him.

"You don't… understand," Andrew continued. "There are sins that I carry inside of me, never spoken unto man, only to God, that deteriorate my bones. My spirit has become brittle because of my sins. I fear they have yet to be forgiven and I doubt that they ever can be."

"How can you say that," Jaylen asked humbly. "You've done so much good, for so many."

"Yes, but so much wrong to so many others," Andrew replied.

"No matter what it is, our Father is able to cover and carry all of our sins, especially when they are too heavy for us to bear. We cannot forget this," Jaylen said, attempting to comfort him.

"I suppose you're right," Andrew said after consideration.

The two of them sat quietly amongst one another for a time, both looking up to an old, graffiti-covered and partially broken, yet still standing cross before Andrew broke their silence.

"All that as it may be, there are other things that haunt me as well," he said.

Jaylen looked over at him, encouraging him to continue.

"That vision, it wasn't the only one."

"What do you mean?" Jaylen asked.

"The same night as the first, there were two others. There was the vision of you going into the Green Zone to find someone that would lend their help, then there was another. I saw a group of men that came here to overtake this place and we were not prepared. However, somehow, I was confident within my spirit that should we be on guard, we will be able to withstand them," Andrew said.

"That sounds like the Barbarians," Jaylen said. "So, they're finally going to pay us a visit?"

"Then, there was one more," Andrew said. "It was difficult to make sense of it but, it appeared to be some sort of war taking place. This one was hazy for me. What was most troubling was that in this vision, they killed someone close to us all. We all grieved deeply, but… I wasn't able to make out who it was. All I could remember was the sadness that we all carried. It was a time of darkness for all of us."

"Was there any sign of how this could be prevented," asked Jaylen?

Andrew slowly turned to him with his eyes red, filling up with tears as the feelings of that moment resurfaced for him all over again.

"I'm afraid not," Andrew said. "This seems to be an evil that has been coming along the horizon for quite some time. Its arrival seems to be one that is inevitable, regretfully, for us all."

22
ROBBERY

Across the street from Flannigan's Groceries was an old black four-door sedan parked alongside a popular coffee shop that had already closed for the night. Inside of the car were three men, one woman, all of which were Barbarians. They all wore their prized custom-made human skull gas masks that had been painted in all black to match their attire. Their breathing was heavy as they peered through the front of the store, eyeing Kaleb and Alicia who'd been closing for the evening.

Without either of them uttering a single word, they all exited the car simultaneously and began walking up the street towards the store. As they approached the intersection, the light turned green for cars to continue, however, neither of the Barbarians stopped or ever once looked into the direction of the cars to see if it had been safe to go, which it hadn't been, as the four of them scrolled across the street. Cars had already proceeded through the light and as the four Barbarians entered the intersection, they were forced to swerve and honk their horns aggressively at them.

"Assholes!" one driver yelled out of his window, holding up his middle finger at them as he sped off.

They were, however, unfazed.

The woman approached the front door of Flannigan's and yanked on the door a few times, attempting to open it. She'd been unsuccessful. The rugged way she'd tried to open the door caught Alicia's attention.

"Hey, obviously we're closed! What's the matter with you?" she asked, clearly annoyed by the woman.

"What's going on out here," Kaleb asked as he walked out from the back office?

"Those idiots out there were yanking on the door when they could clearly feel that it was locked," Alicia replied.

"What the hell is on their faces," Kaleb asked as he squinted to get a clearer look at them?

Outside, one Barbarian pulled out his knife, and with the back end of it, he banged against the door until it shattered some. From there, the other two men kicked in the rest of the glass and then they all stepped inside. Alicia's annoyance quickly turned into terror. Her brother moved her behind him as the four intruders, with the woman up front, slowly walked towards them.

"The supplies, the ones you give to the group in the Red Zone, where are they," the woman demanded in a muffled tone?

"What are you talking about?" Kaleb asked, confused.

The woman pulled out her knife.

"No games, only the supplies, and you will live," the woman said. "This will be my last time asking. Believe me when I tell you I am very impatient. Now... where... are... the... supplies," she asked as Kaleb became face to face with the Barbarian?

Kaleb's mouth became dry and his tongue swollen as he quickly scrambled within his mind to find out what to do.

"Be wise on your next course of action; murder does not bother me. I'm prepared to prove it," she said, reaching around Kaleb to touch Alicia's hair.

"W-we don't want any trouble; we can help you. Just tell us what you need and we'll do whatever we can. We don't mind helping," Kaleb said.

"Everything placed aside already for them, we want!"

"What? The amount that we prepare for them takes time. We haven't had time to pull everything together yet," Kaleb said.

The woman suddenly punched Kaleb in his nose, causing him to bleed instantly. He stumbled back into Alicia's arms as they both collapsed onto the floor, where she tried her best to help him stop the bleeding.

"You're playing a very dangerous game with your lives right now... and you're losing. How could I be so clear in what I'm demanding if I didn't already know every single detail about what I am requesting," the female intruder said calmly as she knelt before them.

"Now, before you make a comment that will cost you and your sister your lives, please understand that we already know everything, such as that you provide them with shipments every other Thursday. This is Tuesday of the 'every other week' which means that you should have their supplies already prepared. You can view this as an early collection day."

"We have it in the back; it's in the back," Alicia said while she held a torn piece of her shirt towards her brother's nose.

The female Barbarian slowly rose as the three men that had come along with her quickly made their way towards the back to locate the food that had been stored for Andrew and his group inside the church.

"Very good, you get to live today," the Barbarian said.

She walked towards the back where the rest of her team had found the three pallets worth of food and other useful supplies. She instructed one of the men to bring the car around to the side alley that was next to the store. As Alicia walked in from the store, the woman turned around towards her.

"You've done well. We will take care of things here," she said.

"I take it that this will be an ongoing thing?" Alicia asked.

"Of course, it will! We're your new clients. Also, you should know that this will be our one and only trip."

Alicia appeared confused.

"Then, how do you plan on getting everything?"

The Barbarian took a few steps towards the visibly shaking Alicia.

"That's none of our concern. That will be left up to you to figure out. Today, we will only take a few things with us, as this was merely our introduction to you. Besides, we only brought one car, so it won't be able to hold everything."

While they were all in the warehouse waiting for the car to come around and working out arrangements with Alicia, Kaleb had still been inside the store and had grabbed a .38 caliber handgun from behind the register.

There was a knock on the side door in front of the stairs that led up to what had once been Melanie and Jaylen's apartment. Alicia was told to go over and open it; it was the Barbarian who'd gone to get the car. Except for the woman, they began taking armfuls of food and placing it inside of the trunk of the car parked in the alley. The intruder stared at Alicia while the men worked.

"Where is he?" she then asked.

"Who?" Alicia asked, although she knew very well who she'd been referring to.

Behind the counter, both of Kaleb's nostrils had been plugged with tissue that had begun to turn red as he loaded the pistol with a box of bullets. He was ready.

She placed the blade to Alicia's neck as she used her as a shield to search around for Kaleb while the men continued. They checked inside of the small office, in each corner, underneath the desk, inside of the large cabinet; he wasn't there. Then she slowly directed Alicia back inside of the store. While on the ground, Kaleb looked up at the security mirror to see the two of them enter back into the store from the back.

"Come out now or I'll kill her. It makes no difference to me," the muffled female voice said from behind the mask.

Looking up at the security mirror, Kaleb observed them checking down the aisles, Alicia still with the knife tightly at her throat. More pressure had been applied now, causing a small amount of blood to trickle down her neck. Alicia grimaced in pain.

Kaleb knew he didn't have much time and that he didn't have room for error. He watched in the security mirror as they came up an aisle and then paused in front of the register. The intruder looked up at the mirror, which reflected a blurry image of Kaleb seated on the floor. Suddenly, the door to the back-warehouse burst opened as one of the other masked Barbarians rushed in.

"We're done!" he came in, announcing loudly.

His surprising entrance caught Alicia, as well as the female intruder, off-guard, but not Kaleb. This was his opportunity. The woman holding Alicia hostage turned her back towards the counter when her partner abruptly entered, causing her to become distracted. Kaleb quickly jumped up from the floor, aimed the gun at the woman's back, and fired twice and got off a shot at the guy who came in as well. Alicia screamed and scrambled down the aisle.

Kaleb ran towards the door, jumped over the guy he'd shot to go after the other two men, but the gunshots caused them to quickly jump into the car, snatch off their masks, and speed away frantically. The driver hadn't managed to fully gain control and when they fled into the street, the tail end of the car swung around, and two oncoming vehicles struck their car. Inside, the driver's body became mangled and lay motionless.

A few hours later at a nearby police station, Trevor entered to meet with an officer whom he'd been speaking with to help him locate Andrew. When he walked in, Officer Askew was seated at his desk when he saw Trevor approaching him from a distance.

"*Great, this guy again,*" Askew mumbled to a colleague under his breath.

"That the advisor from Region Two who's searching for that guy in the Red Zone," the other officer asked?

"Yeah… that's him," Askew replied.

"How the hell are you supposed to find anyone out there; he could be anywhere? He could be dead for all you know."

"I don't know, wish to hell I didn't have to deal with it, but you know, he's a big deal or something."

Trevor reached Askew's desk and made himself comfortable in the chair seated on the side.

"I take it you haven't heard anything since I haven't heard from you," Trevor said.

"You got it," Askew said.

"Well, have you actually gone out there to search for him?" asked Trevor.

Askew paused to look at Trevor for a moment.

"Look, we have no reason to go out on any type of wild goose chase in search of a guy who's not even from this Region in the first place, simply because you say that he is dangerous. Do you understand how insane that is?"

"It's just not me that says he's dangerous, he's a known criminal within Region Two who's liable to create religious underground cults wherever he goes. Now, the last time I checked, that was considered a crime and if he's in your Region, I'd say he's also now a problem that you will have to deal with," Trevor said.

"But see, that's where you're wrong. If he's in the Red Zone, which more than likely he is, then he's completely out of our hair. So, that would mean that he remains none of our concern," Askew countered.

"That's *if*... he's in the Red Zone," Trevor said.

"Oh, please, of course he's out there! If he was inside of the Green Zone, he would've been found and if he was pulling any of that spiritual cult shit that you're talking about, he would be dead. Case closed," Askew said.

Trevor sighed as he dropped his head.

A few feet away inside of a holding cell, the passenger who'd been in the crash earlier saw Trevor speaking with Askew at his desk. He recognized Trevor. He remembered meeting him at the house some time ago when Trevor stopped by inquiring about some guy he'd never seen or heard of. The passenger was the one who answered the door that day. He saw Trevor get up from the desk and he called out to him.

"Hey, suit guy!" He didn't catch Trevor's attention, so he continued walking.

"Hey, you still looking for that guy? I know where he is," the caged and bruised Barbarian said, revealing the bloody smile he'd acquired from the accident.

Trevor stopped abruptly and looked over towards the cell and slowly began walking towards the man.

"*Hey... I remember you,*" Trevor said at almost a whisper.

"Of course, you do," the Barbarian said.

"You're a bit more bloody than I remember you, but I still recognize you all the same. Fancy seeing you on this side of town," Trevor said.

"You can say that it was a rough night for me. Things didn't quite go as planned," the man said. "I'm actually the lucky one."

"I can imagine," Trevor responded. "Have you… heard anything about the man that I was looking for?"

The blood-filled smile spread across the man's face once again.

"I haven't seen him with my own eyes, but… I have a *really* good idea as to where he is."

"Well, that's not very helpful now, is it?"

"Oh, I would say that it is! You see, out there," the man gestured with his head towards the Red Zone, "there aren't too many people that are alive and the ones that are have probably gone insane by now."

"Like you," Trevor asked?

The man ignored him and continued.

"There's a group of people at a… *certain* place that have been able to thrive throughout all of this. They've flown completely under my people's radar, but we finally found them and figured out their scheme of running things. If the man you're looking for is still out there, he's probably amongst those people."

"Where are they?" Trevor asked, now feeling a little more convinced.

"The way of unlocking that answer requires you to go back to the mansion, tell my people that the plan was foiled and that they need to pay the *targets* a visit to straighten things out. Feel free to travel along with them. Be sure to mention that I'm here so that they will come for me," the Barbarian said.

"You expect them to come after you? *Here*?" Trevor asked. "You don't know how this all works, do you? They don't keep non-registered citizens who commit crimes imprisoned for long; there's a no-tolerance policy in place. You'll become magically lost in the system somehow, but in all actuality, they will kill you. You're simply hanging out here until your number's called. Thanks for the tip," Trevor said as he exited the police station.

23
SEVERING TIES

Tensions came to a boiling point inside of every Red Zone Quadrant, as those who hadn't received Hansen's imprint became willing to take the risk of sacrificing their lives for crumbs of bread. Thefts within both Regions rose substantially along with murder rates; those who were imprinted weren't so willing to give up their possessions and their actions were backed by the court systems. The movements of those within the Red Zone against those on the other side heightened the public's already negative perception of non-imprinted individuals. They weren't seen as simply trying to find one good meal for the evening or a warm place to rest and when they were caught, to no one's surprise, they were brutally attacked, beaten, and usually killed. This was justice, as it was seen through the eyes of the public and their government.

Naomi's car pulled up in front of one of the newly constructed homes that was part of the deal for imprinted citizens given out by the government. However, it was obvious that the owner had enough money to upgrade because this neighborhood and the home model certainly weren't part of the standard home packages. Naomi's daughter kissed her mother on her right cheek, the two hugged, and Naomi watched as her daughter exited the car and ran up the steps to her father's house.

Naomi noticed how big she'd gotten; she was almost nine now. Naomi couldn't believe how fast she'd grown. At times, she wished that she and her ex-husband had been able to work things out for Marissa's sake; Marissa was unusually mature for her age, and she somehow understood the two of them separating.

Marissa's father opened the door to let her in, and he stuck his hand out to wave goodbye to Naomi. Earlier, when the two were deciding how to handle Marissa coming over, he offered Naomi to stay over for dinner, but she declined. She told him she had more work to get through. It was typical for her and while they weren't together, her ex was somewhat agitated by her response, because she always seemed to put her work first, which was part of the reason they'd gotten a divorce. He'd informed her he'd made enough money, so that she didn't have to work as much as she had, and with their combined income, they were very well off. However, it wasn't about the money with her; she went in each day to bring about change with everything that she had in her. She watched the two of them go in and then she slowly placed her car into drive.

Inside, Marissa greeted her father. He grabbed her bag, and then she ran off upstairs to her bedroom.

"Geez, what's in this thing, Marissa?" he called out. "This thing weighs a ton!" He slung it over his shoulder and started up the stairs to sit the bag down in her room. "How did you get this thing from the car," he asked?

She didn't answer. She'd already jumped on the phone with one of her friends.

"Yeah, Dad, I'm really glad to be here," he mumbled to himself sarcastically as he walked out of her room.

Naomi had become exhausted from having to attend these hearings repeatedly without there not being much progress within how the non-imprinted were treated. She was coming to her end with her fight against the oppressors of those who'd chosen to continue to stand firmly on their beliefs. Her fight, it seemed, was lonesome, as the limited number of those who once stood beside her had become bought, corrupted, or had simply given up. Alone she sat, once again, facing Congress with one last plea.

"Councilwoman… Councilwoman… we're waiting to hear from you," Ambassador Wells said to a somewhat dazed Naomi.

"Yes, yes, of course," Naomi said, clearing her throat. "I-I just wanted to…" her notes had been before her, but she just couldn't seem to find the appropriate words to express what she'd been feeling. She felt defeated and heartbroken and it had become visible to Congress members, particularly to Ambassador Wells and Moreno, much to their delight.

"Go on, Councilwoman," Ambassador Moreno urged!

"*How*… I just want to know how?" Naomi's voice was shaky as tears fell onto the page of notes that she'd been preparing for days now. Somehow, they just didn't grasp the anger and frustration of what she'd been feeling on the inside.

"Just… how could this government, one that is supposedly for the people, be so completely heartless. None of you… have any resemblance to a soul inside of you, not one. Each one of you on this entire panel is as equally horrible as the one seated next to you. Oh, but, let's not forget the architects of this utopia, Mallory Hansen and Nathan Dunne. I'm not one for spirituality and Gods and devils, but if they exist, I'm convinced that those two evil monsters are the devil himself, twice over."

"Okay, Councilwoman, do you have anything of pertinence to present before Congress today; or is this just all rambling nonsense?" another member on the panel asked.

"In your eyes, I suppose not, Councilman. The human beings that you cut off, left for dead, and treat like wild strays… all I ask is that you just acknowledge them for who they are. They're human beings! You believe in something, just as they do. Why do you see them as nothing? Why are you, we, or I better than them? I ask you and your absent body, mind, and spirit President. This Congress is the one that has failed! We are the ones that have fallen short! We are the evildoers! Can't you all see that? In time… your sins will become obvious to you, but when they do, it will probably be too late to do anything about it. I have nothing much else to say, I suppose. I will be resigning, effective immediately. My last request from you I found to be quite ironic and it will, perhaps, cost me my life for quoting such a thing inside of these walls. As I've stated, I've never been much of a believer, but I've always understood, respected, and admired the path and discipline that it takes to follow a higher power. My ask is that you do what is right and not what is a part of your agendas. Feed the poor, shelter the homeless, and nurse the sick even when they don't believe the same as you. Do unto others as you would have them do unto you and love all man, just as God has loved you. Thank you."

The chambers instantly became enraged as everyone shouted at Naomi for the blasphemous and forbidden words she'd spoken. Everyone yelled to the top of their lungs, threw papers into the air, and at Naomi, protesting their displeasure for what she'd said. It was a criminal act to mention God, let alone cite quotes from the Bible. Her actions were punishable; she understood this. Somehow, as the chaos continued to escalate all around her, she became calmer than she'd ever been in her entire life. Wells screamed to supersede everyone else's yelling and restore order, all to no avail.

Naomi gathered her belongings, placed them inside of her briefcase, and embraced them tightly across her chest as she walked out of the chambers with her held higher than it had ever been. As she walked down the aisle towards the back exit, more paper and insults were thrown at her. Some even took it upon themselves to spit at her and rip at her clothing. She regained her composure and successfully made it to her car, where she cried harder than she ever had before.

One week later while in his office looking over documents on his desk, President Dunne's secretary came in to tell him that Naomi's body was found in one of her vacation homes in the western part of Region One and that her death had been ruled as an overdose according to autopsy reports.

"Seriously," Dunne asked as he dropped back in his chair attempting to be shocked at the news he'd received?"

"I'm afraid so," his secretary confirmed. "They believe it was a suicide."

"Unbelievable," Dunne said, shaking his head. "You just never know with these things. Poor woman, with all the violence taking place, she must've felt that all of her amazing work wasn't leading anywhere. Thank you for letting me know. I'll reach out to her family soon."

The secretary walked out and closed the door behind her. Dunne turned around in his chair and looked out at the view from behind him filled with greenery while he listened to the birds singing. It hadn't been news to him, however; he'd known the exact moment about what had transpired with Naomi. When it happened, he'd received a message that simply read, "done."

"I just don't understand why you'd want to come back out here; something's off with those guys. You can tell that they're into some twisted shit," Trevor's driver said.

"Be that as it may, I'm prepared for them," Trevor replied while sliding his clip back into his handgun.

The two had entered back into the Red Zone to meet up with the Barbarians again so that he could gain further intel on where his father might reside and to tell them that their plan, whatever that had been, hadn't worked out for them inside of the Green Zone. They pulled up to the mansion once again, with everything seeming to be at a dead standstill. It was hard to imagine that there were many people inside. The SUV parked and Trevor stepped out from the back and tucked his gun on the backside of his waist. He put on his gas mask and walked up the steps to the mansion.

"Hey, what do you need," a voice from behind him called out? Trevor turned around. It was Ahmad.

"Hi, I came by here a little while ago and I spoke with a gentleman here at the door about a man whom I've been in search of," Trevor said.

"Yeah, I heard about you; what do you want," asked Ahmad? "We still don't know where he is."

"Well," Trevor began, then snatched off his mask, "I hate this thing, but you can't be too careful with the poisoned air out here, right?" He made a failed attempt at humor, judging by Ahmad's unchanging face.

"The reason I came back here was that I ran into the guy that I spoke with here, during my last visit, inside of the Green Zone. Things weren't looking too good for him, so he wanted me to deliver a message for him which would actually benefit both of us."

Ahmad looked skeptical, but he was very concerned about why his friend hadn't come back from the trip.

"Where is he?"

"Now, before we get into those details, he stated that there is a place out here where you guys need to visit to correct what went wrong on his journey. At this location, he said that I might be able to find the person that I'm looking for, so I would like to travel with you. Does any of this make sense to you?"

"Maybe," Ahmad said. "I asked you, where is he?"

"Unfortunately, he's been arrested. He requested that you all come for him, but that may not work out well for any of you, to tell you the truth."

Ahmad dropped his head.

"I'm on a severely strict deadline so I really need to know where the gentleman is that I'm looking for, like soon, so can you please help me locate this man," Trevor asked?

"I suppose. I don't really care what you do to be honest with you. We're going, whether you come along is none of my business," Ahmad said.

"Perfect! So, when do we go, are we doing this now," Trevor asked, clasping his hands together?

"Hey, I don't know, alright? We weren't planning on going by there today; you just came here with this information, so chill," Ahmad said. "I'll have to let my people know."

"Okay, then. Perhaps I'll wait inside of my truck," Trevor said.

"Man, I don't care what you do," Ahmad said, heading up the stairs into the house as he faced Trevor. "You can wait out here the entire night as far as I'm concerned."

Andrew's eyes suddenly sprung open as he came up from inside of his prayer room. He rushed outside of the door, passing by several members of his group, towards Jaylen's room before bursting inside.

"They're coming!"

Andrew surprised Jaylen upon his entrance, causing him to rise to his feet and reach underneath his bed for an assault rifle that he came across on one of their earlier visits deeper into the Red Zone. He didn't say a word. He walked out of his room, past Andrew, to alert the other runners within his crew. They were armed as well, with assault weapons and semi-automatic handguns that they'd been lucky enough to find. They had been very careful regarding how they moved, so they had been fortunate enough to avoid running into any trouble during their time inside of the Red Zone, but they had been overly prepared. Once Andrew had informed Jaylen of his vision, he prepped the others to stay on guard. Now was the time that they officially had to defend their turf; it was all or nothing. Successfully maintain all that they'd fought so hard for, or lose it all.

Headlights from pickup trucks, SUVs, and various other cars burst through the thick cloud of absolute darkness as the Barbarians made their way towards the mystery church. It had become an unwritten law that any large number of groups of people who'd managed to successfully cope within the land had to relinquish all of their resources to the Barbarians. In this case, there were also personal matters attached to their visit, so it was even more serious.

No one spoke a single word within any of the vehicles. All were masked, focused, and ready to carry out the mission. Up front, inside of the all-black and tinted SUV in the back seat, was their supreme leader, the lion skull. Far back within the distance of the pack was Trevor, trailing along, prepared, after his long journey, to meet the man who'd left him and the rest of his family within the woods that night to become captured by their enemy.

Jaylen and the rest of his small army stood guard upstairs inside of the tattered down sanctuary, looking out through the shattered glass with their guns in hand. They were ready. The possibility of losing what they had gained hadn't been a question for them. Underneath them, below the sanctuary, were families, men, women, and children, who needed their protection. This had been one of their primary motivations to fight.

And then there was the church itself. It had served as a tower of protection from their enemies who'd sought war against them and had become their responsibility to shield it from any form of attacks and defacing, outside of what had already occurred, as well as against its inhabitants. Somewhere, within the hearts of all the men, it was the church, more than anything else, that they were truly defending.

"Here they come," Daniel said, noticing the headlights approaching the church from a distance.

"I say we go out spraying them before they even get the chance to get close," Terrance said. "We don't know if they're strapped or not; don't think any of us want to get into a shootout with them. We can finish 'em before anything even gets started."

Jaylen continued looking on at the rapidly approaching vehicles, thinking of the best strategy to stand their ground.

"What do you think," Daniel asked Jaylen?

"We stay in, let them come to us. I have a feeling they're not expecting us to be as prepared as we are. We'll see how they respond," Jaylen said.

"What if they're hostile?" asked James.

"They probably are," said Matt.

"Then they'll die," Jaylen replied. "We can all go, but I'm not lying down. I've been the victim, helpless, and unable to do a thing about it. This time, if I'm to be a victim, at least I'll go out fighting back and putting it all on the line. I don't mind going out like that, but we'll see how they move first before making any permanent decisions."

His men respected the energy he'd put forth and were as ready as he was.

The cars aligned out front and turned off their engines as each one of the Barbarians all slowly exited their vehicles. Noticing that they'd all come to a standstill, Trevor's driver asked if he should park behind the last car. Trevor just observed the church for a moment, scoped the outside, noticing its massive structure and then looked at the Barbarians parked up ahead of him.

"No," Trevor told his driver, "go around to the back."

Each Barbarian filed behind one another as they headed up the stairs towards the front door of the church. Meanwhile, inside, Jaylen and his men had taken cover behind anything they could find away from the entrance. Downstairs, Andrew and his two watchmen kept the rest of the group away from encountering all that had been transpiring above them.

The door into the sanctuary slowly creaked open as one of the dark figures poked his head inside to check to see if anyone had been on the other side and if it had been safe for them to enter. The area appeared to be clear, so he and the others, including Ahmad, walked in, one by one, and aligned themselves across the back of the church. Once the animal and human skull wearing Barbarians had assembled themselves, they simply stood there, without moving an inch. The men, although they were unseen by the Barbarians, had them clearly within their line of sight.

"Dear God," Matt said quietly to himself upon witnessing the grotesque visual of their enemies for the very first time.

"What are they doing?" whispered Daniel.

"Looks like they're waiting for something," Terrance said.

Then they heard the slow, dreadful, thudding footsteps entering across the eroded wooden floors of the sanctuary. They looked to see who or what else had entered and, upon discovering what it was, chills trickled down each one of their spins. The lion skull, their supreme leader, had walked in and positioned itself directly in the center of the sanctuary with its comrades remaining behind it. For a time, it stood still, looking around, soaking in its surroundings and, somehow, it must have picked up on something.

"Show yourselves!" The chief Barbarian, in a deeply sinister tone, called out to whatever it had sensed within the air to reveal itself unto them.

"What do you want to do?" Daniel asked Jaylen. "We could finish them all right here."

With no warning to his men, Jaylen sprung up, holding the rifle at the leader of the Barbarians from behind an overturned table in which he and Daniel had been hiding behind. Once he'd done so, his men did the same.

Ahmad's eyes widened behind his mask upon seeing Jaylen across from him and the rest of the Barbarians. He wanted to say something that would prevent the standoff from turning into a bloodbath, but he wasn't sure about what would stop either side from standing their ground.

"I don't know why you're here, but we don't want any trouble. Just leave, and there won't be any problems," Jaylen said.

"Perhaps, you should know the reasoning behind our visit before you hand out your weightless threats," the lion skull replied.

"From this angle, it looks like our threats carry a lot of weight," Jaylen said. "Now, why are you here?"

"You have a supplier inside of the Green Zone who provides you with goods; what we require is simple. We want in on this network. You will now bring back goods to us as well on your journey," the leader said.

"Why in the world would we do that?" Jaylen asked. "There's nothing in that for us. Besides, with the number of goods that we bring back, there won't be any room for anything more for anyone else."

"You should consider more trips," the leader said.

"That's too dangerous! It's already risky as is and you're talking about going over there even more? No way! Who the hell are you all anyway for me to do something like this for you?" Jaylen began to sweat. He wasn't sure about what these people had up their sleeves, but he was prepared.

"We decide if you should live or die, that's who we are!" The deep voice from the head Barbarian vibrated within the walls of the sanctuary, striking fear in the hearts of Jaylen's men.

"If you value your life, the lives of your men, and... the others underneath us, you will accept my proposition. This evening you were prepared, but then comes the morning and the next evening, and the morning after and the evening after that. You will never know when we will decide that it is your time. Even if you were to kill us right at this very moment, my promise will still stand. There are legions of us, and we will return in droves until we have your skulls to wear as masks. Look into the empty sockets of those behind me and you'll see for yourself that I have not spoken a lie."

Jaylen was terrified, and he'd known for a fact that the Barbarian meant every word, but he couldn't let his fear show. He thought about Andrew and the others downstairs; he needed to protect them. It was as if he was having a redo at having an opportunity at protecting his mother.

"That all sounds really scary, but I'm prepared to take those chances," Jaylen said.

Matt looked over at Jaylen out of the corner of his eye nervously.

"What a fool," the lion skull said! "Your pride has cost the lives of everyone whom you've ever placed value in. We will take some of you to oversee that the goods are still brought to us, so you see, my plan will still be carried out. Tonight, you live, but the days after, you will suffer greatly as you shed tears of anguish unlike you've never known to exist. You will plead with me to spare the pain with your demise."

"I think it's time for you, your people, and your boogeyman speeches to pack up before we start blasting," Jaylen said. "I don't know about tomorrow, but as far as I'm concerned, tonight, we will be the only ones making all the blood spill if you and your people don't get out of here."

Trevor managed to sneak in through the back of the church while the Barbarians had occupied Jaylen and his crew. He snuck around, hiding when necessary, avoiding Andrew, who had been gathered together with the others. After so much time, this had been the closest he'd been to his father in years. Although he hadn't seen him yet, he could tell that he'd been close.

As he continued to search around, he stumbled upon a prayer room. It was filled with lit candles all around, which cast a shadow against the walls as he entered. The feeling of being near his father grew even stronger; *he could feel him.* Anger and rage elevated inside of him, as he took notice of Bible scriptures inscribed all along the walls in red paint that Trevor assumed was placed there by his father. Even in paint and with all the years that had gone by, he recognized his father's handwriting. He couldn't understand what had been happening inside of him, but his emotions overtook him as he took a seat on the bench facing the door, crying silently to himself.

Inside of the sanctuary, the Barbarians decided to leave but vowed that they would return. Meanwhile, Ahmad remained conflicted as to whether he should make his presence known to Jaylen, his old friend.

"We should've shot 'em while we had the chance," Daniel said to Jaylen when they left.

"We're not trying to start a war, Daniel!" Jaylen became angered with Daniel questioning his decision to allow the Barbarians to leave.

Daniel stepped up to Jaylen, the two became face to face.

"I've been out here longer than you have. I've seen up close what those guys can do! They've done things you couldn't even dream of in your darkest nightmares," Daniel said. "You don't need to worry about starting a war because they'll start it for you and I assure you, there won't be any mercy."

"Whose side are you on, huh," asked Jaylen? "We're not killers! We're not like them! If it isn't necessary, we will not take anyone's life."

"Take my word for it. Killing them would've been extremely necessary," Daniel said before walking off.

Shortly afterward, Jaylen and the others returned downstairs to connect with Andrew and the rest of the group. Jaylen explained to Andrew everything that had gone down and that he and the rest of the team would be on constant surveillance of the church to look after everyone. Andrew trusted Jaylen's word but he'd been somewhat disturbed, so he decided to go and pray in his prayer room.

The door opened and upon walking in, something suddenly startled Andrew.

"Jesus Christ!" Andrew noticed a man dressed in a suit inside of his prayer room seated on a bench facing the door with his head lowered.

"C-can I… *help you*?" Andrew was unsure of whether this man had been with the Barbarians or if he truly needed help. At any rate, he desperately wished that Jaylen and his men were there with him.

Trevor slowly raised his head, revealing his puffy eyes unto his father, whom he hadn't seen since he abandoned his mother and younger brother many years ago.

"*Dear God… it's you*," Andrew said. "*Trevor.*"

Trevor slid over some and patted an open spot on the bench next to him.

"Come, father; catch up with your son. We have a lot of things to discuss."

Andrew was nervous. He wasn't sure if he should've been scared or excited to see his son.

There had been something within his tone that suggested that his request to sit next to him wasn't optional, so he did.

"I-I haven't stopped thinking about you all," Andrew nervously said.

Trevor forced a shaky smile to spread across his face.

"How about that," he said. "We haven't been able to stop thinking about you either."

"Everyone's... okay?" Andrew asked.

"Of course! Everyone is well taken care of... I made sure of that. Someone had to step up, right?"

Andrew dropped his head with guilt.

"When we were captured, I made a deal with the authorities and managed to work things out. After all, we weren't necessarily the ones that they were after. However, part of the deal, and my life's mission, was to find you. And here we are, reunited, father and son." Trevor wrapped one of his arms around his father's shoulders.

"Trevor... I'm so sorry," Andrew said as tears fell down his face. "I regret what I did that night every single day; it haunts me. And I know that the torture is warranted. I deserve it."

"You're... *sorry*?" Trevor chuckled lightly. "You placed us in harm's way, your wife and two children, and abandoned us, like a coward, as we became captured and all you have to say is 'Trevor, I'm sorry'?"

"Truly, I am," Andrew said. "It is my greatest sin and no matter what I do or say can ever replace what I've done. I accept the punishment that God has for me."

Trevor sighed.

"That's good that you're willing to accept God's punishment. I'm happy to hear that, but are you willing to accept my punishment?" Trevor slowly pulled out his gun and pressed it sternly against his father's ribs. "You can worry about His punishment after we're done here."

"Trevor, please," Andrew begged. "I-I was foolish for doing what I did; none of you deserved that. God has dealt with me and has changed me for the better, despite my ongoing punishment of abandoning my family. Please, don't carry this hatred inside of your heart, Trevor. It's too heavy of a burden to carry."

"You're right, dad, it is too heavy for me to carry, so I must free myself." Trevor turned and looked into his father's eyes as the gun fired. "All sins must be paid," Trevor said.

Andrew fell over into the arms of his son as Trevor held onto him, both with tears in their eyes, until Andrew took his final breath.

Everyone looked around, trying to decipher where the loud bang had come from, and everyone immediately became concerned with Andrew, who'd gone off to pray by himself. They rushed to his prayer room and found him lying within a pool of his own blood along the bench. Everyone cried out and screamed at the loss of the man who'd taken them in, sheltered them, fed them, and kept God's words alive within their hearts. The rest of the night they mourned as Jaylen rocked back and forth on the floor with Andrew's lifeless body in his arms.

24
FINAL WARNING

REGION ONE: SOMEWHERE AROUND ~~WASHINGTON, D.C.~~

Inside of a dimly lit office, Cassandra lied down across an expensive handmade sofa as she stared up into the ceiling. It had been one of her weekly scheduled visits to the therapist she'd been seeing lately. There had been no one for her to really open up to since she left her cousin and the rest of her family back in New York.

"How often do you think about him?" the therapist asked.

"Often," Cassandra replied after a deep breath.

"How frequent is often?"

"Every day. I think about him every day it seems."

"What comes to mind when you think of him?" asked the therapist.

"Oh… everything, memories, good times we shared together. But usually, I just wonder if he's okay out there. There's so much going on in the world today and I'm just always finding myself being concerned for him. I think about how I might feel if I found out that he was alive. I like to think that he is; that makes me feel happy, but you just never truly know."

"Do you feel regret?"

"What? Regret? No. I don't think I do," Cassandra said.

"Why aren't you able to let go and move on?"

"It just didn't end well; we were in love, so the way it happened… I didn't exactly tell him I was him to go through with becoming imprinted. I guess, in my mind, I knew it meant the end for us. Basically, I just miss him. I'm still in love, you know? But being in that city just made me constantly feel like an enormous hole was still in my heart; I could still feel him in the air whenever I would go out, even though he was nowhere around me. I don't think I will ever be able to fill that void. There's a part of me that makes me feel as though I betrayed him." Cassandra replied.

REGION ONE: SOMEWHERE AROUND ~~NEW YORK~~

Jaylen stood at the grave where they'd buried Andrew in the field next to the church as he thought about what may be on the horizon for him and the rest of the group. Usually, during these times of uncertainty, Andrew or his mother would be there to lend him some form of advice for him to stand on, but now it was just him. He now had a group of people whose well-being rested solely within his hands.

"How are you doing?" Daniel asked, as he approached Jaylen next to the grave.

"Tell you the truth, I don't really know," Jaylen answered. "I just wish that we could know what happens next. We don't know who killed Andrew, and that bothers me. We could guess that it was the Barbarians, but we don't know for sure."

"Yeah, I know what you mean," said Daniel. "I just feel that it has to be them. I mean, who else could it be? They're the only ones who would make a move like that out here. And besides, they were here."

"Maybe you're right, but people are getting desperate nowadays. People are losing their minds and doing a lot of things you wouldn't expect them to do. We'd be surprised," Jaylen said.

"That's true," Lisa said. She and Jaylen embraced one another once she came out to see him. "Before we were ever shipped out here, people were losing it. Being out here only intensified things. I've seen believers kill other believers with no remorse over a small piece of bread and still feel as though they have done nothing wrong. Times have definitely changed. You can't help but wonder if it is all coming to an end. It's probably for the best, anyway."

"These days… we just have to remain prepared for anything. Anyone who's not with you is your enemy," Jaylen said. "He saw all of this coming, but he just didn't recognize himself as being the victim. He was a seer, but he would always downplay it for some reason, not really embracing it. I told him that the spirit of God Himself was within him. During these times, it seems that the spirit of God is absent, but by us seemingly being stripped bare, being down only to our minimum necessities, we can feel Him feel like we, perhaps, never have before because we need Him more than we ever have. We always needed Him, but we weren't always in place, so He needed to regain our attention. The believers who remained alert and continued to hunger and thirst after Him were able to see this. They have kept their minds on things within the spirit, while others have lost their way and their faith remained in place as long as they could find their next meal. If they went hungry, they cursed God, not knowing that He would provide for them just as He had for us. These were the teachings of Andrew; he made sure that we kept our minds within the spirit. He will be sorely missed."

A floor to ceiling bulletproof glass was put into place inside of the press room at the world headquarters to prevent a situation from happening again such as the attack against former President Mallory Hansen. While the former President's recovery was miraculous, the security simply couldn't take any chances of having their current leader attacked.

The media had been waiting for Global President Nathan Dunne to arrive and address the public regarding current affairs that had been concerning to the citizens inside of both Regions. When he entered, cameras began flashing rapidly from the other side of the glass as he approached the podium.

"Thank you, everyone, I would like to thank you all for being with me today. I assure you I plan on being brief, but very clear with my intentions," Dunne began. "There is no secret as to the alarming rate of crimes that have taken place within our communities and this administration has heard the complaints from our citizens and we have become well prepared to enforce a strategy to ensure that we bring these crimes to an abrupt end. We have strong reasons to believe that these acts of theft and manslaughter against citizens within Green Zones inside of every Quadrant have occurred at the hands of those who have chosen to not be a part of our global rebuild. We have offered them every opportunity to join us and to feel complete freedom and independence to live in a manner that they've always hoped for. The old world rejected those ideals and became overrun with the greed and corruption of their political figures. However, Mallory Hansen was able to dig deep with the rubble and ash of this world and be able to see its potential through the eyes of every single one of you. He gave us all a second chance, a better chance, at life. Yet, there have been those who have rejected these ideals and have entered your communities to steal and terrorize your neighborhoods. They were the ones who decided that they would be okay with living on the outskirts of every Green Zone. But when things became more difficult for them, they took from you! While being our enemy is fine, what we will not do is sit on our hands as we allow our people to become attacked by those who oppose us. My administration will strike back with absolute vengeance! We granted your wish of separating you from our kind, yet somehow, you continue to display the lingering hatred that you harbor towards us in the ugliest ways imaginable. We have grown weary of having patience with you and attempting to understand and accept your ways. This is not an administration that stands on violence, but if this is the only language in which you all understand, we will prove to you that we can speak it fluently. So today, I stand before you to deliver this very simple message: your end is near."

President Dunne turned and walked away from the podium as cameras flashed and everyone yelled out questions to him, despite seeing his departure.

He'd been having trouble sleeping ever since he and the rest of the Barbarians visited the church where he'd seen Jaylen. He hadn't expected to see him there. Although Ahmad and Jaylen hadn't quite always seen eye to eye, Ahmad maintained some level of respect for him deep down inside, which had still been the case. Ahmad stared out of a window in one of the hallways inside of the mansion, still contemplating if he should approach Jaylen as well as what he should say if he did. He ran it over in his head to see it sounded, but none of it made sense.

Hey, it was actually me and my guys who came to extort you and your people a few days ago; I didn't expect to see you there. Sorry about that.

Everything he thought of came off wrong. Then he thought about not telling him that he was there that night at all. He figured he would just go to the church and it would be like two old friends catching up. Every scenario pointed to him approaching Jaylen. That was the start, and he decided he could just go from there. He left the mansion, hopped in a car, and drove off towards the church. Once he got there, he parked the car, got out, and walked towards the church.

"Stop!"

Someone yelled out to Ahmad, causing him to freeze right in his tracks. He wasn't sure where the voice had come from, but understanding how things operated in the Red Zone, he knew that he probably wouldn't be given a second warning.

"Who are you, where do you come from, and what do you want?" the voice which happened to be James asked.

Ahmad determined that the voice had come from above him, so he looked up, but the brightness of the sun prevented him from clearly seeing who'd been speaking to him. He squinted and partially covered his eyes with his hand as he looked up towards the sound of the voice.

"My name is Ahmad. I'm here to see Jaylen."

"He asked where do you come from," a second voice asked from the other front side of the roof of the church from where James was standing? It was Terrance. Both he and James held automatic weapons aimed directly at Ahmad, ready to fire.

"Well… I'm from the Green Zone," Ahmad said. "Jaylen and I have a long, extensive history, probably longer than either of you."

"Do you know us?" Terrance asked.

"No," Ahmad answered.

"Then why are you speaking on who we may or may not know and how long we may or may not have known them for," Terrance asked?

"Listen, I didn't come for any problems. Now, I need to speak with Jaylen; I know he's here. It's really important that I see him," Ahmad said.

James and Terrance looked over at one another in their gas masks, trying to decide what to do. While they were deciding, the front doors to the church opened and Jaylen walked out holding a handgun at his side.

"Ahmad?" Jaylen squinted at the sight of him appearing surprised that he was there.

"What's up? Long time no see," Ahmad said.

Jaylen carefully looked around his surroundings as he strolled down the stairs towards Ahmad.

"You-ah-you by yourself, Ahmad?" asked Jaylen.

"Yeah, man. It's just me," he said.

Once Jaylen reached Ahmad, the two men embraced. When they did, Ahmad noticed over Jaylen's shoulder that Terrance and James were still aiming directly down at him.

"Your bodyguards are too uptight," Ahmad said.

"That's how it's gotta be nowadays," said Jaylen.

"I guess you're right," Ahmad chuckled.

For a moment, the men stood in awkward silence until Jaylen broke the ice.

"So, not that I'm not happy to see you, but I just have to know how did you know I was here?"

Ahmad's thoughts bounced back and forth like a ball in a tennis match as he struggled to figure out if he should tell Jaylen the truth about him being there with the Barbarians a few nights ago. How would he respond? He decided that there was only one way to find out.

"A few nights ago, some people came here wearing skulls attached to gas masks," Ahmad began. Jaylen's eyes stared in his as he tried to follow along.

"I... I was here with them," Ahmad said.

"Wh-what do you... what are you saying to me right now, huh," Jaylen asked, appearing visibly upset?

"I didn't know that you were here. I was going to say something, but things would've gotten out of control on both sides," Ahmad tried reasoning.

"Did you or your people do it?" Jaylen asked.

"Do what?" Ahmad seemed confused.

"Did you kill him? Did you kill Andrew?" Jaylen yelled as he came nose to nose with Ahmad. Terrance and James watched on, waiting to see if they needed to fire.

"I don't know who Andrew is, Jaylen. You have to believe me."

"Why should I trust anything that you have to say; if you're hanging out with them, you're my enemy. I should have my guys spray you until you turn to dust," Jaylen said.

"Then fucking do it, Jaylen! You forget who you're talking to or something? I don't take threats lightly; if you're gonna threaten me, you might as well do it. I've never coward to anyone or any situation, you know that. Now, you don't have to trust what I have to say, but I came here out of respect to let you know that the Barbarians are coming back and it won't be like last time. They're only coming to kill."

"Oh, yeah, will you be with them this time, too?"

Ahmad dropped his head.

"You need to get your people out of here. They won't stop until everyone's dead. You rejected their initial proposal, so now, when they return, it won't be to have a conversation with you," Ahmad said.

"We'll be ready," said Jaylen.

"Jaylen, you don't have enough men, guns, or bullets to outlast them. This is another level we're talking about here. You think you're the only people out here with guns? They have guns too!"

"Well, since you're their little delivery boy, deliver this message back to them. Tell them that whenever they're ready, we'll be right here," Jaylen said before turning and walking away.

"You'll need more than your two little roof guards," Ahmad said as he got back into the car.

"You should get out here before my little roof guards give you a little demo on how they perform," Jaylen said. "And trust me, there are more shooters than what you and your team saw the other night. Make sure you tell them that."

The visit didn't go as Ahmad had envisioned it going and he certainly didn't see himself becoming upset, but he had. After all of these years, their relationship was somehow still the same as it had always been.

"Who was that," Daniel asked once Jaylen had gotten back inside?

"An old enemy," Jaylen said. "His name is Ahmad."

"Ahmad," Lisa questioned, who had been standing alongside Daniel? "Where did he come from all of a sudden?"

"Apparently, he's been running with the Barbarians the entire time," Jaylen answered.

"Really? I'm not so sure if I'm even surprised, to be honest," Lisa said.

"We're going to need everyone, and I mean everyone, on board with us on this," Jaylen said to them. "I wouldn't dare think of putting our people in harm's way, but they're coming back like we kinda suspected they would, and from the sounds of it, they want to go to war. Anyone that has a pair of hands needs any type of weapon that they can find to use against them."

"What if we leave or just give them what they're asking for?" Lisa asked.

"It's too many of us to travel for any long-distance, then you factor in transporting food as well, it'll be nearly impossible. Then, after all of that, they'll probably find us. And giving them what they want means turning us into their slaves. They'll have to kill me before that happens," Jaylen said. "The problem with all of this is that we just don't know when. We have to continue to stay alert, just as we have been, but now, we have to get everyone involved."

"And to make matters even worse, we're running out of supplies. We'll need to make another run soon," Daniel said.

Inside of the back office at Flannigan's, Kaleb and Alicia planned to continue providing for Jaylen while also protecting themselves from potentially more harassment from the Barbarians.

"We have to keep helping them," Kaleb said, "or else they'll all be dead. I don't care how many more of those clowns come here, we just have to fight them off the best we can."

"Kaleb, that sounds really brave of you and all, but to be completely honest, that's a little suicidal. There's no way that you and I can go against them," Alicia said. "We're civilians, they're career thugs; there's an enormous gap there. We got very lucky last time."

"You suggesting we stop helping them, because I'm not?" he asked.

"Look, I don't know! Maybe I am. Everyone loses if we're dead," Alicia said.

"But here's the thing," Kaleb said, "They won't kill us."

"And what makes you so sure about that? You recall what happened when they came here, right?" Alicia asked.

"Yeah, but think about it. You just said it yourself. Everyone loses if we're dead, which includes them. They need us to continue with the distribution, otherwise, with us out of the picture, they'll be right back in the same spot."

"Great point," she said. "But now," Alicia sighed, "the larger problem is with Dunne's new plan. He's heightened security around here and has declared to go to war with non-citizens. He catches them inside of here and they're dead."

"Then maybe... we deliver to them," Kaleb said hesitantly.

25
INVASION

Everyone inside of the church became on edge after Andrew had been murdered. While Jaylen and his men assumed the Barbarians had killed him, they weren't completely sure that they had. Many members within the group came to Jaylen looking for answers and he tried his best to console them the best way that he could, much like Andrew always would, but he wasn't sure if what he'd been offering was really helping them. They would ask him if God had spoken to him as He had spoken to Andrew, but He hadn't, Jaylen would tell them.

"I'm just a regular guy."

He would try his best to remember the words from the scriptures that were taken away from them, burned, and forbidden for anyone to own, and he would remind them of God's promises to those who believed.

"All the things that we are facing, we can handle them, otherwise we wouldn't be going through them. When things become unbearable to us all and when the timing is right, He will come for us. We must remember that," Jaylen said to one woman in their group.

Ahead of their next pickup from Flannigan's, Kaleb had paid Jaylen a surprise visit at the church to deliver the news of a visit from the Barbarians and news of Dunne planning to come after everyone inside of the Red Zone.

"Great, now the entire world is out to get us; literally," he said to Kaleb as they sat inside of the sanctuary. "The Barbarians will be starting a war with us on any given day, and who knows when Dunne will send his people in. We're as good as dead."

"Whatever the case may be, you guys will still need food and I'm not stopping on delivering on my promise," Kaleb said. "Right now, security and surveillance inside of the Green Zone has intensified like you wouldn't believe, so you and your men coming there for pickups will be impossible. This is why I came here. I wanted to let you know that from here on out, I'll be delivering to you."

"What about getting through security?" Jaylen asked.

"I'll manage. I can handle that part. Just as long as you no longer step foot inside of the Green Zone again, everything will be fine."

"Well, on this side, should you make it over here with all the goods, you have to worry about the Barbarians. Where we're positioned, it's almost impossible for you to not have to pass by them," Jaylen responded.

"Look, everything is what it is nowadays, Jaylen. Life is dangerous at any angle that you look at it. That doesn't stop us from doing whatever we have to do. We just move with caution, but if things go bad, I just hope the God that you believe comes through for all of us," Kaleb said.

Once Kaleb had left from meeting with Jaylen, he hit the highway and began heading back into the Green Zone. While he sped along, unknowingly to him, someone off into the distance watched him through a pair of binoculars.

Dunne's military seemed to be ecstatic about the many new upgrades they'd received before they were to head out on their manhunt. Improved armor, headgear with not only imprint scanner technology, but thermal and x-ray vision as well. They studied their tactics and their mistakes during their first interactions with non-citizens and sought after ways to improve their combat methods. Dunne was more than eager to invest any amount of money in the improvement of every Quadrant's military. The time was drawing closer for their surprise attack on the non-imprinted. However, no one knew the day or the hour that they would be deployed, except for Hansen and Dunne.

"I don't know how long we can keep living like this," James said to Jaylen and the rest of the guys outside behind the church. "Things just seem to keep getting worse by the day and the way things are headed, we're probably going to end up dying out here."

"Now we have to wait and pray that Kaleb can bring us food and hope that he doesn't get intercepted by military officers or the Barbarians on his way towards us," Terrance said.

"For me, that's not even the scariest part. We also have the skull guys and the military wanting our heads, for no good reason at all, at a time we are completely unaware of. We're doomed, man," Matt added. "I pray that God just comes and takes us away from this hell; we've been through enough down here."

Kaleb loaded up the truck and attached a trailer behind it so that he could have the space to place more items to carry out into the Red Zone. The sun was setting, and it had been after he and Alicia had closed the store for the evening. She decided she was coming with him, despite him not wanting her to out of fear that it might be too dangerous.

The roads had been flooded with cars, cars flying above them, and pedestrians walking along the sidewalks, but the entire time, Kaleb and Alicia couldn't keep their attention away from the military officers patrolling around and illegally doing imprint scans on citizens unbeknownst to them. Kaleb's grip around the steering wheel seemed to tighten when they came into close proximity to one officer. At a traffic light, the military bot stopped as it was crossing the street, turned, then stared directly into the truck.

"*Oh shit*," Alicia whispered.

Luckily for them, it continued moving along after a moment. They assumed it had done a random scan on them and determined that they were imprinted. After driving several miles outside the center of town, they entered the Red Zone, where they were to meet up with Jaylen for what would be their final time.

As frustrated as Ahmad had been with Jaylen, he still had been somewhat concerned about his well-being simply because he knew just how dangerous the Barbarians were. He was one of them, but his history with Jaylen partially impeded him from being able to look at him with complete disregard.

"Hey, what's the matter with you? You okay, man," one of Ahmad's fellow skull wearing comrades asked him?

"Nothing. I just—nothing. I'm good, seriously," Ahmad responded.

"Then come on, we're meeting inside of the main room before we go handle those wannabe tough guys at the church. If they thought they were the only ones with guns," Ahmad's comrade said, holding up and cocking back his all-black handgun while laughing, "then they have another thing coming."

"I'll be out there in a second," Ahmad said.

"They should've taken the deal, now there is no deal," the Barbarian said aloud as he walked down the hall.

"Dammit, Jaylen," Ahmad said to himself.

"It's like a ghost town out here," Alicia mentioned as they drove past the deserted buildings, homes, and highways. The sight had been unbelievable to her, as it was her first time visiting the Red Zone. She had always heard stories and rumors of what it was actually like, which had given her the worst possible impression of what it was like out there.

Theirs were the only pair of headlights that were coasting along through the night, with everything else being a thick sheet of darkness wherever they would turn their heads.

"It's just so hard to believe that people are living out here; all I can see is… darkness. Nothing. Everything out here appears to be dead," Alicia said.

"Everything is as good as dead," Kaleb responded. "Anything that is living out here is probably hanging on by a thread."

The Barbarians all handled the placing of their skull gas masks over their heads with a careful delicacy, seeing as not to cause it to crack even by the slightest inch. They wore them with great pride and honor as they loaded themselves, along with their blades of various shapes and sizes, and guns inside of their vehicles of all makes and models before departing silently from the mansion. They were on their way back to the church, this time with even more Barbarians and more artillery. But just before they were ready to take off, the driver of the first car pointed out to the lion skull a light traveling along in the far-off distance.

"Follow them," the leader of the Barbarians said, and they pulled off.

Inside the church, the shifts continued, with everyone taking turns to stand guard. When it was their turn, everyone would walk around with guns, knives, sticks, or anything that they could find. Jaylen, however, always remained on guard with his gun always beside him. At the time, he sat on a bench inside of the prayer room, directly where Andrew had been murdered. While he prayed, his automatic rifle remained tightly gripped within the palms of his hands.

Daniel and a few others circled the outside of the church with two more guards standing on the rooftop to monitor things within the distance. During their meeting, Jaylen and Kaleb had arranged for the delivery to be made that evening, so they were all on standby for his arrival.

There was a humming sound that was now heard that Alicia hadn't noticed before. It was strange.

"Do you hear that," she asked her brother as she squinted her eyes with a look of curiosity?

"No," Kaleb said. "What is it?"

"That noise," she replied.

"What does it sound like?"

"I don't know. Sounds like it's coming from…" Alicia stopped mid-sentence, rolled down her window, and stuck her head out.

"I think it's coming from outside," she said.

"I don't hear it," Kaleb said.

"Roll down your window," Alicia said.

He did and leaned his head out some while trying to keep an eye on the road ahead of him.

"It kind of sounds like cars, but... I don't see anything," he said.

They both sat in silence for some time before Alicia brought up the sound again.

"It sounds like the sound is getting louder, right?"

"Alicia, it's probably in another area somewhere. Clearly, we're the only ones out here," Kaleb said, sounding a bit frustrated with their ongoing conversation.

Alicia stuck her head out of the window again, this time turning around to look behind her. When she turned, she noticed enormous shadows in the shapes of cars and trucks bolting towards them, but with the headlights off and the sounds growing louder.

"Umm...Kaleb."

"What?" her brother asked.

"I think we're..."

Headlights from a car behind them suddenly flashed on to the high beam setting and had come directly on the bumper of the trailer, catching them both off guard and blinding their vision in the mirrors. The car swerved backed and forth erratically behind them and began honking its horn. Once this began, all the cars behind it turned on their headlights and began honking their horns as well.

"What the hell is happening?" Alicia screamed at the top of her lungs in fear as Kaleb tried his best to maintain control of the truck.

Kaleb reached down between his seat and pulled out his gun.

"Come on, I'll kill you all right here on the highway. Let's go!" Kaleb said, attempting to psyche himself out of the terror he was feeling.

"Kaleb, no! There's more than one of them. See what they want," Alicia pleaded, now trembling and close to tears.

The first car drove up close to the back of the trailer, honking, causing Kaleb to press the accelerator down completely to the floor. The car continued its pursuit until it bumped against the back trailer and caused the truck to swerve wildly out of control. Kaleb miraculously regained control and continued to speed down the highway.

"They're gonna kill us. They're gonna kill us," Kaleb repeated frantically as he sat upright, close against the steering wheel, with his widened eyes bouncing back and forth from the road ahead of them and the rearview mirrors.

The first car, without warning, pulled away from behind them and sped up until it was directly next to them. Kaleb and Alicia looked over into the passenger side of the car and gazed deep into the purest form of horror either of them had ever encountered, the opening skull of a lion's jaws spiraling down into absolute blackness.

"What the hell is that thing?" Alicia asked.

Then the driver suddenly sat forward, wearing the human skull, to give them orders.

"Follow us!" the Barbarian yelled out from the car.

The car sped up and was now in front with Kaleb and Alicia, followed by the other Barbarians, trailing behind.

The night was quiet while they all waited for Kaleb's arrival, which had been like most nights, except for the night that they were paid a visit from the Barbarians. While the night had been peaceful, the anticipation and anxiety had set everyone on edge.

"What if he doesn't make it?" Matt asked Daniel as he paced back and forth outside.

"He will; just relax," Daniel replied calmly.

"It's taking him a long time."

"It's a long trip."

"I just hope he didn't run into any trouble. But you're probably right though, I'm just overly anxious," said Matt.

"As usual," Daniel muttered.

Daniel hadn't wanted to alarm anyone, but inside, he felt the same as Matt had. The trip was long, but not *that* long. Calculating the amount of time their usual visits to Flannigan's, they would have gone and made it back with the time that it was taking for Kaleb to arrive.

"Hey, Daniel," one of the watchers from the roof suddenly called out to him.

"Yeah?" he shouted back.

"Exactly who all else is supposed to come with Kaleb," the watchman asked as he noticed several sets of headlights approaching from the distance?

"Just him, as far as I know. Why?"

"Either he brought all of his employees from the store and their families along to help him or… this ain't him."

Daniel looked far out in the distance and saw headlights speeding towards their direction as the feeling of his stomach being tied into a knot unexpectedly came over him.

"Shit! Grab Jaylen," he commanded Matt! "NOW!"

Nearly everyone inside of the church rushed inside of the sanctuary holding guns and whatever else they could find as the line of cars all pulled up near the front, along the sides, and the back of the church. Jaylen and the core group of his men walked out onto the landing part of the church, just outside of the front entrance, with their guns pointed at the uninvited guests. They were familiar with the cars themselves without needing to see who'd been inside; they were certain that it had been the Barbarians.

"We shouldn't give 'em a chance, just start spraying right now," Terrance said while fidgeting.

"There's more of them this time," said Jaylen, "we have to play this thing smart."

The men quickly turned to their left and right and noticed the Barbarians who'd parked on the sides and the back, walking around to the front, this time wielding guns and knives. Once they'd reached the front, they all lined up next to one another when the doors to the front car opened up and two more Barbarians stepped out.

It was the driver and the lion skull, their leader. The driver then walked towards the car behind him, pointed the gun at the driver and the passenger, and ordered them to get out. As the door opened, the Barbarian reached in, snatched out the driver and he fell onto the ground.

"Kaleb," Daniel whispered.

Another Barbarian came over. Now Kaleb and Alicia both had guns being pointed at their heads as they became forced down onto their knees.

The lion skull walked slowly towards the front with both of his hands behind his back.

"Last time, you all seemed to have trouble understanding me. Tonight, I come to bring you clarity," the deep muffled rumbling voice from the lion skull said.

Jaylen carefully walked towards the front of the stairs when he became greeted with the sounds of guns being cocked back, causing him to stop within his steps.

"Seeing as though violence is the language in which you speak, I thought we would show you how well we can speak it," the leader said.

"What do you want with us, we don't know you? We haven't bothered you or intervened with anything you have going on out here?" Jaylen asked.

"There was a misunderstanding, during our previous conversation, in you thinking that we were requesting that you bring supplies to us, but I'm afraid to inform you that… it was not a request. However, you do have one last choice that we will leave you with. Either you prove that your life has meaning by ensuring that we have all that we need, or you can decide that the lives of these two mean nothing to you and I will walk away from here with their skinless skulls as a souvenir. The choice is yours."

Jaylen didn't know what he should do; his heart raced against the inside of his chest as his finger remained on the trigger. He looked around again at the number of Barbarians there were and wondered how successful he and his crew would be in taking them all out. He concluded they wouldn't stand a chance.   And now, he had the lives of Kaleb and Alicia within his hands. He wasn't willing to jeopardize the lives of those inside or the lives of these two after all that they'd done for him and his mother.

"Fuck 'em, Jaylen. Don't do what they say," Kaleb said.

One Barbarian suddenly ran up to Kaleb and punched him across his face, causing blood to spray onto the ground.

"Don't be stupid," the Barbarian said.

"You should think extremely carefully about what you say next," the leader said to Jaylen.

"I just need to understand… why does it have to be like this? We can all get through this as one; we don't have to take from one another," Jaylen said.

"Spare me the speeches. We are who we are; we've become what we have become," the lion skull said. "Now, make your choice, while you still have the opportunity to choose?"

Just then, there was a flickering light within the air, which caused Jaylen to become distracted as he pointed his gun at the Barbarians. Whatever it was, Daniel and the rest of Jaylen's men noticed it too.

"You see that?" James whispered to Matt.

"Yeah, but I can't make out what it is," the other responded.

Jaylen's eyes squinted as he tried to figure out what further trouble loomed over them. Surely, whatever it was couldn't have been a part of the Barbarians as well. All he could hope for was that, for once, someone was coming to be on their side.

The invasion had begun.

President Dunne's soldiers flew into the Red Zones of every Quadrant in search of any remaining individuals who were not registered inside of the Global Identity Database. Their mission was simple: Terminate on sight.

There were mixed feelings among registered citizens about Dunne's plan to eliminate all non-registered citizens; some felt that he'd "taken things too far" and was going a bit "overboard" with his actions.

"The rising levels of crime haven't been at the hands of all of those who weren't imprinted and if it had been, their actions could be seen as justifiable," one citizen expressed on her popular social media page. "Let's just think about it for a second here. These people have been bullied to either give up their entire belief system and identity or become homeless and worry about where their next meal is coming from, yet for some reason, no one is concerned about them. Why? It's because it doesn't affect you, personally. That's why!"

During a surprise attack during the night, military soldiers flew in to search for and destroy any non-imprinted individuals. The aircraft scanned the terrain to pick up any heat sensors which would alert them on whether anyone was on the ground. To prepare for a read, robot and human soldiers alike sat inside the back of the aircraft carrier, with some dangling by a rope in eager anticipation of them being able to capture a kill before any of their fellow soldiers.

"You picking up anything," a voice said from the command center to the pilot of one of the aircrafts? "I'm seeing bodies, but they're only dead reads. Not many people are still alive out here after all of this time. So far, all I'm seeing is dead bodies," the pilot answered.

"Well, keep looking for a little while longer in that area. If nothing comes up, you can head to another spot," the voice said.

"Copy that, we'll keep going," said the pilot.

The propellers sputtered around almost silently as the enormous aircraft vessels made their way towards the direction of the church. Soldiers hung out by the rope, holding their guns, ready for any ensuing warfare that they may encounter.

The uncertainty caused Jaylen to question the leader of the Barbarians, "Are those your people too," while motioning his head behind them.

They all turned to bear witness to the four aircrafts approaching them in near silence, filled with military soldiers.

"Who the hell is that?" one Barbarian asked.

"Hang on, I think I'm picking up a reading ahead. Get ready, men," one pilot said.

The attention and the guns of the Barbarians all shifted behind them as they all became startled by the four dark masses hovering over the night sky.

"It's Dunne, he's sent his soldiers again, they're here to finish us off this time," James' wife said to the others, noticing the aircrafts from inside of the sanctuary.

"I have a read. Soldiers, get ready to engage!"

The military bots in all four aircrafts stood up in unison and marched towards the center of the carrier, where they could drop for release upon the door's opening. Their metallic armor glowed against the neon lighting inside of the vessel that accented the otherwise pitch-black aircraft carrier. Once the aircraft vessels became slightly closer, the bottom doors opened and the military bots dropped from out of the sky. As the air carrier lowered, the soldiers dangling from the rope jumped down and followed them.

"I think we have bigger problems on our hands," Jaylen said, hoping he, his men, and the Barbarians were, for once, on the same page.

Before anyone could fully grasp what was taking place, whistling sounds of bullets and lasers flew past three non-citizens as an all-out attack against them had begun to take place. The soldiers positioned themselves behind buildings and trees while they opened fire and launched grenades towards Jaylen and the Barbarians.

The Barbarians took cover behind their vehicles as Jaylen and his crew retreated inside of the church. One Barbarian tossed a fully automatic rifle into the hands of their leader, who'd taken cover. He removed his skull, revealing his eyes, which had been nearly as dead as the empty sockets from the eyes of the lion skull in which he'd been wearing. He stood up, along with several of his soldiers, and they all opened fire in the military's direction.

"Back inside, back inside," Jaylen screamed out to his men as they rushed back in. "Everyone get down underneath the sanctuary to the bunkers. We're under attack!"

Men and women alike screamed in horror as they ran towards the stairs along the side of the pulpit to take cover.

"What should we do?" someone asked Jaylen.

"Take cover and pray," Jaylen replied. "Pray that God saves us."

Meanwhile, Dunne's soldiers continued to march closer and closer towards the church, still firing, as bullets ricocheted off of the cars of the Barbarians and the outside of the church. A few Barbarians ran towards the church for safety. Some were unsuccessful as a hail of bullets ripped through their backs and out of the front of their chest. The others that managed to make it banged on the door, begging for those inside to allow them to enter. They pleaded for mercy and forgiveness, yet the doors remained closed.

"What should we do; should we let them in?" Terrance asked.

"We can't! They were trying to kill us; that's the reason why they came here, remember?" James responded.

"Open the door," Jaylen sighed. "Do it quickly."

"*Jesus Christ,*" James mumbled in disbelief.

Terrance quickly opened the door as several Barbarians came pouring in.

"Thank you, thank you!" They entered, panting heavily, as they removed their masks.

Terrance closed the door and just as he had, another Barbarian came rushing towards the entrance, but a bullet tore through him, causing his blood to become splattered across the church door.

Outside on the ground, Kaleb shielded the body of his trembling sister as the head Barbarian stood next to them, firing round after round towards the soldiers as the empty shells from his gun fell directly in front of Alicia's face. The soldiers pressed forward, continuing to gain ground, as more and more of the Barbarians fell victim to their onslaught. Their lifeless bodies lied on their backs with their human skull gas masks facing up into the air, some possessing bullet holes with blood running out of them.

The upgraded military bots charged forward as bullets bounced off of them, barely causing any damage to their bulletproof metallic armor. They'd finally gotten close when many of them jumped into the air and landed on the cars of the Barbarians and began gazing down at them. Realizing that their bullets had no effect, the Barbarians stopped firing.

"*Damn*," the head Barbarian muttered.

The bots suddenly jumped down from the cars and began to brutally assault the Barbarians through every means imaginable. Their blood stained the church grounds as their skull masks became crushed and their bodies became viciously maimed and mutilated.

The head of their leader was squeezed between the grip of one of the military bots as he yelled in agony until there was a crunching sound heard from his skull becoming cracked, causing Kaleb and Alicia to flinch. The bot then took the head Barbarians' morphed skull and smashed it into Kaleb's driver side window. Glass shattered and the leader of the Barbarians lied slumped across the driver's seat. The bot looked down and noticed Kaleb and Alicia, observing that they were both registered, so its attention shifted towards the church.

Jaylen and the crew rushed downstairs, realizing that there was no possible way for them to fend off their enemy. Everyone had gathered in the center room and had prayed aloud as Jaylen and his men searched for boards to seal off the doorway that led downstairs.

"We're picking up something. There seems to be a large number of them underneath us," a soldier informed the command center once they'd entered inside the church. "We have to figure out how to get down there."

From below, everyone could hear the heavy footsteps marching around in search of a way to reach them. The prayers became reduced to whispers as tears trickled down their cheeks. The back door and the entrance leading down to them were boarded and Jaylen and his men simply sat at the bottom of the stairs bracing themselves for whatever it was to come.

Sweat fell down their faces, their palms were shaking as they aimed their guns at the door, they were prepared as well as they could be. This was their last line of defense. It was Dunne and his agenda versus a people standing fast on what they'd believed in. Whatever the outcome was to be, they all knew that this would be the end.

The sound of the knob of the door being tampered with was heard as the men grabbed onto their guns tighter, then there was a pounding against it, as if they were attempting to burst through. The group clung onto one another as their tears and prayers frantically continued. Then...

It was quiet.

Right after, the door exploded open, along with the boards that were used to block them from entering. The robots headed down first, followed by the human military soldiers, as Jaylen and his men fired at them with everything that they had while they slowly moved backwards. Everyone else ran off screaming to find places to hide and towards the back exit, but the soldiers had broken through that side as well; they were all trapped. Their bullets bounced right off of the bots as they marched towards Jaylen and his small army. Then, after non-stop firing, Jaylen heard a click from his gun as he came face to face with a military bot. He'd run out of bullets.

The bot grabbed Jaylen by the throat, lifted him into the air, and punched him repeatedly in his face as blood flowed from his mouth and nose before he became tossed like a paper doll onto the ground. His vision was blurred as he looked around and noticed his men all lying around next to him. His ears rang, but he was able to faintly hear gunfire. He tried his best to gather his thoughts as he crawled along the floor, but all that he could think about was that he and his people were dying. In his mind, he prayed.

Why have You turned away from us when we are Your people? You have left us to be delivered into the hands of our enemies and now... our fate is sealed. We have never turned away from You. Why have You turned away from us?

Daniel was lying next to him, lifeless. He caught a blurry glimpse of another body not moving; it was Matt. Jaylen's body became weakened as he began to feel as though life was slowly leaving him. He then heard fewer screams and saw more bodies as his heart rate became slower... and slower. This was the end.

A soldier placed a gun to the back of Jaylen's head, placed his finger on the trigger, slowly squeezed... but then his finger stopped moving. He became still, along with the rest of the soldiers, who became frozen in the last motion that they were in. The military bots became motionless, and they began to malfunction as sparks flew from them.

Everything came to a standstill and there hadn't been a scream to be heard or any type of motion taking place. It had been the case in every Quadrant, every Region, every Green Zone, and every Red Zone. The wind didn't blow; the rivers stopped running, planes froze in the sky, as did the military aircrafts. They were stuck in the sky as all of life had come to a complete halt.

There then was a blast that echoed across the skies reaching from Region One to Region Two, followed by a blinding white light that was even greater than the sun's rays. Suddenly, the ground trembled as rocks and stones slowly levitated off of the ground. The ocean waters rose and the foundations of buildings creaked as the structures started to become lifted away from the grounds of the earth.

Daniel's body twitched.

Then Matt's body did the same.

Beneath the sanctuary, all of the dead bodies of the non-imprinted citizens began to move. In every Red Zone across both Regions, the bodies of the non-imprinted gradually began to rise. Somehow, they became awakened as they seemed to float through their garments, leaving them to remain wherever they were. The looks on their faces were one of confusion as they looked around and saw that others were experiencing the same thing as they were.

Soon, they looked down, and they realized they were no longer on the ground. Daniel looked to see the exact spot where he once was.

He could recognize it because he saw the clothing that he'd been wearing still lying there. Matt and the others, in all Quadrants could witness the same. Some became fearful out of not quite understanding what was happening as they continued to rise higher and higher off of the ground.

Were they dead?

It was a question in which they all wondered, but then, Daniel and others began to understand.

"He's come for us," Daniel whispered as a smile widened across his face.

As Daniel rejoiced, he then looked down and saw that Jaylen's body remained.

"No, no, no... there's a mistake," he said. "There's a mistake!"

However, Jaylen, who'd been still alive, gasped as he felt as though someone had poured a renewed amount of energy and life back into him. His senses became greater than he'd ever remembered them being. Then, without warning, he felt as if he were being lifted slowly from the ground of the church floor and into the air.

Seeing this, Daniel became elated, along with Matt, Terrance, Lisa, James, and the others that they all looked after inside of the church. They were lifted high in the sky and could now look down through the ceiling of the church. As they continued to rejoice with a joy in which they'd never known, all became perfect as they witnessed Andrew also rising alongside them within the distance. Glancing over at them, Andrew simply smiled.

26
REVELATION

Not a single second had gone by as the light had vanished and darkness had, once again, filled the sky above the church. The ocean waters fell back to the earth, the rivers began flowing, and the rocks fell back onto the ground. Life had resumed, but something was... *off*.

The military bots all fell to the ground, several planes lost control, with some crashing into the mountains, and the military pilots fought to keep their aircrafts steady inside of the air. Inside of the church and everywhere else within the Red Zones where the invasions were taking place, the human soldiers all looked around in silence and confusion at the robots that collapsed without warning before them.

"Come in," one soldier radioed inside of the church.

"Go ahead," a pilot radioed back.

"Something has ah... happened."

"What is it?"

"Well, the robots seem to be... broken," the soldier said as he kicked one robot, causing more sparks to fly.

"What do you mean, '*broken*'? Were you able to take care of everyone?"

"Literally that, they seem broken. They were standing here and then, I guess, they just dropped. I don't know what happened or what else to tell you, but... about the people..." the soldier continued as he knelt down and picked up the clothing which Jaylen had been wearing, "they're not here anymore."

"What the hell did you just say? Cut the shit," the pilot said.

The rest of the soldiers all picked up and kicked the clothing all around them and searched inside of the rooms to see if the non-imprinted citizens had somehow hidden from them.

"I'm not kidding around here. Check with the command center to see if they've gotten any reports," the soldier said.

"Hang on," the pilot said. "Goddamnit!"

"What the hell happened here guys," the head soldier asked as he and the men continued looking around. All of the soldiers looked around at one another, startled and confused about what had taken place. They walked outside and saw the dead bodies of the Barbarians still there and Kaleb and Alicia pulling the body of the Barbarian leader out of the front seat of their truck.

"Hey, you two," the colonel called to them, "do you have anything to do with what happened?"

Kaleb and Alicia still looked terrified by the ambush that had taken place.

"Did we have anything to do with what? We don't know what you're talking about," Kaleb said.

"Yeah, right. You're coming with us." The colonel grabbed Kaleb, and they began walking back towards the aircraft. As they began heading back, the pilot radioed the colonel.

"Hey… I just messaged the command center and… they're saying that they've been getting the same reports that you told me. There's been a few minor exceptions, but they're reporting there's a massive amount of non-imprinted citizens that have just… vanished right out of thin air. They're saying that they left their clothes behind. Just where did they all go off to naked?"

"Damn. What the hell is going on?" the colonel said to himself.

President Dunne's head was inside of a toilet as he regurgitated everything that he had inside of him. His eyes were flaming red and watery as he stood to his feet and wiped his mouth. On the other side, one of his housekeepers knocked on the bathroom door to check on him.

"Sir… Sir, are you alright, can I get you anything?" the housekeeper asked him.

After a few more moments of sounds of retching coming from inside of the bathroom, the door swung open and Dunne stood before his housekeeper, appearing sick with his disheveled hair and heavy breathing. He leaned against the frame of the door as he tried to catch his breath.

"He came, He came back. I can feel Him," President Dunne said before walking past the housekeeper.

The housekeeper looked back at him with a confused look on his face.

"Who came, Sir? Were you expecting someone?"

Ahmad had broken off from the Barbarians and had managed to escape back into the Green Zone. In a bold move, he simply walked along the streets without fear of being captured by military officers. As he walked along, he overheard several people on the street discussing an abnormal amount of accidents taking place and that there were reports that many people had disappeared from the Red Zone that evening.

He became shocked at what he'd been hearing as he ran into an alley and instantly fell onto the ground. He looked up into the air, as he couldn't help but think that Jaylen and the others were part of the people who'd vanished. Somehow, he knew their disappearance hadn't been a bad thing and as he sat there; he wished that he'd been taken along with them… wherever they'd gone.

The reports of what had taken place had been all over the evening news. As Cassandra came out of the kitchen holding a glass of wine, the television was on and she heard the reports of what happened on the broadcast. She froze mid-track with full knowledge of what had taken place as the glass slipped away from her hands and shattered on the floor.

"*He was right,*" she whispered to herself.

When Trevor arrived back inside of Region Two, the first thing that he'd wanted to do was get back to his mother and younger brother. After the plane finally landed, despite dealing with some of the strangest turbulence he'd ever encountered, he rushed to the car, and his driver sped away towards his home. When he arrived, there were police cars everywhere, causing him to immediately feel dread. He jumped out before the car could hardly stop and he rushed to the front door where police and his housekeeper had been. With his eyes filled with worry and concern, he asked where his family had been, and began to run throughout the home screaming out their names, only to receive no answer. He came back to the housekeeper and the officers asking for an explanation, but all the housekeeper could tell him was that, "They disappeared."

Trevor became enraged as he grabbed his housekeeper and began screaming at him, telling him he was supposed to look after them while he was gone. He was filled with anger and there had been nothing he could do. He was all alone.

Inside of his home office, within the dark, with only the light from the moon shining down through the window, Hansen stared up into the sky with the feeling of disgust, anger, and hatred inside of him. Hansen rested his head on his hand as he peered up as if he'd been in deep thought for what should take place next. He felt that it had now been his move. He and Dunne's plan hadn't gone as they'd expected, and he knew that time had been running out for them both. Slowly, more of the light from the moon started to illuminate the dark room and began to shine directly onto Hansen's face that he'd attempted to keep hidden within the dark. As it had, layers of his flesh peeled back, revealing pieces of his authentic form, and his eyes lifted to face the light of the moon as if he'd been challenging the heavens.

"And so, it begins," Hansen said with a deep snarl before the light of the moon went dark upon his face.

About the Author

Aaron was born and raised in Birmingham, AL, but has lived in California for quite some time. Much of the inspiration for his writing comes from stories from his upbringing, keen observations from everyday life, and deep dives into endless rabbit holes of research on a multitude of subject matters.

He spends much of his free time reading, learning, traveling, listening to music and podcasts, and writing.

Social Media Links

HTTPS://WWW.AARONLUSTERBOOKS.COM

HTTPS://TWITTER.COM/ALUSTERAUTHOR

HTTPS://WWW.FACEBOOK.COM/AARONLUSTERAUTHOR

HTTPS://WWW.INSTAGRAM.COM/AARONLUSTERAUTHOR

EMAIL: AARONCLUSTER@GMAIL.COM